HELEN HARDT

"These two are downright lovable! You are rooting for them to get together from the get-go. The chemistry between them is smoking HOT, and...once they get in bed you will need a fan."
~Guilty Pleasures Book Reviews

"Helen writes these books with such grace and finesse that you feel as though you've been transported back in time and are walking among the characters. You feel every bit of passion, anguish, and love emanating from the pages. It envelops you and leaves you grasping at the hopes that these two wonderfully in love couples get to have the HEA they both deserve."
~Bare Naked Words

"Flawlessly written, and in my opinion a work of art..."
~Girly Girl Book Reviews

OBSESSION

**STEEL BROTHERS SAGA
BOOK TWO**

OBSESSION

STEEL BROTHERS SAGA
BOOK TWO

WATERHOUSE PRESS

For Meredith Wild

*Three years ago you came to me looking for
an editor and the rest is history.*

Thank you for being a loyal colleague and friend.

WARNING

This book contains adult language and scenes, including flashbacks of child physical and sexual abuse, which may cause trigger reactions. This story is meant only for adults as defined by the laws of the country where you made your purchase. Store your books and e-books carefully where they cannot be accessed by younger readers.

CHAPTER ONE

"You *what?*"

My sister, Marjorie, whipped her hands to her hips, her brown eyes wide and angry.

I let out a sigh. "You heard me the first time. I asked Jade to leave."

Marjorie shook her head, her lips trembling. "I don't get you, Talon. Jade is the sweetest person in the world. She's the best friend a girl could have, and she's been there for me every time I've needed her. It gave me great joy to help her when she needed help, to let her come live here and start her life over after she got humiliated on her supposed wedding day. Why in God's name would you ask her to leave?"

How could I answer? Jade had only been gone since this morning, and already an emptiness had surfaced. Even in this sprawling ranch house, the loss of Jade's body, her soul, was measurable—a thickness that was damn near visible. It percolated through me like a cold fog.

"Damn it, Talon, you owe me an explanation."

Marj spoke the truth. I just didn't know how to put my explanation into words without telling my sister things I didn't want her to have to deal with. My brothers having to deal with them was bad enough.

"So you're really just going to stand there with your mouth hanging open like an idiot, huh?" Marj bit her bottom lip. "Fine. I'll call Jade." She stomped off.

My skin tightened around me. Jade would probably tell my sister that I'd been screaming like a maniac before I booted her out of our house, but at least she wouldn't be able to tell Marj the truth. Jade didn't know the truth. She didn't know I'd had a flashback while she was massaging me.

I reached down and gave my mutt, Roger, a pet on the head. He licked my fingers.

Even canine loyalty wasn't going to cheer me up today. Life was about to get hard. Not that I wasn't used to that, but this time, emotion was involved—emotion that was new to me. I sucked in a deep breath. I'd go to the guest house and talk to Ryan. My younger brother's door was always open. After all, I was a hero in his eyes.

What bullshit.

But Ryan would listen. He always listened, and I had to tell someone what had gone on between Jade and me.

I had to tell someone that I had fallen in love.

What else could it have been? Even now, having only been separated from her for twenty-four hours, she still invaded my thoughts. Her golden-brown hair flowing over her creamy shoulders, her ruby-red lips so full and kissable with the taste of strawberries and champagne. The silvery-blue eyes that darkened and smoked ever so slightly when she was turned on. Her beautiful breasts with brownish-pink nipples that were always hard for me. That soft sigh that escaped her lips every time I entered her.

I had hungered for her since the first time I laid eyes on her, and with each kiss, each touch, each minute in her presence, that craving had turned quickly into an obsession.

Jade Roberts was now as essential to me as oxygen, as sustenance, as water.

And I had thrown her out of my house.

"Come on, boy," I said to Roger. "Let's go see Ryan."

I opened the French doors out of the gourmet kitchen onto the redwood deck, followed the pathway half a mile to the guest house, and knocked.

My brother opened the door. "Hey, Tal, what's going on?"

"Do you have a few minutes?"

"Sure."

"I wasn't sure I'd find you home on a Saturday evening."

Ryan let out a laugh. "I put in a twelve-hour day, and I'm too freaking bushed to go out. Why aren't you in the city?"

Good question. My brothers both knew I tended to spend weekends in the city—meaning bedding cocktail waitresses or anyone else who threw themselves at me to release the pressured steam of my life. Maybe Ryan and Jonah hadn't noticed, but ever since Jade moved to the ranch, my trips to the city had been fewer and farther between.

"The city doesn't offer much for me anymore."

Ryan widened his eyes. "Come on in. Sounds like you need to talk."

I entered, Roger panting happily at my heels. Ryan led me through the living area into the kitchen to the laid-back family room. He walked behind the bar. "I'm guessing you could use a drink." He pulled out a bottle of Peach Street bourbon.

I nodded. "That's the God's honest truth."

Ryan poured me two fingers of the whiskey, straight, and slid it across the bar. He poured a glass of red wine for himself. Then he came around and sat next to me on a barstool.

"So what's eating at you?"

Where to begin? Ryan knew my history. So did my older brother, Jonah. But we didn't talk much about it. Neither of them knew the gory details. I had spared them that. Ryan was my little brother by three years. He had gotten away that horrible day. He had run because I'd told him to, and the poor guy harbored a lot of guilt for that.

"Have you ever been in love, Ry?"

Ryan raised his eyebrows and swallowed the sip of wine he had taken. "For a man of few words, Talon, that is certainly not a question I ever expected to hear from you."

I rubbed at my jaw and took a drink of my bourbon, letting the spicy warmth slide down my throat. "It isn't a question I ever thought I'd ask either."

Ryan took another sip of wine and set his glass on the bar. "I can at least answer you honestly. No, I haven't."

"Not even with Anna?"

Ryan shook his head. "Anna and I had a good run, not to mention some amazing sex, but in the end, we both agreed that what we had wasn't anything lifetimes were made of."

"What about Joe? Do you think he's ever been in love?"

Ryan smiled. "I think you'd have to ask him."

My brothers were both married to their work—Jonah to the beef ranch and Ryan to the winery.

"There are a lot of women in town who would like to take one of the Steel brothers off the market."

My brother laughed. "What's the hurry?"

"Well, none of us are getting any younger."

Ryan looked at me pointedly, his dark eyes serious. "What the hell is this about, Talon?"

I wasn't much of a talker, not even to my brothers. They both knew that. What had I been thinking? I was about as uncomfortable as a grizzly in tights. I downed the rest of my whiskey like a shot and set the glass on the wooden bar. "Nothing. Sorry to bother you." I stood.

"Oh, no, you don't." Ryan grabbed my arm. "You're not coming in here and opening up that can of worms without explaining why."

I sighed and sat back down. "Jade left."

"What? Why?"

"I asked her to."

My brother shook his head. "What did Marj say?"

"She's not happy about it. She's probably on the horn to Jade right now, finding out what went on."

"Well, what *did* go on, Talon?"

I picked up the bottle of Peach Street, poured myself another drink, and met Ryan's dark gaze. Time to lay the cards on the table. "I fell in love with her."

CHAPTER TWO

JADE

I grabbed my cell phone off the night table where it buzzed. *Marj.* Of course. I couldn't believe she had waited this long to call, but she had been in Grand Junction last night and most of today in a cooking class. I inhaled. How was I going to explain to her what had happened? We had to have this conversation sooner or later. I just hoped she wouldn't be too angry with me for keeping my relationship with Talon a secret from her.

"Hi there," I said to the phone.

"Don't 'hi there' me. Where the hell are you?"

"I'm in a hotel in Grand Junction. I just got back from the Carlton, where I had dinner with my mother and her current boyfriend."

"Brooke's in town? How in the world— Oh, no, you don't. I won't be sidetracked by Brooke Bailey or anyone else. What the hell is going on, Jade?"

"How was your first cooking class? Is it worth giving up Friday night and Saturday for?" Okay, cheap shot, but Marj was a bit spoiled and might take the chance to talk about herself.

"Nice try."

"Yeah, well..." I had no idea what to say to her. She was my best friend in the world, and we never had secrets. Until now.

"Jade, this isn't funny. Why did you leave?"

"Why don't you ask Talon?"

"I *have* asked Talon. All he would tell me is that you had to leave."

"He demanded that I leave."

"What the hell is going on? Why would Talon ask you leave? I don't get it. Why would he care one way or another whether you're at the ranch?"

I let out a heavy sigh. I didn't want to have this conversation with Marj over the phone. This talk would be best served with a pizza, a bottle of dry red, and a pint of Ben and Jerry's. "Can you come to the city?" I asked.

"Jade, I just got back from the city."

"I don't want to have this conversation on the phone."

"Frankly, neither do I, but we don't have any choice because we are going to have this conversation now. I need to know what's going on with you and my brother."

If only I knew. What I *didn't* know about what was going on between Talon and me could fill up a tome. We were attracted to each other. No, that was way too tame. We had wicked sexual chemistry. No, again. It was more than that, even for Talon. I was sure of it. We had unbridled passion and need for each other. Still not enough. So why not drop a bomb?

"I'm in love with him."

Silence on the other end of the line. An entire minute passed, according to the second hand on my watch. "Marj?"

"Yeah, I'm here."

"I'm sorry I didn't tell you."

"You *should* be sorry." Her voice was rough, strained. "I thought we didn't have secrets."

A lump clogged my throat. "I know. I'm so, so sorry. I just didn't know how to tell you. The thing between Talon and me kind of came out of nowhere."

"Jade, you lived at the ranch for over a month. You don't really expect me to believe that there was no way you could find a minute to tell me in that amount of time."

I bit my lip. Marj had every right to be furious with me. I was furious with myself. I owed her more than secrecy. "I know. I'm sorry. I just didn't know what you'd think of your brother and me..."

"You didn't give me the chance to think anything about it." Her voice was tight, as if the words were strangling her.

Worry choked me. Talon had been more than his usual "off" last night. He'd gone crazy, yelling at me to "make it stop." Make *what* stop? I still didn't know. "I... I think Talon needs help, Marj. I think he needs to see a psychiatrist or therapist or something."

"Jade, you have to help me out here. Which conversation are we having? Are we having a conversation about my brother's mental health, or are we having a conversation about the fact that you and my brother have been falling in love for the last month and I didn't even know about it?" Her voice shook, anger lacing through her words.

You and my brother falling in love, she'd said. The truth was, I had no idea if Talon was in love with me. He'd told me from the beginning that he'd never love me, and my desire for him had been so great that I hadn't cared at the time. I'd told Marj that I was in love with Talon. I hadn't told her he was in love with me.

"Look, I don't have a car. I took a cab here. I really can't talk to you about this over the phone." Tears misted in my eyes. "Tomorrow? Please?" After the dinner I'd just shared with my mother and her boyfriend, Nico Kostas, I was exhausted. Marj deserved better than dealing with me in this state. Hell, I was lucky she was still talking to me after this secret I'd kept.

"Nope. Sorry. We're having this conversation now."

I nodded, knowing full well that Marj couldn't see me. "All right. Where do I start?"

"Start with why the hell my brother asked you to leave my house."

"The answer to that question is a big, resounding 'I don't know.'"

"I don't buy it, Jade. You say you're in love with my brother."

"Yes." I gulped.

"Then why in the world would he ask you to leave? Does he not share your feelings?"

"I have no idea. I never told him *my* feelings."

Silence again. Then, "Is he in love with *you?*"

A jackknife slid into my heart. "No. He's not."

"I'm not understanding any of this."

"I don't understand either. Let me just start at the beginning."

For the next hour, I chronicled my time with Talon. I left out the specifics of our incredible sex, but other than that, I spared no detail to my best friend. I told her how we'd met in the kitchen during the night and talked, how he kissed me, how he told me he'd never love me but that he needed me, craved me...right up until last night, when he'd treated me to an elegant dinner in his room.

"I can't believe all this was going on under my own roof and I had no idea," Marj said.

"Well, it was mostly at night, and you know you can sleep through anything."

"But Jade, why would you keep this from me? We tell each other everything."

I sniffed. "I know. It's just... He's your brother, and something about him... I guess I just didn't feel like I was at liberty to say anything. You know how closed off he is."

"He's not as closed off as I thought he was. Frankly, I'm thrilled that he connected with you. I'm not sure Talon has ever connected with anyone before."

"But that's just the problem. I'm not sure we really ever *did* connect. I mean, he would shut me out at every turn. Even after an...intimacy."

"You mean a fuck? You can say the word, Jade. You were fucking my brother. I can take it. I just don't understand why you couldn't confide in me."

I didn't know how else to explain it to her. I had wanted to confide in her, but Talon was so impenetrable sometimes. He had so many walls built up around him. I didn't feel like I could tell anyone about what was going on between us, not even my best friend. How could I make her understand that?

"Please don't be mad at me, Marj. I couldn't handle

losing you too."

"Oh, for Pete's sake. You haven't lost me. And you probably haven't lost Talon. Just tell me why he asked you to leave."

"I've told you. I don't know. I was in the middle of giving him a massage, and all of a sudden he had this meltdown. He started screaming, and I couldn't make out any words other than 'make it stop.' Frankly, it scared me a little. When I finally got him calmed down, he wouldn't talk to me. He just said that I needed to leave. I told him I couldn't until morning, and he told me to leave then. This morning, when I was done in the shower, I came out to find a red rose on my bed."

"A red rose?"

"Yeah. No note or anything. I assumed it was from him since you weren't home."

"Even if I had been home I wouldn't have left you a red rose. Don't you know what that means?"

I didn't know what anything Talon did meant, and he wasn't exactly the floral type. "No. Do you?"

"Jade, a red rose—a single red rose—means love. Talon loves you."

My cell phone slipped from my hand and clattered to the floor, my heart pounding.

"...where he got a rose?" Marj was saying when I got the phone back to my ear.

"Sorry, what?" My hands shook.

"I'm wondering where he got a rose. We don't grow roses anywhere on the ranch."

I was still stuck on the "Talon loves you." Sweat coated

my palms. I stayed silent.

Finally, Marj went on. "I want you to come back. Come back tomorrow morning, okay?"

"I can't," I said, still trembling.

"Why the hell not? This is my house too, goddamnit."

I still hadn't quit my job at the Snow Creek city attorney's office. I had planned to call my boss, Larry Wade, on Monday. Tomorrow was Sunday. Going back to Snow Creek would keep me from having to find a new job in the city. Plus, I could use all the investigative tools at the city attorney's office to do some sleuthing of my own. But I couldn't go back and live in Marj's house, not with Talon right down the hall. Whatever the rose meant, it didn't mean he loved me. He didn't want me there, and I couldn't do that to myself. Constantly seeing him, wanting him—it would be easier to rip my heart out of my chest with my bare hands.

"Do you know where I could rent an apartment in town?"

"You're not renting an apartment in town. You're staying with me."

"I can't, Marj. Seeing Talon would be too difficult, and he doesn't want me there."

Marj gritted her teeth. Yeah, I couldn't see her, but I knew she was doing it.

"All right. We'll get you set up at the hotel tomorrow. You can stay there for a few nights until we can arrange for an apartment for you."

"I..." God, why was this so complicated? "I can't come back tomorrow. I used up all my cash for the cab fare to get here."

"Cash? You're really worried about cash? I'll pay your fare, for God's sake."

"You've already done too much."

"No, I haven't done enough. My best friend in the entire world kept a serious secret from me. Obviously I haven't been a very good friend."

"Marj, you're the best friend ever. You know that."

She sniffled into the phone.

"Oh, God, please don't cry."

"I'm okay. Please, just let me pay for your cab fare. I'll help you out with the hotel until we can find you a nice place to live that you can afford. Okay? Please?"

"No. I wasn't thinking. A cab here in the city will take a credit card. I'll be fine." I drew in a deep breath.

I was going back to Snow Creek.

CHAPTER THREE

TALON

Ryan's mouth fell into an O as he poured himself another glass of wine. He stopped just before it overflowed. "What?"

"You heard me, bro."

"You're in love with Jade?"

I let out a chuckle. "I am. I mean, I was pretty sure I was, but I'm not sure I knew it for a fact until just now."

"That's great. She's awesome. Really smart, too. She caught on at the winery right away."

Hell, yes, she was awesome and really smart. More importantly, she was giving and caring. And of course, smoking hot. Basically, she was perfect.

"Great? You can't be serious."

"Of course I'm serious. But let me ask you this. If you're in love with her, why in the hell did you ask her to leave?"

"Because, Ryan, you and I both know I have no business loving anyone. Why would she want to be saddled with the mess that is my life?"

"Your life doesn't have to be a mess, Tal. You can get help."

"The last time I tried to get help, I ended up at the ER."

"So? No one ever said this was going to be easy."

"Easy? Aren't I due for some easy at this point? My life has been anything but."

My brother placed his hand on my forearm. We brothers hardly ever touched each other, and though I knew it was for comfort, it only made me *un*comfortable.

"I know you haven't had it easy."

"You know. But you don't really *know*." I downed another gulp of my whiskey. Good stuff.

"No, I don't," my brother said solemnly. "Neither Joe nor I have ever claimed to know exactly what you went through. And you've never really opened up about it."

"Would you have opened up about it, if it had happened to you?"

Ryan shook his head. "Talon, I sure don't know. I'd like to think I would've gotten some help."

I thumped my fist on the bar, making both of our glasses rattle. "You have no idea what you would do."

"Look, I didn't mean to hit a nerve."

No, my brothers never meant to hit a nerve. But they did sometimes. And it wasn't their fault.

"I'm...sorry," I said.

I hated those two words, and usually they had to be pulled kicking and screaming from my lips. They came a bit easier this time. In fact, they had been coming easier and easier since I'd met Jade.

"It's okay, bro. No worries."

I finished my second whiskey. "I've got to get going."

"Oh, no, you don't. You know, Joe mentioned that Jade was getting under your skin somehow. I can see she got under further than either he or I could ever imagine."

I cleared my throat. More even than *I* could've ever imagined.

"I'm going to call Joe. I want him to come over, and the three of us can talk."

I shook my head. "I don't think I can do it."

"Look, *you* came over here. I can count on the fingers of one hand how many times you've gone out of your way to come see me. Which makes me think this is something serious. Let me ask you, Tal. Are you ready to go back to the doc?"

I'd seen a psychologist, Dr. Melanie Carmichael, one time. Twenty-five years had gone by before I'd taken that initiative. Twenty-five years... Why had I done it? For Jade, of course. "Nothing really matters anymore," I said. "Jade is gone."

"You can ask her to come back."

I clenched my jaw. "I can't."

"I don't get it. Did she rebuff you or something?"

"No."

"So she doesn't know you're in love with her?"

"No," I said again.

"Don't you think you should tell her?"

For the third time, I said, "No."

Ryan rubbed his chin. "Is there any chance she might return your feelings?"

How I dreamed of it. Part of me wanted nothing more than the white picket fence and Jade at home, her belly swelling with my child. But any chance of a normal life for me had been erased from my existence twenty-five years ago. Did she return my feelings? How could she? I was a fucked-up mess.

"I doubt it."

"Why would you say that?"

"Well, for one, I kicked her out of my house."

Ryan nodded. "Yeah, there's that."

"And you know me, Ry. I'm a mess. She deserves... better. Hell, she deserves the best."

"Talon, you *are* the best."

I couldn't help a loud scoff. "Don't even go there with me. I am the best of nothing."

"I disagree. You're the best brother I could have."

I rolled my eyes.

"I'm serious. You saved me that day. How many other people would've done that? You could have easily been the one to get away. You were bigger and stronger. But you stayed there, kicking and screaming, getting them off me so I could get away." Ryan shook his head. "I wish there were a way to thank you for that. Some way to let you know just how grateful I am that you're my brother."

I squirmed in my chair like a little kid, belying my thirty-five years. This wasn't the first time Ryan had gone all sappy on me. Truth was, all it did was make me wish I were listening to fingernails on a chalkboard.

"You would have done the same for me."

"But I didn't. I got away. I could've stayed and helped you fight them off."

"For God's sake, Ryan, you were seven years old. They were three grown men. We were lucky one of us got away. They could've easily overtaken both of us."

"My point is, you didn't have to be thinking about me.

We were both just kids. Most other kids would have just thought about saving themselves, but not you. You thought of me first."

Ryan liked to make me out to be some kind of hero, but a hero was so far from what I was. The first day I met Jade, she called me a hero because I'd served in the military. I told her the same thing I told Ryan now. "I'm no hero."

"You are to me, bro."

I squirmed again. Could this get any more awkward? Thankfully, my thoughts were interrupted by a pounding on the door.

Ryan stood. "Who in the hell could that be on a Saturday night?"

The door clicked open. "Is Talon here?"

My sister's voice. *Shit.*

A few seconds later, Marj stormed into the family room. "So *there* you are. It might interest you to know that I just finished an hour-long conversation with Jade. How could you be so cruel?"

My sister, being ten years younger than I, didn't know anything about those horrific events twenty-five years ago. My mother had been pregnant with her at the time.

"What did she say?"

"Nothing I care to repeat. But she's coming back tomorrow."

I opened my mouth to speak, but she held up a hand.

"Don't bother. She will not come back to the house. Oh, I wanted her to, but she refused. Because of *you*, apparently. She's going to stay in the hotel in town until she can find a nice apartment."

Emotions thick as syrup gushed through me. I was being pulled two ways. Joy that Jade would be returning warred with the iron-clawed horror of my past that would ultimately come between us. Relief that she wouldn't be at the house, a constant temptation for me, brawled with heart-wrenching anguish that she would not be where I could see her every day.

My sister was still running off at the mouth. "If you ever come between my best friend and me again, Talon, I swear to God I will never speak to you again." She turned to face Ryan. "And you either."

"Hey, what did I do?" Ryan asked.

"The two of you and Joe are hiding something. My guess is Jade stumbled upon it, or maybe we both did when we found those documents the other night. Whatever it is you're trying to keep from me, I *will* find it. Do not underestimate me." Marjorie turned with a huff and walked out of the family room.

Ryan pursed his lips. "I really don't like where this is headed, bro."

I threaded my fingers through my dark hair. Neither did I.

CHAPTER FOUR

JADE

"It's not the Ritz, but it's better than the place I stayed last night."

Marjorie looked at me, her eyes wide. "Where did you stay last night? Or do I want to know?"

"Some little fleabag called Crazy Hearts Motel."

Marj shook her head. "Oh, Jade, that is the worst. They rent rooms by the hour there, and I've heard they have a bedbug problem."

Crap. Now I was itching all over. Psychosomatic. Had to be. "I'm trying to save for a down payment on a car, Marj."

Marj wrapped her arms around me. "As long as I am on this earth, you never have to stay in a place like that. You read me?"

"You know I hate taking advantage of people."

"You are my best friend in the whole world. I want you to take advantage of me. What's mine is yours."

I smiled, my eyes dewing up a bit. Marjorie truly was the best friend in the world. Even though she was a spoiled prima donna in some ways, she was one of the most giving people I knew. I had no doubt she'd give me the shirt off her back if I needed it. I sat down on the queen-size bed in the modest room of the Snow Creek Inn. I could deal with this for a couple days until I found an apartment.

Marj sat down beside me. "Well, it's Sunday, and as you know, nothing's open in a small town. First thing tomorrow, you and I go apartment hunting."

I laughed. "First thing tomorrow, I have to go to work. I never actually got the chance to quit my job, and now I'm glad I didn't."

Marj give me a friendly punch in the arm. "Touché. Then tomorrow morning, I will start apartment hunting for you."

Yes, Marj was a giving person. However, I wasn't sure that her idea of a suitable apartment for me would match my own. She'd no doubt find someone luxurious place I couldn't afford. "That would be really nice if you did that. It will certainly save me a lot of time. But you know I can only afford the bare minimum. I need to save for a car and my student loan payments start next month." I shuddered to think of the large payment that would be sucked from my checking account.

"All of this would be a moot point if you would come back to the house."

I vehemently shook my head. "I can't."

"But you *can*, Jade. If you're truly in love with my brother, you need to talk to him and work this out."

"It can't be worked out. He was upfront with me. He told me he could never love me, and I believed it when he said it. I have no reason to assume that has changed."

"That is the most ridiculous thing I've ever heard. Talon may be quiet, and he may have some struggles in his life, but he's as capable of love as anyone is. He's a wonderful brother, and he would do anything for me or Ryan or Joe. I know. He has a lot of love to give, Jade. Don't give up on him." She squeezed my hand. "Plus, I would love to have you as a sister-in-law."

I couldn't help but laugh out loud. "That will never happen."

"Never say never."

But I did mean never. "Marj, something is eating Talon. I mean that seriously. Something is constantly gnawing at him, poisoning him. I don't know what it is, and even if I asked him about it, he would clam up like he always does. Until he can face what's eating him alive, he can't love me. He's incapable of it. He was telling me the truth when he told me he wouldn't love me. I went into it knowing. I just didn't expect to fall in love with him."

"I don't think Talon's ever had a girlfriend," Marj said. "Even back in high school. I remember Joe and Ryan dating, but I never remember Talon bringing a girl home. I was just a kid, around five, so I could easily have missed it." She cleared her throat. "And I know he has women in the city."

There went the dagger into my heart again. I knew about Talon's tarts in the city. He'd made that pretty clear when he told me how he had his blood tested every six months for STDs and always used condoms. That was one sexually active person. Why else would he be so obsessive-compulsive about getting his blood tested so often?

I bit my lip.

"I'm sorry," Marj said. "I didn't think about how hard it would be for you to hear that."

I shook my head. "It's not news to me, believe me. He was upfront with me about how he views women. He takes what is offered and then leaves. I knew that when I went into it, as I said. I shouldn't be surprised by any of this. I had just hoped..."

"What? That you could save him?"

A tear trickled down my cheek as I nodded.

"Oh, Jade. I'm so sorry. But you know as well as I do that no one can save Talon except for Talon."

Is that what I had wanted? To be the savior of Talon Steel?

For the first time, I admitted it to myself. Yes. I had wanted to save him. Whatever was eating him up inside, I wanted to be the one to free him from it.

And I had failed.

I turned into Marjorie's shoulder and cried.

★ ★ ★

Larry called me into his office as soon as I got in the next morning. He sat at his desk, blond and balding as ever, wearing a navy blue blazer that looked too tight across the shoulders. I took a seat across from him.

"Are you doing okay today, Jade?" he asked. "Your eyes are a little red."

I cleared my throat. Since I had cried half the night, my eyes looked like hell. "I'm fine. I had an allergy attack this morning, but I took an antihistamine, so I'll be fine soon."

"An antihistamine?"

"Don't worry, the non-drowsy kind."

"Good, good. I have a new assignment I want you to work on. I need some heavy-duty investigation."

New assignment? Sounded great to me. Anything to get my mind off my troubles. "Happy to help. What do you need?"

"I need you to dig up whatever information you can find on the Steel family."

I jerked in my chair but caught myself. So much for getting my mind off my troubles. "The Steel family? You mean Marjorie and her brothers?"

Larry nodded and took a sip of coffee. "Yes."

"May I ask what case this is for?"

"You may ask, but I can't give you an answer. It's classified."

Classified, indeed. I knew well enough that Larry's ethics were bendable. He wanted information on the Steels for some reason, and I would bet it had nothing to do with any current case. He'd mentioned when I first started my job that he'd known the Steels since they were kids. Something niggled at the back of my neck. Larry was up to no good.

After Larry had insisted, despite my myriad conflicts of interest, that I work on the case against Talon when my ex-fiancé had him arrested for assault and battery, I knew his ethics were practically nonexistent. I hadn't squawked too much about taking Talon's case because I'd wanted to make sure he was treated fairly and didn't have to do any prison time. I'd worked him a pretty sweet deal, but I'd made myself a promise as well. Never again would I compromise my ethics for this job or any other.

I was about to go back on that promise.

I didn't delude myself for a millisecond that Larry's reason for wanting me to dig up information on the Steels had any validity, but I had my own reasons for wanting to know more about them, and with the city's sources at my disposal, I'd be in a great position to find out exactly what I wanted to.

So I smiled and nodded. "Absolutely. Glad to do it. Is there any type of information in particular that you're looking for?"

Larry handed me a stack of manila folders. "There's been some speculation that Bradford Steel was involved in organized crime and money laundering."

Talon's father? "I guess I don't understand why that's of any importance. Bradford Steel is dead. Do you have reason to believe the Steels are still involved?"

"That's part of what I want you to find out, Jade. Even if they aren't, a lot of their assets might be seizeable as dirty money. Our evidence goes back further than Bradford. His father, George Steel, was also allegedly involved."

"And what evidence might this be?"

Classified. I heard the word before he said it.

"I'm afraid that's classified."

"Isn't this a little out of our jurisdiction? Shouldn't the FBI be involved? Or at the very least the Colorado Bureau of Investigation?"

"Are you questioning me?"

"I'm just trying to understand exactly what you're looking for."

"Take a gander through the files I just gave you. They'll be a good starting point. I don't want to bring in the Bureau unless we find anything hard. That's why we're keeping this local and under wraps for now. No reason to screw up the lives of nice people like the Steels if you don't have to, right?"

I nodded. "Right. I understand."

I understood all right. Larry wanted to screw the Steels, and I doubted it had anything to do with organized crime or dirty money.

So I'd be doing three investigations. I'd investigate the Steels for Larry. I'd also investigate the Steels for myself. And third, for Marj. Last week, she and I had done a little investigating of our own in the basement of the ranch house. We came across her birth certificate, giving her first name as Angela, something she never knew. Her father had always told her that her first name was Marjorie and she didn't have a middle name. We also found the marriage certificate for Bradford and Daphne Steel, Marjorie's parents. The certificate had listed Daphne's maiden name as Wade, rather than Warren, which Marjorie had always thought it was.

I took the file folders. "I'll get right on it. When do you need this information?"

"As soon as possible, though I don't have any particular deadline. I'm more interested in accurate information, and I think you'll have to do some digging to find what I need. So I don't expect you to be in any hurry. Just do the best you can and keep me apprised every few days."

I nodded. "Understood."

"And in the meantime, if I need you to work on something more important, I'll just pull you off this for a few days."

I nodded again and left. I walked into my office and sat down at my desk. Before I even looked inside the file folders, I decided to do a little investigation of my own.

I keyed in the appropriate passwords to access Colorado records. First, the marriage certificate.

I typed in Steel, Bradford and Wade, Daphne.

Nothing.

My skin chilled. I had seen the original marriage certificate with my own eyes, and it was between Bradford Raymond Steel and Daphne Kay Wade.

I got my bearings and typed in Steel, Bradford and Warren, Daphne.

Bingo. Everything else on the certificate was the same— their birth dates, the date of the marriage, the signatures...

My heart did a jump. Was the marriage certificate that Marjorie and I found a forgery? Or had someone gotten into the Colorado database and changed Daphne's name?

Next I accessed records of birth. I pulled up Jonah's, Ryan's, and Talon's. All were identical to the copies we'd found in the Steels' basement. I inhaled and typed in Angela Marjorie Steel.

No record.

I typed in Marjorie Steel.

Bingo again. Marj's birth certificate popped up, minus her unknown first name.

Why would anyone change these? Again, I wondered if the documents we found were forgeries or whether someone had accessed the Colorado database. That would not be an easy thing to do.

Unless one was a city attorney maybe? I shook my head, erasing the thought. Larry had the same access to the files that I did. He didn't have authority to change them. If he had that kind of authority, he certainly didn't need me to do his investigating for him.

I couldn't imagine who might have that authority and who the Steels—or possibly someone else—could've gotten to make the changes. Or why they wanted the changes made anyway.

I made quick copies of both documents to show Marj later. Then I opened the first folder on the stack Larry had given me.

It was full of bank-account records from the Cayman Islands. Criminals often kept their money in Cayman banks due to the bank secrecy laws and reduced taxation. Those were also perfectly good reasons for anyone with a lot of money to bank there...and the Steels did have a lot of money. More so than I could've even imagined, as I cruised through these bank accounts.

There were bank accounts in all of the Steels' names and many in names I assumed were dummy corporations set up to move funds around. Still, I didn't see anything out of the ordinary. The Steels had money. That was certainly no crime. And just because they banked in the Caymans didn't automatically mean their money was dirty.

The next two folders contained more bank accounts, some of which were hopelessly outdated.

My eyes were bugging out from looking at all the numbers.

I felt like I was working at cross purposes. I both did

and didn't want to find something. I certainly didn't want to find out that the Steels were involved in anything illegal, but I did want to find anything that might help me uncover the secret that Talon was keeping and that Jonah and Ryan were helping him keep. These bank accounts did nothing to help me figure out why the marriage certificate and name certificate had been changed.

I doubted any of their money was dirty, at least not the current Steel money. I had witnessed how hard both Jonah and Ryan worked at the ranch. Talon too, when he was out at the orchards. He knew his stuff, and I couldn't wait until the Fuji apples were ready. And the peaches... Colorado Western slope peaches... Nothing better.

More bank statements in the next folder. Had Larry only given me bank accounts?

At one o'clock, I took a quick break to walk over to Rita's Café and have some spinach quiche, and then I got straight back to work.

At about two thirty, Larry walked into my office. "How's it going?"

I looked up from the millionth bank account I was reviewing, my neck now stiff and aching. "Still looking through the files."

He let out a chuckle. "Yup, there's a lot of them. If there's one thing the Steels have, it's money."

I smiled. "Is there anything specific you want me to look for?"

"Just anything that doesn't look quite right. The fact that they bank in the Caymans and in Switzerland is a red flag, as far as I'm concerned."

I nodded. "It can be. Though they might just bank there because of the laws."

"I thought of that, but better safe than sorry. Let's see what we can find." He walked out the door.

Why did I have the distinct feeling that the city of Snow Creek was paying me to do someone else's dirty work?

★ ★ ★

I left right at five o'clock, my eyes crossing from all the numbers. One more folder to look at, but it would wait until tomorrow. A whole day's work, and all I had learned was that the Steels were loaded. That they'd always been loaded.

I stopped at Rita's again, got a sandwich to go, and headed down the street to my hotel. Living in a small town was great. Everything was within walking distance. I might not like it when winter came, but right now was perfect. By winter, maybe I'd have saved up enough for a car.

Up in my room, I shed my work attire, washed the makeup off my face, and got into a pair of cutoffs and a David Bowie T-shirt. I hadn't brought the extra file home as I normally would have. I really needed a break from those numbers. I grabbed a bottle of water out of my mini fridge and sat down on the bed to eat my sandwich.

Midway through my first bite, a knock sounded on the door. "Hold on," I said, my mouth full of turkey.

I gulped down the bite, took a quick drink of water, crossed to the door, and opened it.

CHAPTER FIVE

TALON

She just stood there, looking luscious in those damned Daisy Duke shorts of hers and a David Bowie T-shirt. I'd have thought she was too young to be a Bowie fan. Whatever. The word "Bowie" was stretched out across her delicious tits.

Had it just been three nights ago that I had kicked her out of my house and out of my life? She stood, her hands on her hips, her ruby lips glistening, her golden-brown hair tumbling over her shoulders, and my groin tightened. How had I ever thought I could live without her?

I loved her. I'd had a hard time admitting that to Ryan last night, because I had actually been admitting it to myself. But did I? Really? I didn't even know what love was, at least not this kind of love. Perhaps I was feeling something else entirely. I probably didn't possess the capacity to love.

Still, the words "I love you" were on the tip of my tongue as I looked into her silvery-blue eyes.

"What do you want, Talon?"

Her. I wanted her. Just seeing her again made my dick hard, but I couldn't just grab her and kiss her, not after how I'd treated her.

"Are you going to actually speak, or are you going to just stand there with your mouth hanging open?"

Then again...

I stepped through the doorway, gripped her shoulders, pulled her to me, and pressed my lips to hers.

She opened for me instantly, as I knew she would. We couldn't resist each other. Was she as obsessed with me as I was with her?

Smack! She broke the kiss and pushed me away from her. Hard. My back hit the wall right next to the door that was still open.

"Stop it," she said, her eyes on fire. "That isn't going to work this time."

"It worked every other time," I said.

"Every other time you hadn't kicked me out of your house and out of your life. This is bullshit, Talon. Nothing more than bullshit. Now I asked you once before. What are you doing here?"

What was I doing there? I couldn't answer her when I didn't know. All I knew is that I had to see her, touch her, know she still existed in the universe. "Do you...want to go to dinner?"

She pointed to half a sandwich and a takeout bag from Rita's sitting on the bed. "I've already got dinner, and I'd like to get back to it. So please leave."

I turned and closed the door to her hotel room, locking the deadbolt.

"I told you, leave." Her full lips trembled.

God, I wanted her. My body reacted to her very presence. I quivered before her, the effect as unsettling as it was arousing. How had I been so stupid to think that kicking her out of my home would make the desire go way?

I hadn't been that stupid. I'd known I'd never be free of her.

Could she help me? Could she heal me?

No one could heal me. I was a broken man, a shattered soul. But when I was with Jade, in her arms, her lips on mine, I became someone different. Someone almost... special. Special didn't make me any less broken or any less shattered, but it gave me something I'd never had before.

Hope.

"I said leave," she repeated.

I owed her that much. I would go, and I wouldn't come back until she invited me. I turned toward the door, my gaze zeroing in on the peephole at eye level. *Please, Talon. Leave her in peace. She deserves that. Hell, she deserves the best.*

But my feet were stuck in blocks of concrete.

★ ★ ★

"Run, boy. Run."

The evil laughter of the three masked men whirled around the boy's head, almost visible—black swirls of smoke morphing into devilish images.

"What are you waiting for, boy? We've left the door open for you. Can't you see the light up there? How long has it been since you've seen light, boy?"

The boy stood at the bottom of the stairs in the cold dark cellar where he was kept. They had finished with him and then led him, his legs wobbly like jelly, over to the landing, where the open door pointed the way to daylight.

To salvation.

His legs itched to run, to scramble up the stairs and never look back.

But they would never let him go. This was a tease, just like all the other teases that amused the three monsters. He'd tried it once before. He'd gotten to this top of the stairs and then been grabbed and forced back down. His punishment had been taking the big one, the one with the tattoo of the flaming bird, into his mouth.

"Go on, boy. You can go. We're done with you."

How he longed to escape. How he wanted to keep running until his legs could carry him no farther.

But his feet were stuck in blocks of concrete.

★ ★ ★

I couldn't leave. I wanted to leave for her sake, but I couldn't. I was too weak. Too weak to climb the stairs away from her. She had a hold on me. I didn't understand it, but it was there. As sure as the sun would rise tomorrow, it was there.

I turned to face her, her hands again on her hips, her red lips swollen from our brief kiss. I walked toward her slowly, taking in all of her sweetness, her goodness, her pure heart. When I was close enough to touch her arm, I looked into her steely blue gaze and muttered only one word.

"Please."

The beautiful lines of her face softened. "That might be the first time I've ever heard you say that word, Talon. Outside the heat of passion, that is."

The fact that she was right hit my gut like a brick. Had I become so hardened by my life that I was incapable of common courtesy?

I had.

I touched one of her cheeks, thumbing the apple. Her skin was soft as silk under my fingertips. She closed her eyes, turning into my hand. She softly grazed my palm with her lips.

I lowered my head and touched my mouth to hers. She opened, as she always did, but this kiss was different. Then it dawned on me why.

I was *giving* her a kiss.

Such simple words. So simple and so apparent, but something that had eluded me for so long.

Instead of taking a kiss from her, I was giving a kiss *to* her.

And it was a sweet kiss indeed.

She slid her soft tongue against mine, infusing me with her strawberry-champagne essence. She melded her body into me, her soft breasts pressing against my chest. Though my dick was hard, as it always was in her presence, my first thought wasn't getting into her pants as it usually was. My first thought was showing her that I could give too.

I had wanted to solely give to her for a while now. Perhaps I had begun that journey, but with this kiss, I gave with all my heart and soul. Everything that I was, broken as it might be, I gave to her with that kiss. I gave it to her without any idea of getting anything in return.

And in all the giving, I received something so much sweeter. The kiss she gave me back was more beautiful and more profound than any kiss we'd shared. It wasn't our most passionate kiss, it wasn't our most ferocious kiss, but it meant so much more than all of those kisses put together.

I love you, Jade. I love—

She broke the kiss, stumbled backward, and crossed her arms over her chest.

"Please," I said again. I pushed her farther back until her legs hit the bed and she sat down. I sat next to her and kissed her again, softly, slowly, sliding my hand down, cupping one of her soft mounds. I pressed my lips to her beautiful mouth, and then I pulled back and simply looked at her for a few scant seconds. Then I kissed her again. I pulled her tank top up and unclasped her bra. God, such beauty. Jade was a goddess. She didn't resist as I licked her nipples. They were hard, but I tamped down the urge to pinch and bite them. I tongued them gently, and then I returned to her face, kissing those full cherry lips once more.

I slid my lips over her neck. She reached up and cupped my cheek, her fingers warm and satiny. I lifted my head and looked into her eyes, her blue gaze melting me. With her thumb, she tugged on my lower lip.

"Take off your shirt," she said.

I shook my head. I wanted this to be about her first.

I stood and pushed her down so she was lying on the bed. I slid off her Daisy Dukes and her underwear and spread her legs as I knelt on the floor. Slowly I stroked my tongue up her slit while I reached forward and grabbed her breasts, squeezing them lightly.

She moaned. God, the sweet sound. I could never live without hearing those melodic sighs from Jade. I gave one nipple a slight tweak. Not a hard pinch like she was used to from me.

"More, Talon. Pinch me."

I shook my head between her thighs and continued to lick her glossy folds. Her musky apple taste tantalized me, and I inhaled, savoring the smell as well as the flavor. My God, she was amazing. Her sighs drifted to my ears, and I couldn't help myself. One arm wandered upward, and I pinched a nipple.

She jerked beneath me. Another soft moan escaped her lips.

I continued to eat her, sucking out her sweet cream. Her juices gushed over my chin.

When she was good and swollen and I could feel her on the edge, I shoved two fingers inside her heat. She climaxed around me. Every one of her contractions convulsed through me, taking me to the highest peak in Colorado. Each tremor, each quake—I felt them as if they were my own, my pulse racing, my cock throbbing.

When her release subsided, she pulled me to her and kissed me hard. The mingling of our saliva and her juices intoxicated me. I swirled my tongue around hers, taking the flavor, the passion...until I remembered I wanted only to give.

She broke the kiss, pushing me away slightly. "Please, Talon, take off your shirt, take off your pants. I want to suck that gorgeous cock of yours."

How could I turn that down? I moved slightly, planning to stand, when again I remembered. *This is about her. Only her. I want to give.* "No, baby. This is about you."

She let out a giggle. "That's sweet, really, but believe

me, sucking you *is* about me. I'm dying to do it right now."

My name notwithstanding, I wasn't made of steel. I'd take her word that she wanted this, because damn, I sure did. I was harder than I'd ever been. I stood and slowly disrobed, her fiery light-blue gaze never wandering from me. When my cock sprang free of its confinement, she dropped to her knees and licked the bobbing head.

Fuck... I gathered every last shred of willpower I possessed. I longed to explode down her throat, but I also wanted this amazing sensation to last. She took such care, raining tiny kisses along the underside and then twirling her tongue over my balls while working me with her fist. Shudders raced through me, boiling my blood in my veins. When she returned her mouth to my cock and plunged onto me, I nearly lost it.

But no, I wanted to come inside that sweet pussy of hers. My heart stampeding, I pulled her off my cock, turned her around, bent her over the bed, and plunged inside her wet heat.

And again that soft sigh—the gentle caress of her vocal cords that I loved—escaped her lips as I entered her. With that sigh she became mine.

Or at least I imagined that she *could* be mine.

Her walls clenched around me, fitting my cock as though the universe had cast her to be my perfect match. As if she had been created for me. Only me.

I thrust and I thrust and I thrust and I thrust and I thrust—trembling, quivering—until I withdrew and flipped her over so her beautiful face was visible to me. Her gaze caught mine, and God, I could drown in those shining eyes.

alled in sick, so he asked her to fill in. He had a bunch of

ling that had to be done with the Secretary of State."

That explained why she hadn't called yet. "No problem.

'll scan the paper tomorrow morning and maybe look at

ome places over my lunch hour."

"I wish you'd come back to the house."

I shook my head. "Believe me, I thought about it. I

an't."

"Why not?"

Sometimes I couldn't believe the things that came out

f his mouth. "Because you kicked me out in no uncertain

rms three short days ago."

He stood, gathering his boxers and jeans and putting

1em on quickly. His gorgeous torso was still bare, still

listening with perspiration from our encounter. He was

beautiful. When I looked at him, when I saw through his

visible walls, I wanted nothing more than to hold him,

take all this pain away. Before I could do that, though, I

eeded to know what the pain was and why he was so closed

f from everyone. I didn't know how to find that out. Marj

dn't know, and if Jonah and Ryan did, they certainly

eren't talking.

"I shouldn't have kicked you out like that," he said.

"But you did, Talon, and you had a reason at the time.

ll me something. Does that reason still exist?"

He didn't speak, only bit his lower lip slightly and let

jo.

"I deserve an answer."

He raked his fingers through his thick head of dark hair.

ou know, I saw a gray hair in the mirror this morning."

I sat up on the bed, she still lying down, and stuffed my cock inside her again. I held one leg of hers up over my shoulder, opening her to take me fully.

She closed her eyes and moaned. "God, Talon, that's so good. I've missed you."

She'd missed me? I grabbed both of her beautiful tits and squeezed, her nipples hard. I pinched them the way she liked.

Words strained at my lips. How I wanted to say I'd missed her, too. That my life had been empty for the three days without her. Instead I leaned down and kissed her softly, tugging on one of her nipples.

She jolted against me. "Talon, I'm coming again. Oh my God, I'm coming."

She convulsed around my shaft, and I cried out. I was on the edge of the precipice, looking down into nirvana, but I wasn't ready to come. I slowed my thrusts a little, willing myself to wait. But it was too late.

One more plunge, and I erupted inside her, giving her everything that I was. Through each spasm that sent me farther and farther into heaven, I gave. And I gave. And I gave her some more. When my climax ebbed, I pulled her up to me, wrapped her legs around me, and kissed her softly, as we had at the beginning of this lovemaking. I looked deeply into those steely blue eyes, aching to give her even more—all that was my heart, my soul.

Could I?

The question was moot. I had already given it to her. I only prayed that she would keep it safe.

CHAPTER SIX

JADE

So tenderly, he kissed me.

How had I let this happen? I had so wanted to be strong, but any fortitude I possessed was useless where Talon Steel was concerned. I would always surrender to him. My only escape would be to leave Colorado altogether and get as far away from him as I could.

But I wouldn't do that. Colorado was my home. I'd lived here all my life. I could go back to Denver, but he would find me.

I *wanted* him to find me.

I love you. Those words sat on the edge of my lips, hungering to spew forth. I clamped my mouth shut. He wasn't ready to hear those words.

And I wasn't ready to say them.

He pulled away from the kiss and gazed into my eyes, his own burning black. I waited for him to speak, but he did not.

"Talon."

He arched his eyebrows.

"That shouldn't have happened."

I expected him to agree with me. He always agreed with

me about that. Had always been the one to say [he would] never fall in love with me, that this would not happ[en.]

But instead, he said, "That needed to happen, [...]"

I had no idea what he meant, and asking him t[o explain] it would do no good. Talon didn't explain things.

"I'm glad it happened," I said, my voice low.

His dark eyes smoldered. "I'm glad you came [back.]"

My eyebrows shot up. Had I heard him correct[ly? Who] are? You kicked me out, remember?"

"I was wrong to do that."

"You were?"

"Yes. You're Marj's best friend. She wants you h[ere,] needs you here."

My heart fell. The barriers had risen once m[ore. He] was glad I was back for Marj's sake, not his own.

I knew better than to try to get through to Tal[on when] he was walled off. I didn't believe him for a min[ute, but] pressuring him would do no good. When the blocka[de went] up, it became impenetrable.

"Well, I didn't want to leave Marj either." I [looked] away. I couldn't stare into his beautiful eyes when [he was] barricaded. It was too painful, like a blade slicing m[y heart] in two.

"Marj would like you to come back and stay [at the] house," he said.

I blew out a breath of air. "As much as I love it [at the] house, I don't think that's a good idea. Marj is going [to help] me find an apartment. In fact, she was supposed [to today,] today, but I haven't heard from her yet."

"She was pretty busy today helping Joe. His se[cretary]

What did that have to do with anything? He was thirty-five. Of course he had a gray hair or two. Jonah had more than a few at his temples. It looked good.

"Please don't change the subject. This is too important to me."

"Maybe my gray hair is important to me."

I shook my head, stood, grabbed my shorts and tank, and threw them on without my bra and underpants. "Leave, please."

He widened his eyes. Did he truly have no idea why I was asking him to leave?

"You hurt me," I said.

He swallowed visibly, put on his shirt, and left my hotel room.

★ ★ ★

The next morning, I sat at my desk, scanning the local paper for possible apartments. The only one within walking distance to work was a room over the local beauty shop, and I didn't relish smelling perm fumes all day. There were a couple of cute one-bedrooms on the outskirts of town, but until I had a car, that wouldn't be feasible. So the beauty shop it was. I called Sarah, the shop owner, and arranged to take a look at the apartment over my lunch hour. Then I went back to work, opening the last folder of the stack Larry had given me yesterday.

The first few documents were still more bank accounts. Sheesh, these people had a lot of cash. Still, from what I could tell, all the deposits and withdrawals seemed legitimate—until something stood out at me almost as if it had been written in glaring red.

Twenty-five years ago, a withdrawal of five million dollars had been made from one of the operating accounts. I couldn't tell from the bank account to whom the payment had been made. I would need to go through a bunch of documentation to find out where it had gone and why. Such a large amount of money had to go somewhere.

I hastily went through the rest of the documents in the last folder, but nothing stood out as important.

A few minutes later, Larry walked into my office. "Any luck?"

"As you probably know, all these folders that you gave me yesterday are mostly bank accounts. Honestly, I didn't see anything that looked untoward until this morning."

He came closer and sat down in one of the chairs opposite my desk. "What's that?"

I pushed the requisite paper in front of him. "See that withdrawal of five million? It's an incredible sum of money, much more than any of these other withdrawals. It just seemed to stand out to me. I wonder what it was for."

"That is worthy of note." He shoved a piece of paper with more private log-ins and passwords written on it. "I'm giving you full access to all databases in the state of Colorado. See what you can find." He smiled and exited my office, leaving the door open.

I didn't know where to start. I doubted I had access to any bank files, so how would I find out? I couldn't ask any of the Steels. Heck, Marj had barely been born and the guys had been kids when this happened. They wouldn't be any help at all. Their father was dead, and as far as I knew, they never had anyone else working around the ranch who would have had access to their accounts. But maybe... Steel Acres was a multi-million-dollar enterprise. Surely they didn't handle all the money themselves. But how would I find out who had been handling it twenty-five years ago? Asking the Steels wasn't an option. I couldn't exactly tell them that my boss, the city attorney, had asked me to investigate them, nor could I tell them I had my own reasons for doing the detective work.

What happened twenty-five years ago? That's what I needed to know.

I looked through the old newspaper archives and so far had come up with dead ends, when the alarm on my phone beeped. Time to go meet Sarah at the beauty shop and look at the apartment. I grabbed my purse, told Michelle I was leaving for lunch, and headed out.

The shop was two blocks over on Headley Avenue. I walked in.

The manicurist looked up from her station. "Hey there, can I help you?"

"Yeah, hi. I'm here to see Sarah about the apartment upstairs."

"Awesome sauce." The manicurist flashed a scarlet-lipped grin. "She's in the back. I'll go get her."

She left her client. Within a few minutes, she was back with a middle-aged woman, slightly plump but pretty, her blond—clearly colored—hair pulled back in a ponytail.

The older woman held out her hand. "I'm Sarah Carter. You must be Jade."

"Yes, I am. Great to meet you."

"I only have a few minutes. I have a client processing. But the place is small." She laughed. "It won't take too long for me to show it to you. Come on back."

The apartment was accessible from the back of the beauty shop as well as from the outside. Sarah led me up a flight of narrow stairs. She unlocked the door and opened it.

"It ain't much, but it's cheap. I'm your landlord. I own the building, and I live in the apartment next door. Just these two apartments. One of my girls was renting it, but she got married last week, so we're vacant again."

I looked around. I liked the hardwood floors, although they were in need of a good buffing.

"No bedroom, I'm afraid, but the living area is huge, so you can use a futon at night. I updated the appliances in the kitchen two years ago, so they're nearly new. Updated the bathroom too. It's small, but state of the art."

"It's actually pretty cute." I was getting a good vibe from it, which surprised me. And heck, a manicure was only a couple steps away. I loved a good mani-pedi.

I looked through the kitchen and then the bathroom. "I assume it's ready now to move in?"

"Yup. All you have to do is sign the lease."

"Are you willing to go month-to-month?" As cute as the place was, I'd be moving into one of those better apartments on the outskirts of town when I got a car.

"Absolutely. Most of my tenants go month-to-month. Because the place is so small, it's really just a starter pad. Usually people are here for six months to a year."

"That sounds perfect to me. I work over at the city

attorney's office, so it's close enough to walk. I don't have a car right now."

"Sounds like you're interested, then."

I nodded. "I definitely am. I don't have any furniture though. I'll have to arrange for a mattress or futon before I could move in."

Sarah nodded. "I can help you there. If you want the place furnished, it's an extra fifty a month. I can move in a sofa, a coffee table, two chairs, and a pullout bed. Lisa had her own stuff, so the furnishings are in storage down in the shop. I can have my boyfriend move them up anytime."

I let out a laugh. "By the end of the day?"

"You betcha."

I held out my hand. "Then, Sarah, you've got a deal. I'll write you a check right now for the first month."

That transaction taken care of, I headed over to the hotel, grabbed my suitcase, let them know I wouldn't be staying another night, and took my stuff over to my new apartment. By then my lunch hour was over, so I stopped by Rita's to grab a sandwich to go and headed back to the office. These sandwiches were adding up and squashing my car fund. I'd need to get to the grocery store and lay in supplies.

No sooner had I logged back in, when my phone buzzed. *Marj.*

"Hey there," I said.

"Jade, I'm so sorry I couldn't find an apartment yesterday. Joe needed some help because his secretary was sick and he had some filings that couldn't wait."

"I know." *Shit!* I cuffed my hand over my mouth.

"You know? How?"

I sucked air through my teeth. I had promised Marj no more secrets. "Talon told me."

"Talon? When did you see Talon?"

I sighed into my phone. "He came to see me last night."

Silence on the other end of the line. In my mind's eye, I could see Marj's mouth dropped into an oval.

"I promised I wouldn't keep anything from you, remember?"

"Yes," she said. "I appreciate that."

"He wanted me to come back to the house."

Marj squealed into the phone. "Yay! That's great."

"I turned him down. I don't think it's a good idea right now."

"Are you kidding? It's a great idea."

"Well, it's too late. I'm bound for at least a month for my new apartment. I just signed a month-to-month lease today."

"You did? Where?"

"The apartment over the beauty shop."

Marj huffed. "That dive? I would've found a much better place."

"Marj, I scanned the ads this morning. The only other places are those apartments on the outskirts of town, and I need a car for them, so the beauty shop it is. It's a cute little place."

"If you say so."

"I say so. Remember, I'm used to living modestly. It won't bother me at all."

"I'm sorry." She sighed. "I don't mean to go all diva on you. If you're happy, I'm happy. But I'd still rather have you at the house."

"I know, but it's probably good for me to be on my—"

I dropped the phone.

CHAPTER SEVEN

TALON

I walked into Jonah's office, needing to talk. What was it with me and talking lately?

His secretary was back today, though she looked a little pale.

"Are you feeling better, Dolores?" I asked the gray-haired woman who had once been my father's secretary.

"Yeah. I look a lot worse than I feel."

"Is Joe around?"

"He just went out to the pasture. I think he's in the north quadrant today if you want to go looking for him."

"Thanks."

I drove out to the stables. Several months had gone by since I'd taken my horse, Phoenix, on a ride. I'd go out and find Joe, maybe help him a little if he needed it. I'd already been to the orchards and taken care of things there for the day.

Phoenix snorted when he saw me. The hands exercised him regularly, but I had been lacking in my attention to him lately. I'd had the horse since I was fifteen. I loved animals. This horse and Roger were my best friends.

I groomed him, saddled him up, and took him outside

the barn, where I mounted and took off. The day was clear, the mountains green and violet in the distance, the sky a bright cerulean. Just another day in Colorado. I didn't appreciate the beauty of my home enough. I needed to bask in it more often. I worked Phoenix up to a gallop, letting the wind ruffle my hair as we sailed through the breeze.

Phoenix. I'd named him after that majestic flaming bird rising from the ashes.

★ ★ ★

The one with the low voice grunted, finishing.

"My turn," Tattoo said, pushing Low Voice away.

Tattoo's rancid breath was hot against the boy's neck. The boy winced, scrunching his nose.

"You're nice and lubed up for me now, bitch. I can slide right in and take what I want."

The boy closed his eyes, detaching himself from the horror surrounding him. Above him, Tattoo pumped, but in his mind, the boy was atop a majestic horse, riding into the wind. Nothing in the world mattered except him, his companion, and the acres and acres of green land ahead of him. He could ride all day and never tire of the beautiful Colorado landscape. The wind whisked through his dark hair. Flecks of dust pelted into his eyes, but he didn't care. He was alone and wild and free. No one could hurt him here. No one could hurt him...

Until that last thrust, when Tattoo socked him upside the head, his forearm dangling in the boy's vision, the flaming bird etched there as menacing as the man who bore it.

"That's it, you little pussy. Take it. Take it all."

* * *

A loud noise echoed around me as I catapulted into the air. In slow motion I descended, and—

Thunk!

My ass hit the ground. Phoenix continued galloping.

When had I let go? I hadn't fallen off a horse in... Had I ever?

Of course I had, when I was learning. When I was a kid.

Phoenix. The horse had been a birthday gift from my father when I turned fifteen. I'd hemmed and hawed over naming him. Nothing seemed right. Joe had suggested Midnight, which would have been a good fit. The stallion was a glossy ebony all over. My father had suggested Zeus, because the male who'd sired him had been named Cronus. Both were strong, masculine names, but they didn't work for me. Marjorie, nearly five at the time, had begged me to name him Barney. I almost caved on that one. I had a soft spot for that little girl. After...the...*incident*, she had been the only good I could find in the world—an innocent baby with pink cheeks, dark eyes, and a smile for everyone. In the end, though, I couldn't saddle this impressive, muscular animal with a purple dinosaur's name. He'd stayed nameless for two months...until I saw a poster of a dazzling, colorful bird rising from vibrant multicolored flames at the local five-and-dime.

Phoenix.

That was my horse's name. It spoke of strength, of rebirth, of second chances.

That poster had graced the wall of my room for a decade. As I sat, my ass numb, my head beginning to ache, I conjured the emotions the image had evoked in me—that it still invoked in me, though the poster was long gone.

My heart thundered as the phoenix, as beautiful as it was terrifying, swooped toward me, its flaming wings heating my face. I closed my eyes, breathed...breathed...

The bird had become a contradictory symbol in my life.

I had to rise from the ashes of my past. I had to *be* the phoenix.

But the phoenix represented...hell.

How had all of that escaped me for so long?

Ahead, Phoenix finally slowed to a trot and then stopped. I whistled, and he turned and walked back to me.

I took him over to a small pool of water nearby for a drink. Fresh Rocky Mountain spring water. Nothing like it. I splashed some of the cool liquid on my face.

I sat down, cradling my head in my hands.

What was I going to do? I missed Jade so much that I physically ached when I wasn't with her. How could I have allowed someone to get under my skin like that? How had I become so obsessed? I could never be with her. This I knew as a solid fact. Yet I wanted her back at the house, at my beck and call. I wanted her in my bed every night, my cock in her pussy every night. I wanted to mark her, make her mine.

But that was never to be.

I took the curry comb out of the saddlebag and brushed Phoenix.

Phoenix.

It had been his name for twenty years. I couldn't change

it now. Besides, it fit him. He was a beautiful animal, black as night and sleek as suede. He stood sixteen-and-a-half hands tall at the withers, not a giant but a darn big horse. He was a Morgan—shiny, fast, and friendly.

I loved this animal as much as I loved that little mutt of mine.

And I loved Jade even more—more than my animals, more than my brothers, more than my sister.

Not only more but in a totally different way—and I didn't mean the physical part.

Jade had now become as essential to me as the blood in my veins.

I wasn't sure I could learn to live without her.

I moved to stand, and the small of my back throbbed down to the crease of my ass. I might've bruised my tailbone. Nothing to be done. Time to get back on the horse.

Get back on the horse. I chuckled to myself. What a cliché. I'd heard it so many times before. *Just get back on the horse, Talon. Don't give in to your fear.*

Truth was, I had no fear. I had enlisted in the Marines, hoping I'd go overseas and get my head blown off. It hadn't happened. Instead I blew a few heads off myself and saved some of my fellow servicemen. People liked to call me a hero. Just like Ryan did.

I wasn't a hero.

Heroes could live with themselves.

I was the one who had gone running into the line of fire to drag fallen men back, to make sure they got medical treatment.

That's what people thought, anyway.

But they were wrong.

I ran into fire, trying to get shot.

I never did.

I'd been back on the ranch for three years now, and I still hadn't truly found my place. I was good enough at running the orchard, and even when I didn't feel up to it, I had the best foreman in the business and several under him who could take care of things.

Axel had taken care of things while I was overseas, and the orchards had flourished.

I really wasn't needed here, but every time I tried to leave, my brothers talked me out of it.

They both felt so much guilt over what happened to me. I wished I could free them from it, but I was powerless. I couldn't help anyone, least of all myself. It would be better for them if I left. They could go on with their lives.

But now...

I couldn't bear the thought of leaving Jade.

True, I had kicked her out of my house myself several days earlier, but nothing had felt right when she was gone. She wouldn't come back. As much as I wanted her to, my actions earlier had taken care of that.

I must've scared her. Hell, I'd scared myself. That screaming—and God only knew what else I had done. It was all a blur to me now.

"Come on, fella," I said, mounting Phoenix and wincing at the ache in my tailbone. "Let's go find Joe."

About twenty minutes later, I found my brother and some of his men checking out some steers on the northern quadrant.

"Hey, Tal," Jonah said when I dismounted. "What brings you up here?"

"I suppose you talked to Ryan."

Jonah cleared his throat. "I have. Let's walk a minute." My brother led me away from his men. "So Jade's back."

"Yes, she's staying in the hotel in town."

"Did you try to get her to come back to the house?"

I nodded. "Marj did too. She won't budge."

"Do you blame her?"

I shook my head. I didn't blame her. I'd fucked this up all by myself.

"Ryan says you're in love with her."

I shuffled my feet in the dirt, scuffing up my ostrich boots. "I am. At least I think I am. I don't really know what it is to love someone in that way."

My brother cracked a smile. "You know when you feel it, Tal. If you feel like you're in love with her, you are."

"I don't know what to do about it."

"Do you think she feels the same way?"

"I have no idea. I know we have what you might call 'really good physical chemistry.'"

Joe chuckled. "That's a good thing."

"I just don't know if we can be together."

"You have to be honest with her, for one."

"I can't be, Joe. I can't be honest with someone else when I have a hard time being honest with myself."

My brother turned and faced me, his eyes serious. "If you don't get help, Tal, and deal with everything that's going on inside you, you're never going to live the life you were born to live."

"Are you kidding me? The life I was born to live? So far it's sucked."

"It doesn't suck. You've had some tough breaks."

"Tough breaks? You make it sound like I missed the winning shot in a basketball game. What I went through was more than a tough break."

My brother rubbed his temple. "I'm not trying to belittle what you went through. But you've never actually told me about it. Ryan and I can only guess."

I cleared my throat. "Believe me, you don't want to know."

"Our imaginations are pretty good. We pretty much know what went on."

"What you think went on? Multiply that by a hundred. Then you might get to where I was."

Jonah shook his head. "Damn, I wish so much it had been me instead of you. I should've been there."

I hated when my brother did this. Ryan too. Acted like they wished it had been them rather than me. That was so stupid. They should be damned happy it hadn't been them. We'd been through all that before. No need for me to rehash it. I stayed silent.

"You could go see that Dr. Carmichael again. She's supposed to be really good."

I cleared my throat. "I thought about it. I was just so... I don't know."

"Were you scared?"

"No." I wasn't scared. Hell, I wasn't scared of anything.

Jonah removed his Stetson and wiped his brow. "What'd you come out here for, anyway?"

I swallowed. "I was wondering if maybe you could talk to Jade. Convince her to come back to the house."

"If Marjorie couldn't convince her, I doubt I could."

He was probably right.

"Tell you what. If I can get Jade to come back to the house, would you do something for me?"

I knew better than to make deals with my brother, but right now I was desperate to have Jade back in the house where I could see her.

"What do you have in mind?"

"I get Jade to move back to the ranch house, and you start seeing Dr. Carmichael. Regularly."

CHAPTER EIGHT

I hastily picked up my cell phone from the carpeted floor where it had landed. I had been breezing through news articles online while I was talking to Marj, and a headline caught my eye. It was a full spread in the *Snow Creek Daily*. "Local Hero Comes Home." Complete with Talon Steel in his full dress United States Marine Corps uniform.

Talk about making a splash. A man in uniform—the ultimate man in uniform.

He had been given the Award of Honor.

The fucking Award of Honor.

Why hadn't anyone told me?

"Jade, are you there?" Marj's voice came from my phone.

I held it up to my ear. "Yeah, Marj. I'm here. I... I'll call you back, okay?"

I clicked the phone off in the middle of her good-bye and I started reading.

Local resident and Award of Honor recipient Talon Steel returned home to Snow Creek this past week. Talon entered the Marine Corps as a second lieutenant and quickly gained the rank of first lieutenant and then captain due to his hard work and heroism. He was deployed first to Afghanistan and then to Iraq. He received the Award of Honor from the governor of Colorado for making six death-defying forays into a killing zone to save six American troops. Captain Steel was thirty-two years old at the time of his return. He was granted an honorable discharge.

"Captain Steel is a hero to us all and a great example of a model citizen of Colorado," said the lieutenant governor. "We are proud to have him home to our great state."

Steel is the son of the late Bradford and Daphne Steel of Steel Acres Ranch outside of Snow Creek and brother to Jonah, Ryan, and Marjorie Steel.

Captain Steel was honored at a ceremony in Snow Creek last Saturday officiated by Mayor Tom Simpson. In front of Steel's brothers and sister and hundreds of Snow Creek citizens, Mayor Simpson said that the former Marine would serve not only as a lesson of courage but as a reminder to everyone that heroism comes from everywhere.

"Anyone, even someone from our small town of Snow Creek, Colorado, can do great deeds as part of this great country," the mayor said. Addressing Steel specifically, he continued, "You did more than your duty as a member of the military and a citizen of the United States. Snow Creek is proud to have such a distinguished hero among our population."

The mayor retold Captain Steel's story the next Monday at Snow Creek K-12 School. Captain Steel, an infantry officer in command of an Explosive Ordnance Disposal Unit, and his troops were ambushed by a group of insurgents in a small peaceful village in northern Iraq after dark. Suddenly, the lights in the village went out, and gunfire erupted. About twenty-five insurgents who had been perched on mountainsides took cover in the village and ambushed Steel's unit and one other under the command of Captain Derek Waters. Steel, a first lieutenant at the time, defied orders from Waters, his superior officer, to reenter the battle zone and save six of his fallen comrades: Pvt. Clancy Brown of Los Angeles, Pvt. Lance Fox of Gahanna, Ohio; Pvt. Myron Jones of Schroon Lake, NY; Pvt. Kevin Dale of Reno, Nevada; Sgt. Corey Jensen of Santa Fe, NM; and 2nd Lt. Megan Cline of Dallas.

Captain Steel made only one comment: "I didn't do it to be a hero."

My eyes glazed over as perspiration erupted on my palms. Damn. I closed my eyes. *I didn't do it to be a hero.* I'd heard those words before, when I first met Talon. He'd been driving me from the airport to the ranch over a month ago.

"I think it's really heroic what you did over there. I really respect our military."

"I didn't do it to be a hero."

"Oh, I didn't mean to imply—"

"I'm no hero, blue eyes. In fact, I'm about as far from a hero as you'd get."

"It really doesn't matter what you think, does it? I think anyone who serves our country is a hero. That's my personal definition, and I'm sticking with it."

He'd resisted being called a hero. Wow. Just wow.

I'm no hero, blue eyes.

What a crock.

There was so much more to Talon than I knew.

Why hadn't Marj told me any of this? The Award of Honor from the state? Why the hell not the Medal of Honor from the president? And why wasn't this national news?

Actually, it probably was. That was where I'd start tomorrow in my research.

For now, I'd call it a day. My eyes were fatigued from staring at the computer screen for eight hours straight, but that wasn't why I had to stop. I had to digest what I'd just read. I printed a copy of the article and slid it into my briefcase.

Time to go home. I'd have to stop at the grocery on the way home because my new fridge was bare.

I gathered everything. I didn't even have to say good-bye to anybody in the office because they were already gone. I made my way downstairs and outside the building. As I walked toward the small grocery, a neon sign caught my eye. Toby's Tattoo Parlor. I'd seen the tattoo place before, of course, but I'd never ventured in. Tattoos had always fascinated me, and I wanted one—a tasteful one—right on the small of my back. However, I hadn't found an image that spoke to me...until a few nights ago.

My mother's new boyfriend, Nico, had a beautiful phoenix tattooed on his forearm—swirls of fuchsia, red, gold, purple, with neon-blue and orange flames shooting out from its wings as it rose from a pile of gray ash. It was a symbol of strength, of rebirth, of a new beginning.

All the symbolism I needed in my life.

That was the image I wanted.

A phoenix.

A girl with spiky black hair and a lip ring sat at the front desk, and two male artists worked in the back.

"Can I help you?" the girl asked.

"Yeah, I like to get a tattoo on my lower back, and I'd like to take a look at your art books. I'm looking for a picture of a phoenix."

"Oh, yeah, those make great tats." She pulled a large book up onto the counter. "Take a look in here. We have lots of phoenixes in our mythological creatures section. Dragons too. You like dragons?"

"Sure. But I want a phoenix." I took the book and sat down in one of the chairs across from her desk. I skipped straight to the phoenixes. Phoenix after phoenix after phoenix. They were all beautiful but not exactly what I was looking for—

Until there it was—a near replica of the one I'd seen on my mother's boyfriend's forearm. A gorgeous tattoo, and the colors were psychedelic almost to the point of mind-numbing. Perfection. I walked back up to the girl.

"I'd really love this one. Can any of you guys do it?"

"Yeah, I can do that one. You want to make an appointment?"

"Actually, could I see some of your work first?"

She nodded. "Absolutely. I wouldn't expect you to let me decorate your skin unless you were familiar with my work. I'm Haley, by the way."

"Jade," I said.

Haley handed me another book, this one not quite as big. "This is my portfolio. If you want to look at the other guys' portfolios, please do."

I opened the book. Haley's work was gorgeous. I wouldn't have to look any further. "You do great work," I said to her. "Yeah, let's make an appointment."

"Actually, if you have time right now, I'm available. The tat will take about two hours and run about two fifty."

Two hundred and fifty bucks. I'd just written Sarah a check, but I had enough money in my account to cover it, and I was employed. Still, the car savings and the student loans that were coming due... But something had drawn me into the shop, and then I'd found the exact image I wanted. Seemed like kismet.

What the hell? I closed the book and smiled at Haley. "Let's do it."

CHAPTER NINE

TALON

I mounted Phoenix and rode away from the northern quadrant. It was early in the evening yet, so I decided to take a ride. Let the wind run through my hair a little more.

I rode for about an hour and then headed back to the house. Felicia would have dinner ready soon, and I was actually hungry. Riding was so good for me. I needed to remember to do it more often.

I took Phoenix back to the stables, asked a hand to groom him, and drove back to the ranch house. I walked in and inhaled—robust pork, corn, and chile. Felicia had made tamales, one of my favorite meals.

"Felicia, smells great," I said, entering the kitchen.

"It's ready, Mr. Talon. Could you tell Miss Marjorie and her guest to come to the table?"

"Her guest?"

"Yes, a young lady came a few minutes ago. I assume she's staying for dinner."

"Where are they?"

"They're in the living room. Didn't you see them?"

"I came in the back way." I walked out of the kitchen through the hallway and into the living room. My stomach was fluttering. God, fluttering. What was I? Some kind of adolescent? Of course it would be Jade. Who else would Marjorie have over?

But Felicia would have said Jade, not "her guest."

My heart sank when I saw who sat across from my sister in the living room—the cocktail waitress I had bedded on a couple occasions. Shit, I couldn't even remember her name. Jenny? Julie?

I backed out slowly. Maybe they hadn't seen me.

But, of course, my sister turned toward me. "Talon, there you are." Her lips were pursed. "You have a visitor."

What the hell was she doing here? And how did she know where I lived?

The woman stood. "Hi, Talon."

"Hi..."

"Julie," she said.

"What are you doing here?" I asked.

"I haven't seen you in a while, and I was worried about you."

Worried about me? She didn't even know me. We'd had sex a couple times. In fact, the last time I had gone to see her, I hadn't been able to perform, so I'd left. Kind of embarrassing.

"As you can see, I'm fine. So you can go now."

"Talon," Marj said.

Yeah, I was being rude. But I had no interest in this girl, and for her to come over here was pretty presumptuous. Marj's clenched jawline indicated that she wasn't thrilled Julie was here either.

"Can I talk to you alone for a minute, Talon?" Marj

turned to Julie. "You don't mind, do you? I need to talk to my brother about some...business."

Julie smiled. "Of course not. I'll just wait here for you."

Before I could tell Julie not to bother to wait, Marjorie yanked me down the hallway nearly to my bedroom.

"What the hell is she doing here?"

"You think I know?"

"Well, she came here to see you, Talon."

"Not at my invitation."

"What do we do with her now?"

"We tell her to leave."

"That would be rude."

"You think I care?"

"She seems to be under the impression that you two are...more than friends."

This was getting beyond irritating. "Her impression would be wrong."

"Talon, who is she exactly?"

"She's a waitress, Marjorie. I met her in Grand Junction a while ago. She and I had...a couple of...dates. And honestly, I'm not really comfortable talking to you about this."

"Look, if you're going to be cheating on my best friend—"

"Your best friend? You mean Jade? Jade and I don't have anything between us."

"Except sex?"

Jesus Christ. Did I really need to be talking to my baby sister about these things? "Look, I know you two are best friends and probably tell each other everything—"

"You got that right."

"But whatever has gone on between Jade and me is none of your business."

"You are my brother, and Jade is my best friend. That makes this every bit my business. Maybe not the relationship part, but the part that affects me. Now who the hell is this waitress chick, and why did she think she could show up at our home?"

I shook my head. "Beats the hell out of me. I didn't even know she knew where to find me."

"Well, I assume you gave her your name."

"Of course."

"The Steels are pretty damned easy to find," Marj said. "I'm going to invite her to stay for dinner."

I jerked my head forward. "What?"

"You heard me. I want to find out what's going on between you two."

"I just told you what's going on between us. A whole lot of nothing. Now either you can get rid of her, or I will."

"Nope. She's staying for dinner." Marj flounced off.

The next thing I knew, I was sitting at the kitchen table flanked by my sister and a woman I'd fucked a couple of times. Could this have been any more awkward? I stayed quiet while she and Marj chattered like a couple of prairie hens.

"So where do you work?"

"The Fox and the Hound Bar and Grill in Grand Junction."

"And that's where you met Talon?"

Julie nodded and swallowed a bite of tamale. "Yeah, couple months or so ago. Wow, this food is delicious."

"Oh, yes, Felicia is a gem." Marj smiled curtly. "Tell me a little more about yourself, Julie."

I rolled my eyes. This dinner had gone on long enough. I listened with only one ear as Julie rattled on and on about how she wanted to start going to night school once she got her GED.

Blah, blah, blah. Sure, that would happen.

"If you'll excuse me, you two, I need to make a quick phone call. I have to check on my cooking class schedule for next week." Marj stood and walked from the room.

Shit. Now what?

"So, Talon, what's going on with you?" Julie asked. "I thought we had something special between us."

CHAPTER TEN

JADE

Haley had drawn up a beautiful image of the phoenix and had transferred the ink outline to my back, when my phone rang.

"You need to get that?" she asked.

"No. Let's go ahead and get this done tonight. I'm really excited."

"Awesome. Let me get the colors I need, and then I'll start the outline. You've never had a tattoo before, right?"

"Nope."

"Okay, it's going to hurt, but it's not quite as bad as most people think it is."

"I've heard it feels like a bunch of pinpricks. I want to do it anyway. I feel really strongly about this image. It resonates with me right now."

"Good enough."

Then my phone started again.

I let out a huff. "Let me just get that and then turn the damned thing off."

I grabbed my phone. *Marj.* "Hey, Marj, what you need?"

"Jade, you have to come out to the house."

"I'm kind of in the middle of something right now."

"Get out of it. This is an emergency."

My pulse sped up. "An emergency? Are you okay? Is everyone okay?"

"Yeah, but Talon's got a girl here, and I need you here."

"A girl?" Jealousy knifed through my body.

"He didn't invite her here. She just showed up. Some cocktail waitress skank from the city. You need to get out here now before he falls in bed with her or something."

"Why didn't he just kick her out?"

"Well...I invited her to dinner."

"*You* invited her to dinner? Why the hell would you do that?"

"Because I wanted to find out what was going on between her and Talon."

I shook my head and rolled my eyes. "Marj, I don't have time for this. I'm in the middle of getting a tattoo."

"A tattoo? I thought we were going to do that together sometime."

"We've been saying that for seven years. We haven't done it yet. I was just passing by Toby's, and I got an itch. I saw a tattoo a couple nights ago on my mom's boyfriend that I really liked, and I wanted to duplicate it. It's perfect for me right now and matches how I'm feeling about myself."

"Have you started yet?"

"No, she just put the image on my back with the transfer. Nothing permanent."

"Okay, then please, please reschedule. I need you to come to the house now."

"I haven't even eaten yet tonight, Marj."

"You can eat here. Felicia always makes enough to feed an army. You know that."

I let out a heavy sigh. There was no arguing with Marj when she got like this. I would either have to go to the house or pay for it later.

"How the hell do you expect me to get there? Hitchhike?"

"Take a cab. You know George is always out in his cab. I'll pay for it."

I was getting pretty tired of Marj offering me money. I could pay my own cab fare, for God's sake. But she clearly needed me there. Fine. I hung up and turned to Haley. "I'm so sorry, but could we reschedule? That was my best friend, and she has an emergency."

"Sure, no problem. I've already got everything ready to go, so all we need to do is book you for a couple hours some other time."

"Do you need me to make a payment now?"

"No. I'll just collect it when we're done."

"Great. I totally appreciate this. I'm really excited about getting this tattoo."

"Well, you have it in black and white right now, although it'll wash away when you take a shower in the morning." Haley laughed.

"I'm looking forward to having it for real with all the vivid colors. Thanks so much, Haley. I'll give you a call and be back in sometime next week."

"Awesome sauce."

Awesome sauce? The manicurist had said that. What the fuck? I found George over at Murphy's Bar, and he was only too glad to drive me out to the Steels' ranch. Ironically, he was also the one who'd driven me to Grand Junction the previous Friday.

"I thought you were moving to the city, sweetheart," he said.

I cleared my throat. "Change of plans."

A little over half an hour later, I was back at the house where everything had started.

"Thank God!" Marj ran up to me as soon as I came in the door. "Wait here while I go take care of George."

I shook my head at her. "Oh, no. I already paid him. Now tell me. Why exactly am I here, Marj?"

"You'll see. I've had to keep the ditz talking for the last half hour while you got here. She has the IQ of a spaghetti squash."

"Why didn't you just get rid of her?"

"Because I have a plan. For you. And Talon."

Oh, Lord...

Marj led me to the family room where Talon—*my* Talon—sat with a blond and blue-eyed curvy vixen.

His face was tense, his lips thin. He looked uncomfortable as hell. Of course, uncomfortable on him was still sexy. His burgundy button-down was open at the neck, a few black chest hairs peeking out. His hair was a mess—a dark, sexy, tousled mess.

"Talon, look who dropped by for a visit." Marj yanked me by the arm into the family room. "Julie, please meet my best friend in the whole world, Jade Roberts."

The blondie flounced up and took my hand. "Wicked awesome to meet you."

Wicked awesome, indeed. This chick couldn't be more than nineteen or twenty, though she talked like she was thirteen.

"Same here," I said. Why was I here again?

Talon stood. "Hi." The word came out gruff, forced.

"Hi, yourself," I said, turning to his companion. "What do you do, Julie?"

"I'm a cocktail waitress."

Okay, twenty-one, then.

Julie grabbed Talon by the hand and pulled him off the couch. "Let's go for a drive. I'd love to see your ranch."

Oh, hell no...

"I don't think Talon has the time tonight," Marj said. "I believe he and Jade have plans."

My eyes nearly popped out of my head. "I don't have any—"

Talon grabbed my arm. "That's right. How could I forget?"

What the—

"Remember," Marj said. "You and he were going to take care of that thing for me?"

"Sure...the thing."

No way in the world could anybody buy this...unless she had the IQ of a spaghetti squash.

Blondie stood on her tiptoes and kissed Talon on the cheek.

And my blood boiled.

"Oh, well. Please call me the next time you're in the city." Julie smiled, showcasing ultra white teeth. "And I'm gonna come back and visit you real soon. I want to see your ranch up close."

Marj grabbed Julie's arm. "We're terribly glad you stopped by, Julie, but I'm afraid we're going to be totally overworked on the ranch for the next few months. Harvest time is coming and all. So please don't drop by unless you're invited." She led Julie out of the family room toward the foyer.

I couldn't help a laugh. I couldn't believe Marj had actually said that, especially after keeping her there until I arrived. I still wasn't sure what that had been about.

Talon looked at me. "So what are you doing here, anyway?"

"Marjorie called me. Said it was an emergency."

Talon cocked his head. "I can't say I'm not glad she's gone, but I don't think this is an emergency."

"Clearly it wasn't. So I guess I'll be going."

Marj ran back in. "Oh, no, you're not leaving. You said you hadn't eaten, so you're going to have a big plateful of Felicia's tamales."

"Haven't you guys already eaten?" I eyed the plates in the sink in the kitchen.

"We have, but we would love to sit down and have a glass of wine with you, wouldn't we, Tal?"

The left side of Talon's mouth quirked up. A pseudo-smile. "Sure," he said. "We can sit down and have a drink."

"Why did you insist on keeping her here, Marj, and then unceremoniously kick her out?" Talon asked.

Marj dodged the question and feigned a yawn. Right. "I just realized I'm exhausted. So why don't the two of you go out on the deck, and maybe you can get in the hot tub later?

Jade, you eat your meal, and Tal, pour her a glass of Ryan's Rhône blend. It's her favorite." She made a quick exit.

Subtle, Marj.

I looked at Talon. His lips were still quirked up.

"Some kind of setup, huh?" I said.

"You don't have to stay."

"Are you kidding? She dragged me away from an appointment, and I'm starving. I can't resist a plateful of Felicia's tamales. But honestly, you don't have to sit with me and eat. I'm perfectly happy eating alone. I was going to be alone tonight anyway."

"This is stupid. I'll go get Marj to hang with you."

My heart sank a little, but I hid it from Talon. "That's fine. Tell her I'll be out on the deck."

I went to the kitchen, where Felicia presented me with a plateful of yummy tamales drenched in green chile "Here you go, Miss Jade. I've missed you around here."

"I haven't been gone very long yet."

"I know. But I miss you anyway. It was nice to have another body around."

I smiled. "Thanks. And thanks for dinner." I took my plate out to the deck and sat down at one of the patio tables.

I dug into the tamales. Felicia made them in a Venezuelan style, with black and green olives, pork, and some carrots and peppers. They were then smothered with her green chile sauce. When I first came to the ranch, I had assumed Felicia was Mexican, because her Mexican food was so delicious and she had the darker Hispanic coloring. Turned out she was Puerto Rican, but she knew how to cook so many wonderful things. Her Italian cuisine was as good as anyone's.

I didn't look up when the French doors opened, assuming it was Marj.

Turned out it was Talon. He set a glass of wine in front of me and then took the seat across from me at the table.

I swallowed my mouthful of tamale, my pulse quickening. "Where's Marj?"

"She wouldn't come. Insisted I come out here and keep you company."

I nodded. "That doesn't surprise me. I...told Marj about us."

He bit his lip. God, sexy.

"I know."

"She hasn't...talked to you about it, has she?"

"No. She's my baby sister. It's not really something brothers and sisters talk about. But she made it pretty clear when Julie showed up today that I wasn't available."

"Really? And how did you feel about that?"

"I have no interest in Julie, blue eyes. I never did."

My skin tingled all over and I suppressed a smile. "But you fucked her."

Talon let out a chuckle. "I've fucked a lot of women, Jade. You know that."

"Have you fucked any since you and I..." I wasn't sure how to finish that sentence. Since he and I *what?* I could've said fucked, but what we did was so much more than fucking. Was it making love? It was on my end, but I had no idea how he felt.

He cleared his throat. "No, I haven't."

I widened my eyes. Warm happiness blanketed me,

along with some surprise. "All those nights you went off to Grand Junction? None of them ever ended in..."

He shook his head. "Honestly? I went to see Julie one of those nights. To try to take the edge off of my desire for you. It didn't work out that way."

"You didn't go through with it?"

"No, I...couldn't." His cheeks pinked a bit. "And I'm glad I couldn't."

My palms got clammy and joy surged through me. He *did* desire me—I knew that—but now I knew it was different for him than it had been with anyone else. I'd known that for a while in my heart, and even by what he told me, but to hear him say the words—the actual words. They were more captivating than the western slope orange-and-pink sunset before us.

I took a sip of my wine, the spiciness a wonderful complement to the sweet corn and robust pork of the tamales. Talon watched me eat, but I had long gotten over being self-conscious around him. He'd seen me in every position possible.

"Those tamales are the bomb, aren't they?" he said.

I nodded, swallowing another mouthful. "I do miss Felicia's cooking. That's for sure."

"You can always come back."

"We've had this discussion, Talon. You kicked me out."

"And I told you, I regret doing that."

"I believe you. I really do. But something happened to you that night, and until you deal with it, I don't think I should be here. At least not on a permanent basis. I mean, I'll come by. To see Marj."

"Just to see Marj?"

Did he want me to say I wanted to see him? Of course I always wanted to see him. But I still didn't know where we stood. Other than the amazing sexual chemistry, I wasn't sure what was between us. I knew *my* feelings, but I didn't know his...and I wasn't sure he did either. "I'm always happy to see you. You know that."

"Good. I'd like for us to have dinner sometime."

The last time he asked me to dinner... That was the night he went crazy on me and kicked me out of this house. So I decided to play it light. "Isn't that what we're doing right now?"

"Touché," he said. "Seriously, I'd like to take you to dinner."

"You mean in your bedroom, like last time?" I said boldly.

He cleared his throat. "No. I want to take you out on..."

He really couldn't even say the word, could he? "A date? You want to take me on a date, Talon?"

He looked down at the table, his head bobbing.

"Is that a yes?" Damn it, I was going to make him say it.

"Yes," he said under his breath.

"Fine. Then look me in the eye and ask me out. Like a man."

He lifted his head up, and his dark eyes were blazing with fire. "What is that supposed to mean?"

"I want you to ask me out."

"You said 'like a man.'" He clenched his hands into fists.

"Well...yeah."

He rose with such force that the wrought-iron chair

he'd been sitting in toppled over. He advanced around the table, grabbed my arm, and yanked me to my feet.

"I'll show you what a man I can be." He crushed his lips down onto mine.

I opened for him without meaning to. I would always respond to him, whether I wanted to or not. He plunged his tongue into my mouth and took. This was the kind of kiss I was used to getting from Talon. And even though I'd loved the kisses the other night that had been soft and giving, this kind of kiss fueled my desire for him like no other. He broke the kiss with a loud smack and trailed little nips and bites on my neck and up to my earlobe, where he tugged. "Look at what you do to me, blue eyes," he whispered. "Do you want me to be a man for you? You want me to show you what a real man can do?"

I sighed, groaned, as he continued his assault on the outer shell of my ear, nipping, biting, the pleasure-pain bursting through me in sparks of fire.

"Answer me, blue eyes. Tell me what you think a real man should do to you."

Something was bothering him. Something about me telling him to ask me out like a man. Those words had gotten to him, and where they were rooted I didn't know, but right now, I didn't care. He'd asked me what I wanted, so I would tell him.

"I want you, Talon. Take me to your bed and fuck me."

In one fell swoop, he gathered me into his arms and lifted me. He stalked to the French doors, kneed them open, and took me through the kitchen and down the hallway to his suite.

I didn't know where Marj was, and I didn't care. If she had seen us, I wouldn't have stopped this. Nothing could stop this. Fiery passion raged through me, my heart thundering, my body quivering. I wanted him like I'd never wanted him before. He opened his door, walked swiftly through the sitting room to the bedroom, and deposited me on his bed. Then he went back to the door and clicked it locked.

He turned to me, his eyes blazing. "Undress for me, Jade. Show me that succulent little body of yours."

I undressed slowly, achingly slowly, because I wanted to make this good for him. If I'd had my way, I would've stripped everything off both of us in sixty seconds and had him flat on his back on the bed, me riding his cock.

I was still wearing my work clothes, but I had dressed more casually today in black leggings and a gray tunic. I proceeded leisurely, performing a strip tease, despite the fire in his eyes begging me to go quickly. I pulled the clip out of my hair and let my waves fall around my shoulders. I shook my tresses and then started unbuttoning my tunic. When enough buttons were undone, I let the gray fabric slide over one of my shoulders, baring it. I continued unbuttoning, and I finally let the garment fall to the floor in a gray heap.

My black lace bra was a demi cup, showing lots of cleavage, and my full breasts were plump from arousal.

I unclasped it in the back, slowly removed the bra, and let it fall to the floor on top of the tunic. I cupped my breasts, giving each nipple a quick pinch. The jolt arrowed between my legs.

Talon sucked in his breath, his erection a bulge against his jeans.

I flipped off my mules, pushed my leggings over my belly and hips, and slid them down both legs at the same time, removing them from each foot one by one. I stood only in my black lace panties.

I stopped for a moment to let him look at me.

His gaze was lascivious as he scanned me from top to bottom with his dark eyes.

My pussy was wet, the moisture warm against my silky underwear.

"The panties, baby. Ditch the panties."

I smiled at him and then bit my bottom lip. He sucked in another breath.

I slowly eased the panties over my hips and down my legs, and then I tossed them to him. He caught them and brought them to his nose, closing his eyes and inhaling.

I'd always found panty sniffing disgusting, but seeing Talon—big, strong, gorgeous Talon—being mesmerized by the odor of my cunt nearly shattered me into climax.

He paced toward me, backed me onto the bed, and pushed me down. Still fully clothed, he hovered over me, taking one nipple between his teeth and tugging.

I gushed fresh juice. My whole universe became my pussy, and everything Talon did cascaded through me, culminating in that bundle of nerves between my legs. Fuck, he was hot.

"Such gorgeous tits, baby. Never seen such beautiful tits before." He squeezed them, pinched the nipples, sucked on one and then the other.

I came undone.

My nipples had always been sensitive, but Talon

brought them to new heights. He was simultaneously rough and gentle with them, a sensation I'd never known before him.

He let one nipple drop from his lips. "I bought you something, baby."

My eyes still closed, still biting my bottom lip, I didn't respond. A moment later, my right nipple was held in a clutch so hard, so full of pain and pleasure, that the sensations spiraled through me like psychedelic arrows.

I opened my eyes. A nipple clamp. A goddamned nipple clamp.

The sight of it drove me crazy. My cunt throbbed for attention.

He looked into my eyes. "Okay?"

I nodded.

"Verbal," he said. "You have to tell me okay."

I nodded again. "Yes, okay."

"Good, blue eyes?"

I nodded again. "God, yes, Talon. I could never imagine it would feel this good."

"You want one on the other?"

Still biting my lip, I nodded.

"Verbal, baby."

"Yes."

He clamped my other nipple, and I nearly exploded.

"Squeeze your breasts, baby," he said. "Squeeze them and let the clamps do their work. And spread your legs for me. I'm going to lick that gorgeous pussy of yours."

He didn't have to ask twice. I spread my legs and held them open. He dived into my heat, tugging at my labia.

"You're so beautiful," he said. "I love your pussy lips. So pink and engorged. I can suck them into my mouth."

His teeth grazed my clit, and my whole body tingled.

"You're so beautiful and red. Like a ruby rose." He tugged on my folds again, worked a finger inside.

And just when I was about to splinter into a million pieces, he unclamped his mouth, rose, and spread my legs.

"And now, blue eyes, I'm going to fuck you. *Like a man.*"

CHAPTER ELEVEN

TALON

I plunged into her with force. She moaned as I took her.

"That's right, baby, like a man. Fuck you like a man."

She gripped me with sweet suction, as she always did. Every time with her was like the first time. She was a drug I could no longer live without. The noises she made, the way she smelled, tasted, like fresh apples from my orchard...

"God, Talon, I need to come..."

She shattered around me, her walls grasping me. But I wasn't ready for it to be over yet. I leaned over, removed her nipple clamps quickly, and licked her tight buds to soothe the sting as she continued bucking with her orgasm.

When she came down, her eyes closed, her facial features peaceful and serene, I withdrew. I quickly discarded my clothes and turned her over. "Get on your knees, blue eyes. I want you this way now." I grabbed her hips and plunged into her sweet pussy once more, and—

My flesh went cold. Icy shards of glass worked their way into my spine.

On the small of her back was a black outline.

She was getting a tattoo. And not just any tattoo...

I withdrew and walked backward, my back finally

hitting the wall. I slid down and hugged my knees.

It can't be... It can't be...

★ ★ ★

"You keep your eyes open, boy. You do as I tell you."

The boy coughed and choked, trying desperately not to gag.

Failing.

The colorful tattoo on the devil's forearm drew the boy's gaze. He stared hard at the image. And even though it laughed, the maniacal heckling not unlike that of the three demons, the boy could at least focus on it and not close his eyes. Its beak was yellow, like a canary, its body the red of a candy apple. Its wingtips bright pink, blue, and orange, ending in white-blue flame. Swirls of gray smoke surrounded the bird as it rose from burning embers.

The bird rose toward a five-pointed star.

"That's right, boy, take it all. You'll never be a man. Never."

Eerie cackling danced around the boy, visible as black swirls around the tattooed bird.

You'll never be a man. Never be a man...

★ ★ ★

The phoenix rose toward a star. I had forgotten until now, when I saw a near replica—the image etched onto Jade's back.

She was kneeling before me, touching my cheek. "Talon, what happened? Are you all right?"

96

I couldn't speak. I tried, but the words wouldn't come.

Had I screamed, like the last time? I didn't think so. Jade would have been acting differently if I had.

"Talon," she said again. "Talk to me, please. What happened?"

I opened my mouth. This time a tiny croak emerged.

"Please, tell me what's the matter."

I inhaled and exhaled slowly, willing my drumming heartbeat to slow. "When did you get a tattoo?"

"I haven't yet. I was about to get it tonight, but Haley only got the outline done before Marj called me with this 'emergency.'"

I swallowed. The lump obstructing my throat didn't budge. "What do you mean she only did the outline? So it's not permanent, then?"

"No, of course not. It's a simple ink drawing for her to follow. It'll come off in the shower."

I stood. A man on a mission. A strange whooshing met my ears. "It's coming off right now."

Her silver-blue eyes held compassion but also determination. "Talon, no. I like it."

"I hate it."

"It's perfect. I saw it—"

"Where?" I grabbed her forearm, gripping tightly.

"Stop. You're hurting me."

I refused to loosen my grip. I couldn't. My fingers were frozen. "Where did you see a tattoo that looked like that?"

Her eyes glazed over with tears ready to fall. "It was in Haley's art book."

"What do you want a tattoo for anyway?"

"I-I've always wanted one. I love tattoos when they're done tastefully. I just never found the right image, and when I saw the phoenix—"

"Why the hell would you want a phoenix?"

She shivered before me. "It spoke to me. It's perfect. I'm starting a new life here, rising from my broken engagement. It made sense to me, and the colors were so beautiful—"

"What colors were they?"

"I don't know. Red. Orange. Some blue."

Colors. I squeezed my eyes shut and tried to visualize the colors... I'd dulled them in my mind years and years ago—but in my flashback, they had been vibrant.

I opened my eyes. "You're not going to get that tattoo."

"Of course I am."

"I don't want you to have a tattoo."

Still shivering, she bit her lip and then visibly stiffened. "I don't recall asking your permission."

I nearly snapped but held myself in check. She was right. She was not my slave, my property, even though I sometimes wished she were. "Fine. Mar your body if you want to, but not with that image."

"But the image is perfect."

A calculating need to control surged through me like rocket fuel. "Trust me, the image is far from perfect. It's not you at all."

"I disagree."

"I don't care. You're not getting that fucking tattoo."

Her eyes darkened to a smoky blue. "I am."

I grabbed her, gripping her upper arms harshly.

She grimaced. "Let go of me."

"Not until you promise me not to get that tattoo."

She kept her mouth shut.

Fucking stubborn woman! No phoenix tattoo. Not on my watch. I dragged her into my shower and turned it on with a swoosh of water. Once it was steamed up, I pushed her inside.

She cowered under the spray, her arms crossed over her chest as if to hide herself. She looked over her shoulder at me, her blue eyes glassy. "Why does this bother you so much? I don't understand."

I turned rigid, raking my fingers through my hair. "You'll never understand. Why did I think you ever might?"

"Understand what? You haven't given me any reason to—"

I grabbed a washcloth and squirted body wash onto it. I stepped in the shower behind her and started scrubbing the small of her back.

"Talon, not so rough, please."

Rough? Hell, I didn't care. I'd burn that shit off if I had to.

Once her skin was free of the outline and the last traces of black were swirling down the drain, I finally started to relax a bit. I slunk against the wet shower wall, closed my eyes.

I opened them when the water patterns changed. She had turned to face me.

Was that shower water running down her cheeks? Or were the tiny rivers tears?

The whites of her eyes had reddened.

Tears.

My heart fell to my stomach. I could bear anything but her tears.

She sniffed. "I don't understand, Talon."

No, she didn't understand. And she never would.

I dried myself off and walked out of the bathroom. I hastily put on a pair of jeans, a T-shirt, and my socks and boots.

Walked down the hallway, out the door to my car, and drove off.

CHAPTER TWELVE

JADE

My wet hair was plastered to my face and shoulders.

Still weeping, I scrubbed at my face. I looked down. My nipples were red and swollen from Talon's attentions and the nipple clamps. What had I done now? Did he really hate tattoos, or was this something else entirely? Oddly, none of the Steels had any tattoos—at least none that I knew of. Maybe they were actually against them for some weird reason, though Marj had often spoken of getting one.

I had wanted one for so long, and that phoenix image perfectly fit how I was feeling and what I wanted to convey through art on my body. I had every intention of rescheduling the appointment with Haley.

But Talon... What was I going to do about Talon?

He needed to get some help. Maybe I could talk him into going back to his therapist. I would talk to Marj about it, Jonah and Ryan if I had to.

I grabbed the washcloth and did a quick once-over my body. I squeezed some of Talon's American Crew shampoo into my palm and quickly washed my hair, tearing up again at the masculine fragrance I recognized from his gorgeous hair. Then I turned off the shower, dried off, and squeezed the excess water out of my hair. I expected to walk out and find Talon waiting for me.

But I was alone in his empty bedroom.

Roger ambled up to me and licked the drops of water off my ankles. If Talon were anywhere in the house, Roger would be with him. Hell, if Talon were anywhere on the ranch, Roger would've gone along. The fact that Roger was here, with me, alone in Talon's room, gave me pause.

Talon was gone.

I dressed, walked down the hallway to the other wing of the ranch house, and knocked on Marj's bedroom door. At her command, I entered.

She was lying on her bed reading. "Hey," she said. "What did you do? Take a swim?"

"It's a long story," I said. I couldn't go into it. I was sure my eyes were red and swollen, but if Marj noticed, she didn't say anything.

"How did things go with Talon? I hope you got that little slut off his mind."

"I don't think the slut was ever on his mind. I'm not sure why you kept her here waiting for me."

"Maybe not my best move, but I needed to get you here."

"You could've just asked me to come over."

"You wouldn't have come. Stop—"

She held up her hand to keep me from talking.

"You know I'm right."

I nodded in defeat. She was right. I wouldn't have come.

"Seriously, what's going on?" she asked.

I shrugged. "Your guess is as good as mine. He's gone."

"Tal? Where did he go?"

"Again, your guess is as good as mine."

"Oh my God. What happened?"

"I have no idea. He freaked out that I was going to get a tattoo."

She shook her head. "That doesn't sound like Talon."

"Well, it dawned on me none of your brothers have any tats. You guys have something against them?"

Marj shook her head. "Of course not. I've known you wanted one forever. We were supposed to get one together, remember?"

I let out a sigh. "Yeah. You're right." It sure made more sense than what I had just been through.

"I thought you stopped before you got the tattoo."

"I did, but Haley had already put the transfer on my back. You know, the temporary outline of the tattoo, for her to follow while she's doing it."

"Is that how it works?"

"Sure. Didn't you ever watch *Miami Ink?*"

"I'm not the tattoo-head that you are, Jade."

"Well, anyway, he freaked out. Threw me in the shower, made me wash it off, and then he left."

Marj closed the book she'd been reading, her eyes troubled. "Makes about as much sense as anything Talon does."

That was for sure.

"I think I'm going to go ahead home, Marj. I'm exhausted. Thanks for dinner."

"I wish you'd stay."

"No. I don't want to. Besides, I have to unpack. But you

have to drive me home."

"Ha! I'm exhausted too. Please just stay tonight. You can sleep in your old room, and I'll drive you to work in the morning."

I sighed. "Marj, I can't wear the same clothes to work tomorrow that I wore today."

"That's no problem. I'll lend you something."

I looked at my nearly six-feet-tall and slender best friend. "Right, because we're so similar in size."

"Look, those black leggings you're wearing are classic. No one will know you wore them yesterday. I'll give you a long, stretchy top. You'll be fine."

I relented. I couldn't ask Marj to drive me home at this hour, and I didn't really feel like going through all my luggage tonight. I'd do it tomorrow.

"Agreed," I said. "And good night."

★ ★ ★

After Marj dropped me off at the office in the morning, I started some coffee in the drip coffee maker I'd purchased for my office. I had picked up some great Arabica beans from Costa Rica while I was in Grand Junction for those few days. Decent coffee for a change, and I sure needed it this morning.

Larry was in court all day, so I had the office to myself except for Michelle and David, who were happy to leave me alone. I went back to the computer to do more research on the Steels.

Where to start? The article about Talon's heroics, of

course. It had been in the local paper, but it was such a huge deal, I figured I could find national or at least state coverage. A search proved nothing. The Award of Honor wasn't worth a bit of national news? And why not the Medal of Honor?

I went back to the original article. No byline, but at the bottom was a name.

Wendy Madigan, NNN.

The National News Network? If this story originated from the National News Network, why hadn't it actually been in the national news?

Maybe this Wendy Madigan would know.

I did a quick database search. Turned out she had been a NNN correspondent until about two years ago, when she retired.

Her image was easy to find, and I recognized her. She had been a staple on the news, and I was surprised I hadn't remembered the name. She was an attractive older woman with short light-brown hair and blue eyes.

Since she was no longer with the National News Network, I had to find her on my own. I found a few e-mail addresses and phone numbers but decided against e-mail. I wanted to talk to her.

The first number I tried had been disconnected.

The second number, however, rang until someone answered. A Denver area code too. What luck.

"Hello?"

"Hi, I'm trying to reach Wendy Madigan."

"May I ask who's calling?"

"Sure. My name is Jade Roberts. I'm a city attorney in Snow Creek, Colorado."

The woman cleared her throat. "May I ask what this is regarding?"

"I'd rather keep that between Ms. Madigan and myself, if you don't mind."

"All right." A short pause. "Wendy, phone."

"Thanks, Mom." Then, "Hello?"

"Ms. Madigan?"

"Yes."

"This is Jade Roberts from the city attorney's office in Snow Creek, Colorado."

"Snow Creek? Where did you get this number?"

"It's one of your numbers of record."

"This is my mother's landline."

"I don't know what to tell you. At some point, it became a number of record for you."

"Look, Ms. Roberts, I'm sure there's nothing I can help you with. You know I'm no longer with the news."

"Yes, I know. But I'm doing some investigation on the Steel family. There's precious little information out there about them, but your name did pop up on an article about Talon Steel."

Silence on the other end of the phone.

"Ms. Madigan?"

"Yes, I'm here. I guess I should've expected this phone call eventually."

My heart thumped. What had she meant by that? "So you know why I'm calling, then?"

"Why don't you tell me why you're calling."

Smart woman. She knew what she was doing.

"I'm doing some research on the Steel brothers and

their ranch here in Snow Creek."

"Why would a city attorney be interested in the Steels?"

"I'm afraid that's classified at the moment, Ms. Madigan." I hated the words as soon as I'd uttered them. I sounded like Larry. Sleazy Larry.

"Then why should I answer any questions?"

"You're certainly within your rights not to. But I'm most interested in an article that appeared in the local paper about three years ago, when Talon Steel was discharged from the Marines and returned to Snow Creek. Clearly the man was a hero, and he received the Award of Honor, but this news did not appear anywhere else. I found your name at the bottom of the local article."

"I'm afraid I don't know what you're talking about."

"Perhaps you didn't want your name there, but it was, Ms. Madigan. Why didn't this appear in the national news? You were a national news correspondent. This man was a hero. Shouldn't this have been sprawled on the front pages of all of the national papers? Shouldn't it have been on the network news? Shouldn't he have gotten the Medal of Honor?"

A throat cleared on the other side of the line. "The Steels are very private people, Ms. Roberts."

That was the understatement of the year. "Do you know how the story ended up in this little local paper, then?"

"I'm afraid I don't."

"Well, it was obviously your story."

"Perhaps my name was a misprint."

I couldn't help a soft chuckle. "Ms. Madigan, you're an

accomplished newswoman. Now, I may be a new attorney, but I know better than to believe the bull you're spewing at me. There's a reason why this story was not on the national news."

"I'm sorry. I sympathize with your plight, but I really can't help you." The line clicked dead.

I had only been investigating for a couple of weeks, but already I knew when someone was lying to me. That number had a Denver area code, and with the databases at my disposal as a city attorney, I easily found the address for the landline. Now, how to get to Denver? The easiest way would be to fly, since I didn't have a car. I buzzed Michelle.

"Yes?"

"Michelle, could you get me on the first flight to Denver, please? And call George to drive me over to the airport, as well."

"You mean you want to go today?"

"If possible. It's early yet. I should be able to get there by midafternoon if there are any seats left. Get me on a return late tonight."

"Should Larry okay this?"

"Larry's not here, and he wants me to get information on this case. I think he'd probably be okay with it. The fare's pretty cheap." I hoped she'd buy the lie.

"All right. I'll take care of it, Jade."

Fifteen minutes later, I had a seat on a flight leaving in two hours.

Wendy Madigan, here I come.

CHAPTER THIRTEEN

TALON

"Yeah?" the heavily tattooed bald guy at the front desk said to me. "What can I help you with?"

"I need to see Toby."

"He's not in today. Just Haley and me."

"All right." I sighed. "Last night, a woman named Jade Roberts came in for a tattoo. Were you helping her?"

"No, that would've been Haley."

"Get her up here, then."

"She's in the middle of a project."

My ears burned. Surely smoke was coming right out of them. My skin was on fire. I threw a couple of twenties on the counter. "Get her up here. I need to talk to her."

The guy played with his lip ring and took the cash. "Haley, there's a guy up here who needs see you."

"I'm busy," a voice called.

Baldy lifted the corners of his lips into a smirk. "I think he'll make it worth your while."

A couple seconds later, a Goth girl with tattoos everywhere appeared. "Yeah? I'm Haley."

"A woman came in here last night wanting a tattoo. Jade Roberts?"

Haley nodded. "Yeah. Uptight businesswoman type, but she was wearing leggings. Go figure. I was really surprised she wanted a tat."

"You're the artist she was working with?"

Haley nodded again, popping a wad of gum.

"She wanted a particular image. A phoenix. Can you tell me where you got that image?"

"She found it in one of our books. It wasn't anything I had done before, but I was pretty easily able to copy it for her. We were about to get down to business when she got a phone call last night."

Thank God Marj had called her. If Julie hadn't shown up at my house last night, Jade would have that damned thing on her back right now. Permanently. I shook my head. I never thought I'd be thankful for my sister's meddling.

"Listen, I need you not to do that tattoo on her."

"Dude, I tattoo anyone who wants me to tattoo them. It's kind of what I do for living. You know, how I pay my bills?"

I pulled a couple hundreds out of my wallet and set them in front of her. "Is this enough to convince you not to tattoo her?"

"Well, it's enough to convince me not to tattoo her once. I charge about two fifty to three per tattoo."

Was she serious? Three hundred bucks to draw on someone's body? Unreal. Time to attack this from a different angle. This woman wasn't the only tattoo artist in Colorado. Hell, she wasn't even the only tattoo artist in Snow Creek. I knew Toby. I could go straight to the top and tell him not to tattoo Jade. Of course, that would piss Jade off. I seemed to be good at that.

"Okay. You can keep that. It's for your time that was wasted last night. What I need you to do now is show me the book where Jade found that phoenix tattoo."

"No prob." Haley pulled a couple thick books onto the counter. "Phoenixes are under mythological creatures, and there might be some under birds. Take a look. I gotta get back to work. I'm in the middle of a tat."

I nodded. "Understood. Thanks. I'll take a look at these." My heart beat rapidly as I started thumbing through the book. I turned to the birds section. A psychedelic peacock nearly jumped off the page. There was even a chicken and a turkey. Who the hell tattooed a turkey on himself?

No phoenixes, though. Why hadn't I begun with mythological creatures? I found the requisite section and began perusing, my fingers sweating. Some of the dragons were pretty cool. I slowly turned pages, finding nothing.

A couple minutes later, Haley trotted back up front. "Dude, I forgot. I wrote down the page number of the book when I drew the image. It should be on page 307, mythological creatures."

Page 307... Ice penetrated my skin.

I gripped the sides of the book, my knuckles whitening with tension. The red bird, colorful wings ending in orange and white-blue flames... My stomach dropped, and acid crawled up my throat.

Identical, or nearly so...and the photo was of a forearm.

I gulped down a giant lump that had lodged in my throat.

Was it the same?

The same?

My knees buckled beneath me, and I grasped the counter for support.

I cleared my throat, desperately trying to dislodge the caustic lump. *Keep it cool. Keep it cool, Talon.*

Images whirled into my mind, conjuring themselves from the blackness. The walls filled with photos of tattoos inched forward, the colors pulsing, vibrating. *No. No flashback. Not here. Not now.*

"Hey, Haley!" I yelled, the room spinning back into focus.

She trotted back up to the counter, looking pissed. "Yeah?"

"Are all these photos from tattoos that were done here in Snow Creek?"

"I haven't the foggiest. Some of the photos are really old."

"Maybe over twenty years old?" I asked.

"Oh, yeah, probably. Toby bought this place from some dude a while back. He'd know better than I would."

"When's he coming in?"

"Probably later this afternoon. I think he's got an appointment scheduled." She strode quickly back to her client.

Quietly, I pulled the photo out of the book. The colors had faded. Yes, it was an older photo. Toby and I would be having a chat.

"What's Toby's cell number?" I yelled back to Haley.

"Not sure I should give that out."

I pulled out another twenty and waved it at her. "How

about now?"

Haley laughed and returned to the counter. She wrote a number down on the back of a business card. "Here you go. Pleasure doing business with you."

★ ★ ★

The boy emptied his stomach.

He wasn't sure why they bothered to feed him. He didn't keep much down anyway. His wrists were noticeably skinnier than when he had been brought to the cold, dark cellar.

They laughed at him, taunting him. "Makes you puke? You can't take it like a man?"

No man should have to take what the boy took. No woman, either. Especially no little boy or girl. No, nobody.

Nobody but him.

He'd been forsaken. No one had come for him. No one would. Did he deserve this? This horrific fate that had been thrust upon him?

He must. Because no one came.

Tattoo clocked him upside the head. "You know you get hit whenever you puke, boy. But still you insist on puking."

The boy gagged again and heaved, the sharp pain from the punch making his eyes water. Nothing remained in his stomach to come out.

Cramps churned his gut. One of them kicked his bare ass, and his head hit the concrete wall.

Blessed blackness, where no pain existed. No masked men. No flaming bird.

Just nothing.

Nothing was good.

* * *

I quickly keyed in the number Haley had given me.

"Yeah?"

"Hey, Toby. Talon Steel."

"Steel, what's up? I'm not sure you've ever called me before."

"I got your cell from Haley at the shop. I need to talk to you. In person."

"Yeah? What about?"

God, my heart was going to fly out of my chest any minute. "A tattoo in one of your books. It's a phoenix on someone's forearm. I want to find out who you tattooed it on."

"I respect my clientele's privacy, Steel."

"I'll make it worth your while to give me the information I want. Can you meet me over at Rita's?"

* * *

"I honestly wish I could help you," Toby said, his blond hair falling into his eyes. He sat across from me at Rita's, sipping on some coffee. "But that's not one of mine. I bought the place fifteen or so years ago, and that tat was done by one of the previous guys."

"Do you know when it was done?"

Toby shook his head. "Sure don't. But I can tell you who I bought the shop from. That might help you."

I racked my brain, trying to remember the name of

the tattoo shop fifteen years ago. I'd been twenty, spending most of my time in the city drinking and fucking. Shit. "I'll take whatever information you have."

Toby grinned, a gold tooth glinting on the edge of his smile. "So how worth my while are you making this?"

I slid a hundred across the table. "How's this for a start?"

Toby nodded, pocketing the Benji. "I'd say that's a great start, Steel. Here's to the beginning of a beautiful business relationship." He chuckled.

Money. Never stopped surprising me how cooperative people got when money was involved. So often I had been willing to give up my entire fortune just to have a normal life, to erase the horrors of my past, but at times like these, I was grateful I had a boatload of the green. "When can I get this information?"

"I've got all the records at the shop. Come on over now, and I'll show you what I have."

Perfect. Absolutely perfect.

CHAPTER FOURTEEN

JADE

My pulse raced as I stood on the front porch of the address where Wendy Madigan lived. *Get a grip, Jade. This is work, nothing more.*

I drew in a deep breath, let it out, and then rapped on the door.

A few seconds later the door opened, and Wendy Madigan herself answered.

"Yes?"

"Ms. Madigan, hi. I'm Jade Roberts from Snow Creek."

She arched her eyebrows, but other than that, didn't look overly surprised. "You've got to be kidding me. You came all this way?"

"It's business, ma'am. You have information I need."

"I'm not sure I do. I'd really rather not discuss the Steels with you."

"Look, you can discuss it with me, or I can subpoena you to a deposition and force the information out of you under oath. I really don't want to have to do that, Ms. Madigan."

I was bluffing. Without a suit filed, I had no right to depose her. I still had no idea why Larry was pursuing this. At this point, I had my own agenda.

She let out a sigh, the laugh wrinkles around her eyes becoming more apparent. She looked old. Old and tired. "I guess I should've expected this sooner or later. Come on in. And call me Wendy, while you're at it."

I smiled, my panic finally easing. "I appreciate it. I really do. And please, call me Jade." I stepped into the modest household.

"This is my mother's home," Wendy said. "I moved in a couple years ago when I retired. Her health is still good, but she needs a lot of help with things, considering her age."

"I really don't mean to intrude," I said. "But I need to get this information."

She nodded again. "Would you like anything? A cup of tea? Coffee? Bottle of water?" She paused for a few seconds. "Scotch?"

I let out a laugh. "Actually, a bottle of water would be perfect. Flying always dries me out."

"Good enough. I'm going to have a stiff Scotch. If I'm going to talk about the Steels, I need it."

"I assume that means this might be uncomfortable for you. I'm sorry about that."

"Uncomfortable? I'm not sure that's the right word."

"What would be the right word?" I asked.

"Hell if I know. The Steels... They do carry their share of secrets."

She was standing with her back to me, opening the fridge, so I couldn't see the expression on her face. Her voice, though, indicated exhaustion. Exhaustion because she was fatigued or at the thought of discussing the Steels?

I had a hunch it was the latter.

Wendy moved to the counter, opened the cupboard, and pulled out a bottle. She poured herself a generous portion of the amber liquid. "Have a seat." She gestured to the kitchen table.

I sat, and she joined me, placing a bottle of water in front of me.

She took a swig of her Scotch. "So what's going on with the Steels?"

"Unfortunately, most of this is classified at this point, so I can't tell you why they're under investigation." Especially since I didn't know. The Steels were not involved in organized crime, as Larry claimed. I'd stake my life on it. "I can only ask questions."

"I hope you understand that I can't divulge certain stuff. A lot of it is confidential between the Steels and me."

"Understood. But the more you can tell me today, the better off it will be for you and the Steels in the future."

She nodded. "Understood as well. What you need to know?"

"Right now, my biggest question is why Talon Steel's heroics overseas were covered up."

"Ms. Roberts...err....Jade, let me be honest with you first off. Talon's heroics being covered up is really a small part of what you're dealing with here."

I nodded, swallowing the drink of water I'd taken. "That doesn't surprise me."

"All I can tell you is that the story was covered up at the request of his older brother, Jonah Steel."

"You mean Talon himself didn't ask you to cover it up?"

"No. But if Jonah hadn't, Talon would have."

"Why do you say that?"

"Talon likes to keep to himself."

Boy, was she right about that. "Why do you think that is? I mean, he was a hero of mega-proportions."

"He has his reasons."

"Do you know what those reasons are?"

"I'm not at liberty to discuss what his reasons might be."

"But you do know what they are?"

Wendy pursed her lips and cleared her throat. She said nothing as she stroked her cheek with her index finger.

Yeah, she knew.

"Can you give me any information on those reasons at all?"

"It would help me a lot, Jade, if I knew why you needed this information."

I didn't know or care why Larry was investigating the Steels. I wanted to know more about Talon Steel and why he was the way he was because I was in love with him, and I wanted to help him. But I couldn't tell Wendy that, so I gave her my canned response. "I wish I could tell you, but it's classified at this point."

She nodded. "Of course. I understand. As a reporter and correspondent, I've used that line more times that I can even remember. I also know what it really means."

I smiled and let out a little small laugh. "So I think you know where I'm coming from, then."

"I do. I do. But I made a lot of promises a long time ago."

"Promises to whom?"

"To Bradford Steel and his wife."

"You knew Daphne?"

She nodded. "We weren't close, but I did know her. She was a very troubled woman."

"Just how far back does your relationship with the Steel family go?" Daphne had died soon after Marj was born, about twenty-five years ago.

"I'd known Brad forever." She got a wistful look in her eyes, as if she were going back in time, to a happier place.

So that was how it was. She had been in love with Talon's father. How could I get her to admit it?

"I see. What does that mean exactly?"

"We went to school together for years. I actually grew up on the Western slope."

"I see. So you and Mr. Steel were friends."

She nodded. "Very...close friends."

I smiled. "I think I get the gist of what you're telling me."

"We were childhood sweethearts, but my family moved to Denver when I was sixteen and Brad was seventeen. We promised to stay together, but you know how that always works out. Long-distance relationships and all."

"I actually do know. Been there."

"Plus we were just babies ourselves." She smiled. "I gave him my virginity before he left." She shook her head and laughed. "Now why the hell did I just tell you that?"

"Because you're strolling down memory lane, Wendy. Don't worry. It won't go any further than me. I'm interested in everything you can tell me about the Steels, but trust me, the fact that Bradford Steel took your virginity will not go into the report to my boss."

She wiped one eye and sniffed. "I appreciate that. Anyway, we went off to different colleges, and Brad ended up married to Daphne. I'm not sure he loved her. She was smart and gorgeous but really troubled. She'd fly off the handle for no reason sometimes, or so it seemed, according to Brad. But she got pregnant with the oldest, Jonah. Brad was nothing if not gentlemanly, so he married her."

"Are you saying the Steels were never in love?"

"My guess is that they weren't. Or at least Brad wasn't. When I started work for NNN, he found me after I did my first piece as a field reporter. He saw me in the news, and he got in touch with me."

I had a feeling where this was headed. "Go on," I said.

"Can I consider this off the record?" she asked.

I nodded. "Sure."

"It didn't take us long to pick up where things had left off." She smiled, shaking her head. "Brad was so handsome, big and strong like his sons are. I had missed him. I'd had a string of boyfriends, but none of them ever measured up to Brad, so I never married. Now and then when I met him again, even though he was married... Well, I'm not proud of it. But then again, I do treasure those memories." She laughed a bit. "I really don't know why I'm telling you all this. I'm not sure I ever told anyone, and here I am, telling my innermost secrets to an attorney who is investigating my onetime lover's family."

"Sometimes it's nice to be able to talk to someone, even a stranger."

She nodded. "I could never tell my mother this. She'd think I was some kind of Jezebel. She'd probably want to brand me with a scarlet letter."

"So when was it," I asked, "that you and Mr. Steel rekindled your affair?"

"About thirty years ago. All the boys had been born. Little Ryan was only a toddler. Brad gave me the old 'my wife doesn't understand me' routine, and I fell for it because I was so crazy about him."

I nodded. "Was he sleeping with his wife at that point?"

"He said he wasn't, and I believed him. Until she got pregnant again with the daughter. He claimed it had meant nothing, of course. That she was going crazy, and he did it to calm her down. I didn't believe that then, and I don't believe it now. But he had a hold on me, Jade. I couldn't let him go. So when he wanted to continue seeing me, I obliged."

Wow. I got it. Truly got it. Talon had a hold on me that I wasn't sure would ever go away.

"So you saw him while Daphne was pregnant with Marjorie?"

Wendy nodded. "Like I said, not proud of it. But if you could only understand how he affected me. Those Steel men..."

I understood better than she knew, but I couldn't tell her that, at least not yet. "I'm honestly not here to judge you, Wendy. I just want information."

"If Brad were still alive, I wouldn't be telling you all this."

"Understood. But since he isn't, I'm glad you feel you can talk to me."

"It does feel good to get it out."

"But none of this explains why certain things are going

on that I can't quite put together. For example, why Jonah and Talon would want to keep Talon's heroics a secret. And why didn't he get the Medal of Honor? It's crazy that this wasn't a big deal."

Wendy quirked her lips. "He was nominated for the medal."

I widened my eyes. "And?"

"And they squashed it before anyone ever found it. Didn't want it."

"Who squashed it? And why?"

"The Medal makes you a celebrity, and Talon didn't want that. He wouldn't have been able to handle it."

I didn't bother asking why. I knew I'd get the same response, that she didn't know why, even though we both knew she did. I cleared my throat. "Moving on, there are a few documents I can't make heads or tails of."

"What documents are those?"

"One is a birth certificate for Marjorie, my...the youngest Steel child." *Don't spill the beans, Jade. Right now, she needs to think of you as an attorney looking for information, not the best friend of one Steel and the lover of another.*

"What about it?"

"I found it in some boxes of old documents at the Steel home."

"Why would you have access to documents at the Steel home?"

Shit. And I'd just told myself to careful...

"They were...subpoenaed for discovery in a different case." Good save. "Anyway, Marjorie's birth certificate and the marriage certificate for Bradford and Daphne pose some confusion."

"Why is that?"

"First of all, the marriage certificate is between Bradford Raymond Steel and Daphne Kay Wade. All the Steels remember their mother's maiden name as being Warren, not Wade. What's even more curious is that when I search the database of Colorado records, the marriage certificate has been altered. It shows Daphne as Daphne Kay Warren."

"Maybe the one you found in the Steel documents was a forgery."

"I'd thought of that. But why would someone forge a marriage certificate, and if they did, why would they change the bride's maiden name? Seems more likely they'd forge a date, maybe for reasons of inheritance. Or forge the whole certificate itself, not just a maiden name. It doesn't make any sense."

"Let me think on that. What about the other document? You said it was a birth certificate."

"Yes, Marjorie Steel's birth certificate. It shows that she was born Angela Marjorie Steel, yet she was always told by her parents that she had no middle name and was just Marjorie Steel. Again, when I checked the Colorado records database, her birth certificate is shown just as Marjorie Steel. This is another change that makes no sense to me. If you're going to forge a birth certificate, why not change the date or the whole name? But to take away a first name? I can't figure it out."

Wendy cleared her throat and stroked her cheek. "I'm

afraid I can't help you with either of those things."

I didn't believe for a minute that she didn't know anything. I was pretty good at reading people.

"These are both pretty innocuous items. Why can't you share any knowledge with me?"

"Maybe I don't know anything." She stroked her cheek with her index finger. Again.

"I don't mean to be disrespectful, Wendy, but I don't believe that."

"Well, it's immaterial whether I know anything or not. I made promises a long time ago."

"To whom?"

"To Brad."

She really wasn't going to budge. The stern lines of her jaw made that more than apparent. So I'd have to do a little budging.

"Look, Wendy, I'm going to be honest with you. Yes, I am a city attorney, and yes, I am investigating the Steels for my boss, but what you don't know is that Marjorie Steel is my best friend. She and I went to college together, and up until a week ago, I was staying with her on the ranch. I respect the fact that you made promises that you feel you need to keep. But if those promises were made to a dead man, what's the harm in telling me the information I need now?"

"It's for the good of the Steel children." Her eyes misted up again. Did she actually have feelings for the Steel siblings?

I cleared my throat. I would have to go slowly with her. "All right. I can accept that. Can we at least talk about the birth certificate? Marjorie is beside herself. She feels like she doesn't even know who she is."

"That's silly. The name on a birth certificate doesn't say anything about who a person is."

She had a point. But Marj also had a point. "She's twenty-five years old, and she just found out she was born with a different name."

"All right." Wendy sighed. "I guess it wouldn't hurt to tell you about the birth certificate."

Thank God. I could at least go home to Marj with a tiny bit of information.

"Marjorie was born prematurely. At twenty-four weeks. She wasn't expected to survive, so Daphne named her Angela Marjorie, Angela meaning 'angel.' Daphne was sure that Marjorie would be an angel soon. Then, when the baby survived, Daphne wanted the name changed. I told you she was troubled. She thought if the baby carried the name Angela, she'd become an angel."

"I guess that makes sense in some convoluted way. Especially for a troubled woman. But how was Daphne able to have the birth certificate changed in the Colorado database? Normally, when you file a name change, your birth certificate doesn't change."

Wendy shook her head. "I don't how that happened. Or why."

She was lying again. She had a tell. She stroked her cheek with her index finger when she was lying or telling a half truth. Good thing I'd taken that course on body language in trial at law school.

"All right. The Steels obviously had an 'in' with

someone who worked in the records office, and they were able to make changes in the database itself. Which might've had to be done manually back then. I'm not sure when the system became computerized. It was twenty-five years ago."

"They were just beginning to computerize everything back then."

Yup. She *did* know something.

"Look, Wendy, I care about Marj very much, and I care about her brothers. Is there anything else you can possibly tell me?"

Wendy licked her lips, seemingly lost in thought. Then, "Maybe it's time. I did some things at Brad's request, things I didn't necessarily agree with, but I loved him and I wanted him happy. I can only tell you this much. Around twenty-five years ago, something happened in the Steel family."

Twenty-five years ago. That was about the time of the five-million-dollar transfer that didn't make any sense in the documents. "What happened exactly?" I asked.

She closed her eyes for a few seconds and then re-opened them. "Something abominable, appalling. Between my clout with the media and Brad's money, we were able to keep it quiet. I didn't agree then, because it meant a lot of sick people got away with some really heinous crimes, but I agree with him now." She regarded me, her blue eyes sunken and pleading. "Please don't dredge up the past, Jade. So many people will get hurt."

CHAPTER FIFTEEN

TALON

The next day I drove to Grand Junction to meet with Robert Prendergast, otherwise known as Biker Bob, who owned one of the top tattoo parlors in the city. Safe in a Ziploc was the photo of the tattoo that I remembered from my past. I'd put it in an envelope so I didn't have to see it. Seeing it was...bad.

I had called Bob ahead of time, and he'd agreed to meet me at his shop. Of course, I'd had to promise to make it worth his while. Wave a few dollars around, and most people ended up exactly where you wanted them. Surreal.

This shop was state of the art, nothing like the little hole in Snow Creek. I walked in, and several artists were working in the back, their tattoo guns buzzing.

The receptionist, platinum blond and heavily tattooed, nodded at me. "Help you?"

"I'm here to see Bob. He's expecting me. Talon Steel."

She smiled and stood. "I'll get him for you."

The receptionist returned with a massive mountain of a man wearing a leather vest, a studded leather belt, and jeans. His hair was wrapped up in a do-rag, and a graying braid hung out from it all the way down to his ass crack, which was, unfortunately, visible when he turned to whisper something to the receptionist.

He held out his hand. "I'm Bob."

I shook his meaty paw. "Great to meet you. Is there a place we can talk? Maybe get a cup of coffee?"

"How about a beer?"

I twisted my lips. "Even better."

We walked a few shops down to a little Irish pub. When I found out they didn't have Peach Street or Breckenridge, I ordered a Jameson. Biker Bob went Guinness all the way, along with an order of onion rings. It was early yet, so the place wasn't too rowdy, and we could actually hear each other talk.

"So what can I help you with?" Bob asked.

"It's about the tattoo parlor you used to own in Snow Creek. Toby Jackson owns it now."

"Yeah, good guy, Toby. Talented artist, too."

"I wouldn't know."

"You mean you're a virgin?"

What the hell? I must've looked as confused as I was, because he let out a guffaw.

"I mean a virgin body. No tats."

"Nope, no tats." And it was going to stay that way.

"I could fix you up. A good-looking guy like you, all those muscles. You got a special lady?"

I kept myself from nodding. "Nope."

"Shoot. She'd love her name on one of those triceps."

The way Bob was eyeing me freaked me out a little. My guts started to churn. "I don't think so. And stop staring at me." I looked away from him.

"Cool down. I'm a ladies' man all the way. But I look at

everyone's body. It's a canvas to me, ya know?"

Whatever. I wanted to get back to the subject at hand. "I was going through one of the books from your old place, and I found a tattoo that I remember seeing a long time ago. How long did you own the shop in Snow Creek?"

"About five years."

Shit. Then he might not know who the hell this guy was either.

"But I worked there from the time I was eighteen and an apprentice."

Eureka.

"Cool. So how long were you there altogether?"

"Fifteen years, all told. Bought it about ten years in, sold it to Toby about fifteen years ago."

Thirty years ago. Interesting. The timing was right. I pulled the photo safely ensconced in its plastic bag out of my pocket. "Do you recognize this work?"

He pulled the photo out of the envelope and his eyes lit up. "Recognize it? That's *my* work. One of my finest designs, if I do say so myself."

My heart raced. "Did anybody else in the shop do that particular design?"

He shook his head. "Nope. Most artists don't use other artist's designs, unless someone comes in wanting that particular tattoo and the originating artist isn't available. Kind of a professional courtesy. But I left copies of my work with Toby at his request, in case someone came in looking for something I was known for. It was part of our deal."

That explained why Toby had the photo. "Do you remember the guy in this photo?"

"That was a long time ago, man. Lots of people loved that design. I used it a lot."

"Did they all have it done on their forearm like this?"

He shook his head. "Most of them had it on their shoulder or lower back. Some on the upper arm. I'm trying to recollect..."

The waitress came by and took an order for another drink for each of us. Bob ordered another plate of rings.

"There was one guy who wanted it on his forearm. That might've been the first time I did this particular design. But then I think there was one other guy who wanted it on the forearm because the picture showed it that way. Obviously. Then there might have been another, too."

And maybe another. Was I wasting my time here? "Do you remember the names of any of the guys who had it done on the forearm?"

"Man, I wish I could help you. But it was a damn long time ago."

"Have you come across this design anytime else in your career?"

"This exact design? Nope, can't say that I have. I do keep it in my own portfolio, as well as the one I left with Toby. But the phoenix seems to have died out. They were real popular some twenty-thirty years ago. Got a new life a while back, with the Harry Potter craze. But since then, not much."

I took out a Benji and slid it across the table to him. "Does this help you remember?"

He swallowed the drink of beer he'd taken and let out a raucous laugh. "I wish it did. But I'm an honest man, Steel."

"Keep it," I said. "I appreciate your time, Bob. If you remember anything, please call me."

"I sure wish I did, because I could handle a few more Franklins thrown my way. I'll think on it, but at the moment I sure as hell don't remember much. I spent a lot of those early years stoned."

I was pretty sure he was stoned now, considering how he was inhaling those onion rings.

I sent another hundred his way as I finished my second Jameson. "To jog your memory a bit."

Bob fingered the Benji and laughed. "I'll do my best. Stop by my shop anytime if you change your mind about the tat. I'll be happy to hook you up."

I chuckled. "Not in this lifetime."

"How'd you come across that tat anyway? Just looking through Toby's books? That doesn't make a lot of sense if you had no interest in getting tatted yourself."

"It's a tattoo my—" The word "girlfriend" sat on the edge of my lips, threatening to eject itself of its own volition. But Jade wasn't my girlfriend. And if I was honest, girlfriend didn't begin to describe what Jade was to me. She was so much more...my everything, my soul. I cleared my throat. "A friend had. Or was going to get. She won't be getting it now."

"Why not? Great tat for a chick. Makes a nice tramp stamp on the back. I remember doing a lot of those."

"She won't be getting this one. Or any tat if I have anything to say about it."

"What do you got against tats, boy?"

Invisible spiders crept up my neck and onto my scalp. My ire rose. "Don't call me boy."

"Hey, meant no disrespect. But seriously, why don't you like tats?"

"I have my reasons."

"Why are you so interested in that particular tat? Or should I say, why are you so interested in the person who *has* that particular tat?"

I pulled one more Benji out of my wallet and slid it across the table and into Bob's meaty hands. "Don't ever ask me that again. Just contact me if you remember anything about who you tatted that on."

"Will do."

I threw a few more bills on the table. "This should cover the drinks and rings."

"Obliged." Bob gave me a salute, downing the rest of his Guinness.

I turned and walked out of the bar.

My whole body trembled, itching, wanting to convulse. I sat down on the bench outside an ice-cream shop a couple of doors down.

And a movie began playing in my mind.

★ ★ ★

Sometimes the bird emerged on the walls of the cellar, most often at night, when they were closing in on the boy. The bird had become both a menace and a sanctuary. It gave the boy solace, something to focus on when the unthinkable was happening, but because it was representative of one who inflicted the horrors on him, it was also a plague that haunted him at night, jeering at him.

You're worthless, boy. Insignificant. Meaningless. Trash

to be used, abused, left to die...

Its flaming wings now gray and white in the darkness, the bird flapped to him, edging toward him along with the pulsating wall.

Worthless... Insignificant... Left to die...

But as much as the boy wanted to die, he never did.

CHAPTER SIXTEEN

Please don't dredge up the past, Jade. So many people will get hurt.

Wendy's words haunted me as George dropped me off at the Steel ranch house. It was Saturday, so I didn't have to go into work. I would tell Marj what I had found out about her birth certificate. I didn't want to tell her, yet, about Wendy Madigan and the affair with her father, but she deserved to know about her name.

I paid George. Seemed like all my extra cash was being used to shuttle me back and forth from the ranch. I had to get a car.

I trudged up the long walkway and knocked on the door. Roger, Talon's mutt, appeared behind the glass. He looked at me, cocking his head through the oblong window next to the door. He was such a cute little fellow.

A few seconds later, the door opened, and Talon's muscular frame greeted me.

My body throbbed. Just being in close proximity to him affected me. As much as I wanted to interrogate him about the tattoo ordeal the other night, I knew it would be futile. I said simply, "Hi. I came to see Marj."

"She's not here. Cooking class, remember?"

Crap. I'd forgotten. Marj had signed up for a weekend cooking class in Grand Junction that met Friday night and all day Saturday.

"I'm really sorry. I forgot about that."

"You want me to give her a message for you?"

I looked at him, shaking my head. Was he really going to stand there and pretend we didn't know each other intimately?

Roger panted at my heels. I bent down to give him a scratch on the head.

"No, no message. But I will take a cup of tea if you have one."

"Here's a deal for you. I'll make the tea if you make up a couple of your patented cheddar and tomato grilled cheese sandwiches."

I couldn't help a smile. "I'll take that deal."

I walked into the foyer as he shut the door behind me. I knelt down and let Roger jump up on me. He covered my face with doggie kisses.

"Funny. Other than me, you're the one he's taken to the most."

"I love dogs. I've never met a dog that didn't love me back. I think dogs just sense dog people."

The late summer day was cooler, and I'd put on a pair of skinny jeans and a sleeveless pink sweater. Talon looked luscious in his boots, dark denim jeans, and a green T-shirt.

"I'll get started." I made my way to the kitchen and looked through the fridge. "I don't see any cheddar in here, but there's some Colby Jack. That'll be good."

I pulled out the cheese, grabbed a tomato from the basket on the counter, took a knife and cutting board, and started preparing. Once the sandwiches were in the pan frying, I turned around. Talon was sitting at the table, watching me.

"I thought you were going to make the tea."

"Sorry, I was just enjoying the view."

My skin heated. The view of him was mighty fine as well. He stood and came toward me, like a wolf stalking his prey. I knew he was going to kiss me before he was even close to me. And when his lips crushed onto mine, I nearly shattered then and there. I swirled my tongue out to meet his. Electricity sparked through my body. The kiss was unyielding, drugging, a kiss of souls meeting and joining.

We ate at each other's mouth for a couple of minutes until I broke away quickly.

"Sorry, the sandwiches..." I walked quickly to the stove to turn them. "Oh, good. They're brown but not burnt."

Talon grabbed me from behind and pulled me back to him. "Fuck the sandwiches."

"Talon," I said against his lips.

But he plunged his tongue inside my mouth.

We kissed with intensity and passion, mindless and demanding kisses that left me breathless and yearning, anticipating, tightening the invisible coils that bound us.

Until I broke away again. "Sorry, but I really don't want the smoke alarms to go off."

Damn. That kiss alone could have set the things off.

I went to the stove, took the sandwiches off the pan, and set them on plates. I grabbed a napkin for each. "So where's the tea?"

Talon didn't answer.

I went to the fridge and pulled a couple bottles of water. "No worries. This will work just fine." I set the waters and the sandwiches at the table. "Come on, sit. Eat your lunch."

He grabbed the sandwich and was about to take a bite when I stopped him.

"Remember what happened last time? Let it cool a bit first." I removed the bread from mine and let the smoke emerge from the hot cheese. Once it had cooled off, I took a bite. "Nothing like it. I may not be able to cook like your sister, but I make a mean grilled cheese."

He tried his. "Yep, pretty good."

Why did I feel like we never had anything to talk about?

Maybe if we weren't in bed, ripping each other's clothes off, we could actually have a conversation. I'd try a tactic, maybe find some answers.

"I found an interesting news article last week."

"Yeah?"

"Yeah. It was about you."

Talon's eyebrows jerked upward almost to his hairline. He didn't say anything.

"About when you got back from Iraq. Why didn't you tell me you got the Award of Honor?"

"Where the hell did you find that?"

"In the local paper archives."

"Why were you looking in there?"

I swallowed a bite of sandwich. I couldn't very well tell him that Larry had told me to investigate him. "I was actually looking for something else on an investigation, and your story happened to pop up."

He put his sandwich down, reached for his water, but didn't take it. "They shouldn't have printed that story."

"Are you kidding me? They totally should've printed it. It should've been national news, Talon, not just a people piece in the local news of a small Western town."

"I didn't want anyone making a big fuss about me."

"A fuss about you? You were a goddamned hero."

"I wasn't a hero, blue eyes. Trust me. I was never a hero."

"You saved those people. At great personal risk to yourself. You could've been killed."

He slammed his fist on the table. "Did you ever think about why I did it? Maybe I didn't do it to be a hero."

I eased backward into my chair, my tension rising. I was used to Talon's outbursts by now, but still they affected me. "I'm sure you didn't. I'm sure all you were thinking about were your fallen troops. Your adrenaline was probably in full force. You were thinking about getting your friends out."

He let out a wry chuckle, his lips twisted into a shape I couldn't read. "Trust me, I wasn't."

"Then what *were* you thinking about?"

"I was thinking about getting my ass *killed*, Jade."

CHAPTER SEVENTEEN

Her beautiful mouth dropped into that oblong shape I had seen so often. She would never understand. I was no hero.

They gave me the damned award—tried to give me the medal, but I didn't want it—for saving six people that day. I was glad I had saved them. Their lives were worth a hell of a lot more than mine. But every time I dragged another one out, still free of bodily injury myself, I carelessly dumped him on the ground and ran back in, hoping to get my fucking head blown off instead of bringing another one to safety.

The time finally came when Waters and a few others literally held me down and wouldn't let me go back in for yet another man. Little did they know, I wanted to go in and never come out.

Jade sat next to me—her steely blue eyes that haunted me, the beautiful golden-brown hair that cascaded over her milky shoulders, those ruby-red lips I had kissed so many times—and for the first time in a long time, maybe ever, I was actually glad—fucking *glad*—I hadn't gotten my head blown off that day.

How I loved her. My mouth wanted to form the words right at the moment and say them.

What would she think if she knew I loved her? She would probably ask how I knew, given the conflicting messages I'd sent her over the last couple months.

"Are you going to say anything, blue eyes?"

She drew her lips into a semi-smile. A forced smile. "I'm not really sure what to say to you, Talon."

"Say the first thing that came into your mind."

She arched her eyebrows and shook her head. "What can I say? I'm glad you didn't die, Talon. Fucking ecstatic, actually. You mean something to me. You may not understand that, but you do. And you mean something to your brothers and Marj. Did you think about what you coming home in a body bag would have done to them? Do you ever think about anyone *but* Talon Steel? Why would you want to die? I don't understand."

I didn't respond. I *couldn't* respond. She was right on two counts. She didn't understand, and I hadn't been thinking about anyone but myself. Truth was, I knew in my heart that the guys and Marj would be better off without me.

She continued, "And honestly? I was surprised."

That got me. "Why should you be surprised?"

"Because most people have a survival instinct. It's one thing to go in and rescue people when you care about your men, feel a responsibility toward them. It's quite another altogether to go in with no regard for your own life."

The survival instinct.

The fucking survival instinct.

The concept was nothing new to me. God, the things I'd said and done to simply survive, to continue to exist in a nightmare. But after two decades of living with the memories of that horror, my survival instinct had been shot to hell.

Since I couldn't voice any of this, I again said nothing.

"Really? You're going to sit there and not respond to me?"

"There's nothing to say, blue eyes."

She shook her head. "Fine. At least tell me why you didn't want this to be national news."

That was easy. "I didn't want anyone making a fuss over me about what a selfless act it had been when I knew damned well it wasn't selfless. It was fucking selfish."

She slid her hand onto mine. "Talon, whatever your intentions were, the end result was the same, and all those servicemen and their families are beyond grateful."

Her touch both soothed and agitated me. So much she didn't understand. "I know. Believe me. I received so many thank-you notes and care packages..." I rolled my eyes.

"And that was a bad thing?"

"Yeah, it was a bad thing, Jade. These people were thanking me, wanting to do things for me, wanting to somehow repay me for saving their loved ones, and all I had been trying to do was get my ass killed."

"But as I said, the end result was the same. You *saved* those men."

"Not all men. One was a woman."

"You saved someone's mother maybe. That's a great thing."

"She was young. No kids." I heaved a sigh. "Having the local story was bad enough. People came to the house bearing gifts. Produce from their farms, wine, booze, cakes and cookies, and casseroles. It was never-ending. Jonah and Ryan played hosts, and once Marjorie got back from school, she helped as well. I just wanted to be left alone."

Damn, if it had made national news, the networks would've been after me for interviews, the fucking talk shows... I wouldn't have been able to take it.

I'd told Jade before, and I'd told my brothers countless times. I was no hero.

Jade stood, still holding onto my hand. "I didn't know you then, and I don't know why you were so determined to get yourself killed over there, but let me tell you one thing."

"What?"

"I, for one, am damned glad you're alive. I wish I understood why you felt you had to end your life, but I thank God you're here. With me. Now." She pulled me out of the chair to my feet and wrapped her arms around me, snuggling her face into my chest. "You smell so good."

For the second, I echoed her sentiments. I was damned glad I hadn't died that day. I inhaled the coconut scent of her hair. "So do you, blue eyes."

She just held me. She didn't try to kiss me, didn't grab the bulge in my pants, which was now visible. She just held me close to her.

And damn, it felt good.

It felt fucking good to be held.

I kissed the top of her head, her silky hair tickling my nose. Oh, I wanted her. I wanted to strip her down and shove my cock into her wet heat right this minute. But I also wanted this closeness, this tenderness.

I squeezed her harder, trying to prolong this moment

for as long as I could. "I..."

She let out a sigh. "What is it?" she asked.

I wanted to say "I love you." I wanted to say it so badly. The words ached to spill out of me.

But I couldn't bring them forward.

Then the strangest thing happened. She pulled away from me and pierced my gaze with her blue one.

"Talon, I love you."

My knees nearly buckled beneath me. My lips trembled. She must've mistaken that for getting ready to speak, because she covered my mouth with two fingers.

"You don't have to say it back. I know you're probably not ready. You may never love me. I understand that, and I don't want to pressure you into anything you're not ready for. I know you said you won't love me. And that's okay. But I want you to know that I love you. I want you to know that you are worth something to me. Not because you saved someone I love. Not because you're a hero. Not because you're my best friend's brother. And not because you're gorgeous and muscular and physically perfect." She smiled. "Just because you're Talon Steel, and I'm really glad I met you and that you're in my life. And if what I have with you lasts no longer than the next minute, I will still be glad I met you, and I will never regret falling in love with you."

My eyes stung. Yes, tears threatened. My body was simultaneously numb and coursing with every emotion imaginable. *I love you too, Jade. I love you too.*

She continued, "And now, I really want to go to your bedroom and make love with you."

My hard cock thought that was a great idea, but what I

really wanted was to savor her, to make this about her, good for her, more than I had the other night. And maybe, just maybe, I would be able to repeat the words she had said to me. Never before had I longed so much to say those words, but I was truly scared. Scared that I wasn't what she thought I was...and I knew I was not. When she found out about me, she would no longer love me.

I cupped her cheek and stroked it softly with my thumb. "You didn't need to say all of that, blue eyes. I'll be happy to make love with you."

"I didn't say it for any other reason than I wanted to say it. Although I do think that's the first time you've referred to the act as making love instead of fucking." She let out a giggle.

"Come with me." I led her down the hallway to my suite, Roger following along.

I would take her slowly this time, even though my cock was straining.

I pulled her pink sweater over her head and tossed it on the chair. I unclasped her bra and freed her beautiful breasts. Her nipples were hard and taut, and I pinched one of the pink-brown nubs.

She jolted. "God, I love it when you do that."

So did I. Her nipples and breasts were a fucking work of art. The finest sculptors couldn't have carved anything more beautiful.

She reached for my T-shirt, but I swatted her hand away.

"Let me," I said. "Let me take care of *you* this time."

I pushed her down on the bed, removed her sandals,

and then unbuckled her jeans and slid them over her hips. Only her leopard-spotted panties remained between me and her luscious body. I didn't want to go straight for her hot pussy, even though I knew it was wet. I could smell her musk, and it was making me crazy. No, I would do something for her. Even though I hadn't been able to give her the words she had given me, I could at least give her tenderness with my body.

I leaned over her, still fully clothed, and kissed her softly on the lips. She opened her mouth to meet my tongue, but instead of taking it, I moved to her cheek, raining tiny kisses over the apple, up to her temple, and then down to her earlobe. I tugged on it lightly and nibbled around the outer shell of her ear. She sighed softly. I probed into her ear with my tongue and then continued down the side of her neck, kissing little trails across her jawline, her cheek, to her other ear, where I repeated my action. Then I kissed her neck, giving her little love bites, refraining from sucking hard and marking her, even though I yearned to do so.

I kissed across her chest to her shoulders, down her arms to her hand, where I sucked each of her fingers into my mouth. I kissed back up her arm and across her chest again, reveling in the soft sweetness of her flesh. Ignoring those amazing breasts demanded all my willpower, but I did it, determined to show her all the tenderness I never thought I could. I kissed over to her other arm, grazing over the soft skin with my lips.

"Talon, please. My nipples."

"Shh," I said against her skin. "In good time."

I kissed a spiral pattern around her breast, not stopping until I made it to the areola. Then I gave the boob a squeeze and moved to the other one.

She squirmed against me. "I'm going crazy here. My nipples need you."

I chuckled against her silky skin while spiraling around the other breast. Her skin was like the finest silk under my lips as I kissed it, swirled my tongue into it, tasted the sleek texture of her.

She squirmed more but didn't ask me to pleasure her nipples again. I slid down to her abdomen and rained kisses over it. When I got to the beautiful pussy between her legs, I summoned every ounce of self-control I had to make a detour and kiss down her thighs, knees, all the way to her beautiful feet, toes painted light pink. I kissed each toe and glided back up again, avoiding her pussy and sliding down the other leg.

My cock was ready to burst out of its confinement. But I was single-minded. She had done so much for me, had tried to make it about me so many occasions. This was her time.

I kissed back up to her abdomen.

Finally, I flicked my tongue over one turgid nipple.

"Oh, God, yes," she sighed. "I've been waiting for that, needing that. No one sucks my nipples like you do, Talon."

"No one's nipples are as beautiful as yours, blue eyes." I sucked one into my mouth while pinching the other one between my thumb and forefinger.

She writhed beneath me, and her musky scent drifted upward. I inhaled deeply, still sucking on her nipple. God, I was so fucking hard.

I ached to free my cock and sink into her moist heat,

but I was determined to give her what she wanted, and right now she wanted the nipple treatment. Not a hardship to focus on her beautiful nipples. I sucked, nibbled, bit, kissed... and underneath me she continued to writhe, convulsing, sighing, moaning my name...like candied nectar for the ears.

She gripped two fistfuls of my T-shirt and tried to pull it forward over my torso.

I gave her nipple a hard bite. "Not yet, blue eyes."

She tried to pull my shirt up again, and I bit her again.

Ah... She liked the hard bite. She had liked the nipple clamps the other night. She liked harsh nipple play.

I certainly had more of that in store for her, but I was trying to be tender today. No more bites on her nipples. Even if she tried to pull my shirt off.

Finally, when her nipples were good and worked over, I slid her panties off her and let my hand drift between her legs and part her silky folds. God, so wet, so juicy. I pushed two fingers inside her and massaged her G spot.

She jerked beneath me. "God, Talon. I want to come so bad."

"Oh, you will, baby. You're going to come a lot today."

And right after I said those words, I found her clitoris and sent her over the edge.

She gripped the comforter as she screamed her release. "Oh, God, Talon, I love you, I love you."

Had she realized she said those words?

She was in another world, a world of nirvana, of rapture.

But even so, the words soared into me, giving me strength, hope.

I knelt between her legs and pressed my mouth to

her wet cunt. It was still pulsing after her orgasm, and her juices warmed my mouth. I shoved my tongue into her deep recesses. Her flavor was like a juicy apple laced with female musk. Not even the finest Western slope apples from my orchard could rival Jade's intense flavor after an orgasm. I lapped at her, feasting on her, determined to suck every last ounce of ambrosia from her mouth-watering body. Then I turned to her clit, wrapped my lips around it, and sucked.

And she flew into another climax.

She grabbed my head, grinding my face against her pussy. "God, yes, Talon. Just like that. Eat me. Eat me raw."

Her words fed my desire, as I sucked at her clit again, this time thrusting not two but three fingers deep within her channel. I massaged that special spot, sending her over the edge again and then again.

She writhed, shivered, shattered, begged me to stop. "Enough, Talon. I need your cock. Now, please."

But I was not to be deterred. My woman wouldn't just come today. She would keep coming and keep coming until her body was so sated, so exhausted, she could do nothing except fall asleep against me.

After that orgasm though, she scooted herself upward, breaking my suction on her pussy with a loud smack. "Talon, I can't take it anymore. I have to have your cock. Please. Now." She sat up and grabbed fistfuls of my green T-shirt, pulling it up my torso.

This time I couldn't say no. I raised my arms and let her rid me of the shirt. Then she unbuckled my belt, unsnapping and unzipping my jeans before pushing them and my boxer briefs over my hips.

Her silvery eyes turned a smoky gray as she glared at me. "Now," she said through clenched teeth.

Without even taking off my boots and jeans, I pushed her back on the bed and thrust into her welcoming warmth.

Oh, the glory, the glory of finding the one who had been sculpted just for me. For that's what Jade was. No one gripped me like she did. No one gloved me like she did. I thrust inside her, and then I had to wait, willing myself to hold off. I wanted to plunge into her one more time and release my seed inside her.

Like an animal, I wanted to spread my seed, impregnate my mate.

She was on the pill, so that wouldn't happen. I had never wanted children before, but the thought of her swelling with my child excited me, surged through me like primal joy.

I pulled out and thrust in again, and she sighed beneath me, that soft sigh that always escaped her like a sweet breeze when I entered her.

I brought my mouth down to hers and kissed her deeply, our tongues twirling together, letting her taste her own flavor from my mouth. She kissed me back with so much fervor, so much passion, that I thought I would come right there.

But again I held off. Determined to make this last. Determined to make this about her for once—not about me.

She moved her thighs upward so her knees were right at my armpits. God, the angle was so deep, so perfect. I thrust and I thrust and I thrust once more, and then, with an explosion of stars behind me, I released into her honeyed pussy.

My breath came in rapid pants as I held fast, not moving, just letting my cock stay embedded in her wet heat.

Emotion swirled thick around me, gutting me. And when I finally opened my eyes, hers were piercing me with that silvery-steel gaze.

I could no longer stop the words.

"God, Jade, I love you. I love you so much."

CHAPTER EIGHTEEN

JADE

The warmth of a summer day burst through me. Had I heard him right? I didn't want to ask, for fear he might take the words back. Perhaps they'd only been said in the throes of his orgasm.

No. That couldn't be. Talon was too closed off, too walled in to bring forth words he didn't mean.

As I stared into his dark, blazing eyes, I knew he had spoken the truth.

As much as I wanted to ask him to repeat the words, to say them over and over again until I tired of hearing them... What a crock. I would never tire of hearing them.

But I wouldn't ask him to repeat them. They had been hard for him to say, I could tell. The last thing I wanted was for him to take them back or regret saying them. I wasn't going to be one of those needy women who had to hear her lover profess his devotion over and over again.

I had been that way with Colin.

But with Colin...

Things had never been like this with Colin.

As much as I'd thought I was in love with Colin, those feelings paled next to what I felt for Talon now. Never had such a primitive force taken me over, demanded obedience... demanded Talon. It was lust, it was desire, it was passion, and it was...*love*. Love like I'd never known or imagined.

I simply smiled at Talon and hoped the smile said what I feared my words couldn't.

He stroked my cheek and pressed his lips gently against mine. Then he rose and sat on the bed next to my supine form. He removed his boots and socks and then his jeans and underwear, which were still down around his knees. He lay next to me, still silent. For once, the silence seemed natural. I reveled in it, in the emotion that was thick around us, in the love we shared.

I didn't delude myself into thinking this could be something permanent...even though I wished with everything in me that it could be. Talon still had too much he needed to work out, and plus... What would he think when he found out I was investigating him and his family for Larry?

What a conundrum. I didn't want to quit my job. I needed it, even though I didn't have a lot of respect for my boss. And on a personal level, I wanted to know more about Talon and his family. I wanted to know why he had tried to get himself killed overseas when he was saving all of those troops.

Something poisoned him inside, and he needed to work through that before we could even think about being together in the long-term.

But for now, I simply wanted to lie next to him, feel his closeness, his warmth. With all my soul, I wanted to help him through whatever was nagging at him. I just wasn't sure he was ready for that yet. I would have to be content to do for him what I could at the moment, and that was to be here for him. To love him. To let him know how important he was to me.

"I meant it," he said.

I smiled again, looking to the ceiling. "So did I."

He turned to me, got up on his shoulder with his head in his hand. "But I don't know if I can..."

I pressed two fingers to his lips. "Don't worry about anything right now. Just know that I love you, and I don't have any expectations. All I need to know right now is that you love me. We don't have to think about anything past the end of today. At least not yet."

He cleared his throat. "Well, there is one thing I do need to talk to you about."

His gaze was intense and fiery, his eyes serious.

"All right. What is it?"

"I don't want you to get a tattoo."

The calming love permeating me morphed into a defensive knot in my gut. "Why not?"

"I just don't."

I sighed, willing the calm to return...and failing. I had been dreaming of a tattoo for years. I loved them, and I really felt that they could tell a story, be a part of me inherently. "I don't understand. Why would you have anything against a tattoo?"

"I hate tattoos."

"Then you don't have to get one."

He sat up, clearly agitated, gripping the bed clothes. "I would never mar my body like that."

"That's your choice, Talon. And I respect it. I just need you to respect mine. I think tattoos are beautiful when done tastefully. And I do plan to get one."

"I forbid it."

This time *I* sat up, the defensive knot rising into indignation. "Did I just hear you forbid me to do something?"

He looked at me, his eyes glaring. "That's correct. I forbid it."

I let out a laugh and shook my head. "I really can't believe you just said that. You can't forbid me from getting a tattoo."

"I just did, didn't I?"

I stood and gathered my clothes. "I do love you, Talon." Oh, I did. In spite of everything. "But if this is how a relationship with you is going to be, I'm not sure I can participate."

He grabbed me and tossed me down on the bed. He turned me over so I was facedown, and he slapped one cheek of my ass hard.

He covered my body with his and bit into my neck. I jolted, the pleasure-pain so intense, it rolled through me like a whirlwind.

He whispered into my ear, "I won't have your beautiful body marred by that horrible image."

Horrible image? A phoenix rising from ashes? It was a beautiful image with meaningful symbolism. Why did he hate it so much? He had reacted so violently to the outline the other night. Something about the phoenix bothered him. What could it be?

I would find out, but right now, with his warm body

covering mine, my pussy was starting to get wet again.

His rock-hard cock jabbed against the crease of my ass. God, what his body did to mine. My skin tautened, and my core throbbed. I knew he was ready to take me again, and I also knew I wouldn't resist.

He slid his cock slowly into me.

"You will not get that tattoo, do I make myself clear?"

I didn't answer, my body so full of heat and desire.

"Your body is mine, Jade. Mine. You will not ink it up."

He thrust again, filling me, completing me.

In that moment, I might've agreed to anything. But I kept my lips shut. The throes of passion would not overwhelm me.

Before I knew it, I was releasing into an explosive orgasm. I bit my lip, moaning, grasping fistfuls of the comforter.

"Mine," he chanted. "Mine, mine, mine."

He kept fucking me, harder and harder, and my pussy began to burn. I wanted more and more and more and more...until another climax overtook me.

Again I fisted the comforter, molded to the sheets.

"Take it, Jade. Take me. Take all of me. You're mine, Jade. Mine."

He pushed hard once more, and then, my pussy so sensitive from two explosive climaxes, I felt every spasm of his cock as he released into me.

His perspiration dripped on my neck, my shoulders, and I relished it as the droplets rivered down my skin.

When he finally pulled out, he rolled off me and lay on his back with his arm over his forehead, his standard postcoital position. I turned onto my back as well but slid the other way so that our bodies were not touching.

As much as I wanted to roll into his arms, I had to figure out a way to deal with this tattoo business. I had every intention of still getting a tattoo. Was it just the image that he objected to? Or was it a tattoo in general?

Surely he had come across tattoos before. He had been in the military, for God's sake. Frankly, I was surprised he didn't have one himself.

I kept quiet for now, breathing in, still relaxing in the afterglow from my two orgasms.

My feet were dangling at the end of the bed, and soon I felt a warm tongue on them. I let out a giggle, sat up, and found Roger licking at my toes. I pulled him up onto the bed and gave him a hug. "Such a good boy. So cute." I stroked his furry little face.

Talon still lay faceup, his arm across his eyes. I released Roger, and the dog bounded straight to his master, licking at his chest and face. No doubt he was nice and salty from all the perspiration.

With his free hand, Talon reached out and petted Roger, still not opening his eyes or moving his other arm.

I loved how much Talon adored this little guy. A man who loved dogs—was there anything better? I had never trusted people who didn't like dogs. I personally loved them, and I'd missed having one in my life the last seven years during college and law school. I doubted that Sarah would let me have one in that tiny little apartment I rented above beauty shop. If I still lived here, I'd have Roger to greet me every day when I came home.

If I still lived here, I'd have a lot of things that I missed.

Talon didn't appear to have any intention of moving. Now probably wouldn't be a good time to bring up the tattoo again. I leaned over and kissed him on the cheek. "I should go now, Talon," I said. "It's Saturday, and I have tons of errands to run."

He grunted.

I put my clothes on, gave Roger another quick pet, and—

Crap. I had no way to get home.

I sat down on the bed again and nudged Talon. "Talon, can you drive me home?"

He didn't move his arms. "Just take the Mustang. The keys are in the little ceramic pot in the kitchen where they always are. I don't mind you using it, and I know Marj doesn't."

"Really, I don't want to impose."

Eyes still covered. "Look, I wish you were still staying here, okay? I asked you to come back. At least take the car. You need transportation."

I swallowed. He was right. I did need transportation. I was spending way too much on cab fare, although George was probably deliriously happy.

"All right. Thank you. That's very generous."

He grunted again.

I went to the kitchen, grabbed the keys, and left.

★ ★ ★

Before heading back to my apartment, I decided to stop

at Toby's. Maybe I could find a different image, one that wouldn't upset Talon so much. Haley was at the front desk.

"Haley," I said, "I'm really sorry I had to dart out of here the other night."

She looked at me oddly, biting her lip, playing with the dangling hoop. "Let me go get Toby."

"What for?"

She didn't answer, just walked to the back and returned with a young blond guy.

"This is Toby. Toby, Jade, the woman who was in the other night wanting the phoenix tattoo."

"Hi, Toby," I said. "I wanted to look through the books and see if I could find a different image for my tat. I had some...issues with the first one."

Toby shook his head. "I'm sure Haley explained things to you."

I raised my eyebrows. "Haley didn't say anything to me. What do you mean?"

Toby cleared his throat, his features uneasy. "I'm sorry, Ms. Roberts. We can't."

"Can't what? What do you mean?"

"What I mean is...we can't help you with a tattoo here."

CHAPTER NINETEEN

TALON

Roger curled up next to me, his warm little body a comforting presence. I missed Jade. Why hadn't I asked her to stay? I wanted her here all the time, with me. I wanted to take care of her.

But who was I to take care of anyone when I couldn't take care of myself?

She'd be after me with more questions—about the tattoo, about the news article that wasn't released anywhere but here, about why I had wanted to...

God, I hated going there. Hated it so much.

★ ★ ★

Iraqi insurgents had ambushed us. Caught after dark in a copse of trees adjacent to a small northern village, I was one of the officers in charge of two Explosive Ordnance Disposal units, all enlisted men except one nurse. The other officer was my superior, Captain Derek Waters.

Shells began exploding all around us, the blasts deafening, and enemy fire erupted from the mountainside. The whoosh of the blood in my veins overpowered the explosions, turning into white noise. I yelled at my troops to run, my voice vague and far-off, and I ran like hell.

Once I escaped the woods and the gunfire, I looked back. No one was behind me. Why the fuck hadn't they run?

More to the point, why had I bothered to run? Fuck, why had I done a lot of things in my life when I'd have been better off dying?

Why hadn't I just stayed, stood stock still, closed my eyes, looked to the heavens...and gotten my ass shot off?

An end to all my problems...

But here I stood. Like a fucking imbecile.

Waters and two troops rushed at me.

"Steel! You okay?" Waters asked.

I nodded. Waters and the two troops crashed to the ground, panting. Still, I stood.

And the answer hit me.

I would go back in.

I would go back in under the guise of saving my men and hope that I got shot to hell. I bolted in, instinctively dodging fire. The first troop I came across was one of my enlisted men, Clancy Brown. He was screaming, his foot having been shot. He couldn't get up, and blood was spurting from his lower limb. I grabbed him by the shoulders and got him onto my back, running like hell to get him out of there. When I finally cleared the copse of trees and the enemy fire, I put him down and went running back in, ignoring Waters, who was now sitting up, yelling at me to stay put.

I charged back in and found my sergeant, Jensen, my second-in-command. I grabbed him and pulled him out, and he too begged me not to go back in there.

"Lieutenant, we need you! You're fucking crazy! Don't do it!"

But I ignored him as well, darting back through, again instinctively dodging the fire when I should've been putting myself in harm's way. All told, I got four more out, including a woman, Cline, one of the nurses who had been with us.

I turned and rushed back toward the woods.

"Damn it, Steel, no!" Waters grabbed me around the neck.

I broke his choke hold easily, but Forrester, one of the men who had escaped with Waters, tackled me to the ground.

"We need you, Lieutenant."

I broke free of Forrester with little effort and surged forward.

Waters stopped me again, with help from Jensen, Forrester, and the nurse, Cline. That woman had a motherfucking strong grip.

"I outrank you, Steel," Waters yelled. "You're not going back in there."

I struggled to regain my freedom. "Your men are in there too, you son of a bitch!"

Somehow, with all the adrenaline pumping through me, I broke free and thrust my body forward again.

Forrester tackled me again.

"Let me go, Forrester. That's a fucking order!"

Waters ran at me, throwing himself on top of Forrester and me. "You're staying put, Steel. And that's a fucking order, you dumb shit. Don't you think I care as much as you do about those troops? Half of them are mine. But damn it, you're no good to anyone dead."

Once more I struggled free, my strength unimaginable. But then—

Thud!

Forrester punched me in the nose, and Cline—yes, Cline, her forehead spewing blood—popped me upside the head. I didn't feel any pain. Too much adrenaline still coursed through my veins. But I went down. I fucking went down. When my head hit the ground, things went black.

Other than a minor concussion, I got out of it unscathed. I was taken to our military base for patching up.

There I sat, healthy as a horse, still fucking alive.

I had done my best to get my ass blown to bits, and it hadn't worked.

★ ★ ★

As I lay in bed, still petting Roger, my body went cold. I was truly no hero. I hadn't risked my life for my men. I'd gone in seeking my own demise.

My eyes shot open.

I was glad I wasn't dead. Fucking glad.

Jade had done that for me, and I needed to do something for her. I needed to work through this chaos that was my life so I could be worthy of her.

I scoffed. I would never be worthy of her, of her love. I did love her, but did she really love me? Jade wasn't the type to lie. She truly thought she loved me. But the fact of the matter was, she didn't know me. She didn't know the real Talon Steel. She didn't know the man who had killed overseas...and who still dreamed of killing three men from his past.

No, she didn't love *that* Talon Steel.

That Talon Steel was unlovable.

★ ★ ★

The boy sat on his ragged blanket, shivering. They hadn't come in over a day, and he had long since finished the meager meal and small glass of water they had left him.

The bucket was full of his waste, and the rancid stench made his eyes water. He should've been used to it by now, but he wasn't. Wasting away in the midst of his own filth... He truly was nothing.

But he dreamed sometimes, when he was able to sleep. He dreamed of escaping and growing into a big strong man... and hunting those masked demons...plunging knives into their hearts... and laughing into their blurred faces as they drew their last breath.

But the walls... In the walls, the face of the phoenix emerged.

"That will never happen, you piece of filth," the bird chided, laughing. "You are worth nothing. Nothing more than that little gray blanket they've given you. You will die here, and they will never pay for what they've done to you. You deserve every bit of it."

And then, even though the boy would close his eyes and cry on the inside, tears would not emerge.

He was too dehydrated to make tears.

He unclasped his hands around his knees and lay down, shivering. As the walls came ever closer...closer...closer.

Until the walls swung back to their normal positions when the door at the top of the stairs opened. The boy squinted at the sliver of light. Footsteps echoed, and one of the three descended, wearing only shorts and a T-shirt...and the black ski mask, of course.

The boy huddled in the corner. Please, please not again. Normally they all came together when they decided to abuse him. But the boy was never sure what would happen when one of them came alone. The demon didn't wear shoes. Normally they did. When the lone beast turned toward the boy, he carried food. The boy had stopped getting hungry a while ago, but still he knew he needed to eat. His stomach was raw and empty.

He needed to eat to survive. Always to survive.

"Here you go, bitch."

The one who brought the food. Not Tattoo or Low Voice. This one was almost invisible most of the time, rarely talked, but he took his turns like the others. He set the tray down.

The boy looked up. The man's eyes glared, but the boy couldn't tell the color in the darkness. He looked down the devil's body, all the way to his ugly bare feet. One, two, three, four, five, six, seven, eight, nine...

Nine toes. No pinky toe on his left foot.

No pinky toe...

★ ★ ★

I shot upright.

One of those bastards was missing the pinky toe on his left foot. Was that unusual? He could have been born that way, or he could have lost his toe in an accident.

I didn't care. I threw on my robe, ran down the hall to

my office, and fired up the computer. I was about to put out a search for men missing a small toe on the left foot.

And one of them was going to answer to me.

CHAPTER TWENTY

JADE

"Excuse me?" I looked to Toby and then to Haley.

The Goth girl was biting her lip ring again.

"Are you in the business of turning away customers?"

"Any business has the right to refuse service to anyone," Toby said.

"But why me? I'm nobody."

"I'm afraid I can't help you." Toby stood awkwardly, adjusting his weight between his two legs.

"You're the only tattoo shop here."

"There are plenty in Grand Junction. I'm sure you can find what you want there."

"But I've seen Haley's work. I love it."

"Haley is a fine artist, but there are many others who will serve you just as well."

I shook my head. "What the hell—"

And it hit me. Talon had been here. He had waved his money around and convinced these people not to tattoo me. He hated the tattoo. He'd made that abundantly clear. But to go so far as to pay off the only tattoo shop in town *not* to do business with me?

Only one way to find out. I turned in a huff and walked

out the door, slamming it.

I drove back to the ranch, anger coursing through me. How dare he?

It was nearly dinnertime by the time I got back, and Marj was pulling up just as I was.

"Jade, great to see you. What are you doing driving the Mustang?"

"Talon loaned it to me."

"Oh, good. Although I'm sure George will miss all the fares."

I wasn't in the mood to make nice, even with Marj. "I've got to see Talon."

"Sure. He's probably inside. Why don't you stay for dinner?"

Dinner? I was hardly hungry. I stalked inside behind Marj. "Talon!"

"Calm down, Jade. We'll find him."

I went running to his bedroom and opened the door, not bothering to knock. Roger looked up from where he was sleeping at the foot of Talon's bed. Talon was nowhere in sight.

Roger panted and ran to me.

I gave him a quick pet. "Come on, boy. Let's put you outside." I let the dog out and then turned to Marj. "Where the fuck is he?"

"Settle down. I have no idea."

"He was here a few hours ago."

"Oh, you were here?"

I nodded. "Is his car here?"

"I don't know. I didn't look," Marj said.

I ran outside. His Mercedes was there, but his pickup was not. He had driven off somewhere. "Damn it," I said under my breath.

Marj came outside and grabbed my arm. "Jade, what the hell is wrong with you?"

"Your brother is what's wrong with me, Marj." I let out a huff. "He has really overstepped his boundaries this time."

"What are you talking about?"

"For some reason, he doesn't want me to get a tattoo. He won't tell me why, except that he doesn't want me to mar my body. I had the greatest image all picked out—a phoenix similar to what I saw on my mom's boyfriend. It truly spoke to me, and after so many years of searching for the right image, I thought I'd found it. But Talon went crazy, forbidding me to get a tattoo, and especially *that* tattoo. I don't take kindly to orders, as you know, so I went in today to make an appointment at Toby's, and I was told that they won't tattoo me. Can you fucking believe that?"

"I'm sure there's a very good explanation."

"Really? You think so? He's a businessman, for God's sake. I'm a client willing to pay good money to get a tattoo. And he turns me away. That has Talon Steel written all over it."

Marj bit at her lip. "Why would Talon care if you get a tattoo?"

I rolled my eyes and threaded my fingers through my hair. "Tell me, and we'll both know. Your brother's just crazy. Simply crazy. There's no other explanation."

Marj sighed. "I don't know that he's crazy, but he does have issues."

"Issues? This goes way beyond issues. Your brother's just going to have to understand that he doesn't own me. I'm going to go into Grand Junction and get my whole fucking body tattooed to spite him."

Marj let out a giggle. "No, you're not."

"Fine. Okay, I'm not." I drew in a deep breath and let it out, trying desperately to calm down. "But I *am* going to go to Grand Junction and get a tattoo. No matter what he says."

"That's certainly your right. Normally, you know I would never tell you not to do something that you want to do, but..."

"But what? Surely, you can't be telling me that you agree with him."

"I'm not saying that." She smiled. "And don't call me Shirley."

I burst into giggles. Trust Marj to pacify me with a stupid-ass joke.

"See, I knew I could make you laugh. Let's go to the kitchen and have a glass of wine. We'll talk this out."

While Felicia was busy in the kitchen getting dinner ready, Marj poured two glasses of wine, and we went out onto the deck.

"Now," Marj said. "Spill it. What the hell is going on?"

I sighed. "I wish I knew." I looked down at my glass of wine and swirled the liquid a little. "He told me he loved me today."

"Oh my God, that's fantastic!" Marj clapped her hands. "I don't believe it."

"I didn't either. I mean, I believe it, I just couldn't

believe he said it."

"Did you say it back?"

"I actually said it first."

"Wow."

"I told him he didn't have to say it back. That I understood if he couldn't, and it was okay, but I just needed him to know how I felt."

Marj took sip of wine. "Talon wouldn't say he loved you unless he meant it."

I nodded. "Yeah, that's what I was thinking. I didn't push it. I didn't even mention it. I didn't ask him to repeat it. I just wanted to savor it, and I didn't want to give him any chance to take it back."

"It's weird to think about...you and Talon."

"I know." I understood what she meant. Her brother and her best friend—it had to be strange for her. But even more strange was the fact that Talon was so...walled off.

Time to change the subject. I hadn't yet told Marj about her birth certificate and what I had learned from Wendy Madigan. I bit my lip for a minute and then took a sip of wine. I couldn't tell her that Larry was investigating her and her family.

I took in a breath and then exhaled. "By the way, I was doing some routine investigation at work last week when I came across an article in the local paper when Talon returned three years ago."

"Yeah, there was quite a to-do about it," she said.

"How come you never told me he was such a hero?"

"He wanted us all to keep it quiet. He begged us to. I'm still not sure why, but I felt I owed it to him. It was his story to tell, not mine."

Ryan had said those exact words to me when I went to him months ago, asking him about Talon. It wasn't his story to tell.

What story? Was Ryan talking about Talon's heroism? About his time in the military? I had no idea.

"I thought we didn't have secrets, Marj."

Her cheeks pinked. I had embarrassed her.

"I know, Jade, but Talon felt so strongly about this..."

"You don't need to explain. And I haven't forgotten that I just kept a whopper from you up until about a week ago."

She smiled.

"Anyway, when I read the story, I got to thinking about those documents we had found. So I did a database search for your birth certificate, and the weird part is that your birth certificate shows you only as Marjorie Steel. This is the official document at the Colorado records department."

"Okay, then why does the one downstairs say my first name is Angela?"

"Well, I researched that a little. There was a name at the bottom of the article about Talon, Wendy Madigan. She used to be a field correspondent for NNN. Do you recognize the name?"

"Wendy Madigan? No, I don't."

I wasn't about to divulge the fact that her father had engaged in a decades-long affair with the former newswoman. True, we weren't supposed to have secrets, but that... Marj wasn't ready for that.

"I called her because I was curious why the news story was only shared locally. Turns out she had used her clout to keep it out of the national news at Jonah's request."

"Doesn't surprise me."

"Anyway, I asked her about your birth certificate, and she told me quite a tale."

I quickly relayed what Wendy had said about Marjorie's mother naming her Angela and then removing the name when she survived.

"No kidding? I was premature?"

"You didn't know?"

She shook her head. "You sure can't tell to look at me. I'm damn near six feet tall."

"Were you ever small for your age?"

"Nope, always the tallest girl in the class. God, it was painful before the guys in school shot up. And even after, I was still taller than half of them."

I smiled. "You were always the most gorgeous too, I bet." But I had to change the subject yet again. "I know this is a hard topic for you, but what exactly do you know about your mother?"

"I don't know a lot. At least not firsthand, because I don't remember her. I've seen pictures of course, and I look a little bit like her, though I have my dad's coloring, same as the boys, but my face is shaped like hers, and my lips."

I nodded.

"I know she was troubled. I mean, why else would she have killed herself?"

I nodded again. Marj was probably not the best person to be asking about Daphne Steel. The boys remembered her and would be able to tell me more. But so far, they had been tight-lipped about anything concerning family.

"Crazy," Marj continued. "So I was supposed to die?"

"Yeah, and I'm sure glad you didn't."

"Me too."

We laughed together and drank some more wine.

"Out of curiosity," I said, "I also checked out your parents' marriage certificate. The official version in the Colorado database says your mom's maiden name was Warren, like you guys always thought."

"That is curious."

I swallowed a mouthful of wine. "I don't really know what to make of it all. Somebody somewhere got into the records database, probably a long time ago, and made those changes in the permanent records. It had to be someone pretty high up in the government to have that access."

"Or my father paid for that access."

I had wanted to say that, but I was glad she had. "I have given that a bit of thought. Especially since I'm pretty sure Talon paid off Toby's Tattoo Parlor not to work with me."

"Well, I'm not particularly proud of it, but one of the benefits of having this kind of money is that we can afford to *buy* certain things."

Felicia opened the door and stuck her head out. "Dinner is ready. Is Mr. Talon coming home?"

Marj sighed. "Beats the heck out of me, Felicia. I think Jade and I will have our dinner out here, if you don't mind."

"Not at all. I'll bring it right out. You want some more wine, ladies?"

Marj giggled. "Of course."

Felicia brought us two plates of spaghetti and meatballs along with the bottle of wine we had opened and left in the kitchen. I inhaled. Mmm. Rustic tomato and beef. Nothing better.

We dived into our meals and were chatting about nothing in particular when Felicia came back.

"Pardon me, Miss Jade, but there is a Colin Morse here to see you."

CHAPTER TWENTY-ONE

TALON

"What is it, Tal?" Jonah stood in his house, wearing nothing but a pair of swim trunks. "I was just about to take a dip."

"Great. I'll join you. We need to talk." I walked past him into the foyer and through the kitchen out to his backyard, where his kidney-shaped pool was waiting.

"You brought your trunks?"

I shook my head. "I'll wear my boxers. You know I don't care about that." I gulped down the lump that had formed in my throat. "I... I told Jade I love her."

Jonah slapped me on the back. "Really? That's great, Tal."

"Really? Is it really great?" I tunneled my fingers through my hair. "You know I don't have any business loving anyone, getting involved with anyone."

"You have just as much business as anybody else. Especially if maybe you go back to see Dr. Carmichael again."

"I don't know if I can. I need to resolve so much. Which reminds me, I had a really weird revelation today."

"Yeah? What was it?"

"One of those guys. Remember all that I ever remembered before was that one of them had that fucking phoenix tattoo on his forearm? Oh, and you'll never believe this. Jade wants to get that exact same tattoo."

Jonah jerked his head forward. "Say what?"

"Yeah, she saw it in a book at Toby's. Out of all those fucking tattoos, she chose that one. Unreal. So I did a little research. The guy who designed the tattoo can't remember who he gave it to, but said it was a fairly popular design twenty to thirty years ago. He only remembers putting it on someone's forearm a few times. I'm going to see if I can get his records."

"If he still has them."

I let out a sigh. "Yeah. I know. He's this old biker guy who says he was stoned half the time back then. I'm going to get a court order or something to go through his records."

"Why don't you just ask him to see the records?"

"I should have. I was freaking out so much over the whole thing that I didn't think of it." I rubbed my chin. "Now that you mention it, that's what I'll do. He's very cooperative when I throw a few bills around."

"Most people are, bro." Jonah chuckled. "Is that what you wanted to tell me?"

I shook my head. "No. I had a revelation, like I said."

"What was it?"

"One of the guys, not the tattoo guy, and not the one I remember having a really low voice. The third guy, the one who seemed to be more of a follower. Anyway...he was missing the littlest toe on his left foot."

Jonah's eyes bugged out. "How did you remember that all of a sudden?"

"Damned if I know. Things just come to me sometimes. Like a couple weeks ago, I had a dream or flashback or something, and I remembered those guys taunting me with a full glass of water that was just outside my reach. All of a sudden it made sense why I wake up in the middle of the night, pour myself a glass of water, and then stare at it and don't drink it."

"Talon, don't you realize that if you went back to see Dr. Carmichael, she could help you with all of this? She could probably bring more memories to the surface."

I scoffed. "You think I want to remember that shit? I remember enough of it as it is."

"But don't you see? These are clues. We could still catch these guys."

"Are you kidding? Those guys have got to be long gone if they know what's good for them. Not all criminals are stupid, you know."

"Then why are you chasing the tattoo clue?"

Hell, I didn't know. Because...because I had to do *something*. But why? I'd never had any urge to do anything about this before. It had been my cross to bear, and I lived with it. "I don't know."

"I think I do," Joe said.

Not surprising. My older brother thought he knew everything. "You don't know shit."

He laughed. "Maybe not. But I think I know why you're raring to do something now, why you're following that tattoo lead. It's because you want to move forward. Finally. Because of Jade."

Jade. Somewhere, stuffed into the recesses of my

mind, did I actually think I could heal? Become worthy of her love?

Did my brother know everything?

I chuckled to myself. No, he didn't. But he might be right about this. Damned if I was going to admit it though.

"You got nothing to say to that?" my brother asked.

"Nope."

Jonah let out a guffaw. "Means you think I'm right."

"No comment."

He shook his head, laughing. "Have it your way. But back to these leads. Any lead is better than none. So far we have a phoenix tattoo on the left forearm and a missing pinky toe on a left foot. That rules out the majority of the men in the world."

"Yeah, I thought of that. So I ran to the computer and did a search, but nothing came of it. I'm not sure what I was thinking. There's no database of guys missing toes out there."

"I know you never wanted to do this before, but maybe it's time we hire a P.I. Those guys could still be found. They could still pay for what they did to you."

If I ever found any one of them, he'd pay. At my own hand. I couldn't say that to my brother, though. "Maybe. I'll think on that. But what are the chances of catching those assholes this late in the game? It's been twenty-five years, Joe."

"Yeah, I know. But I've been thinking about something else."

"What's that?"

"I think it's time we tell Marjorie the truth. About

everything."

Marjorie? Jade's best friend? From whom she had no secrets? Oh, hell, no. "I don't think that's a good idea."

"Why not?"

"She's just...not old enough to handle it."

"She's twenty-five. The rest of us had to handle it when we were half that age."

"Well..." And the truth came out. "She'll tell Jade."

"Not if we tell her not to."

"Look, Joe, you and Ryan and I decided a long time ago that the past was best left buried and we weren't going to unearth it. Just as much for your sake as for mine."

"But *you're* unearthing it, don't you see? By following this lead about the tattoo and now about the missing toe. Are you planning to just let that go? And if that was your plan, why did you go chasing all over to Grand Junction to find the designer of that tattoo?"

I sighed. "Pour me a Peach Street, will you?"

Joe headed to the kitchen and returned a minute or so later. He handed me a drink. "Come on. Let's go outside and sit by the pool."

We situated ourselves in a couple of chaise longues, and I took a slow sip of my bourbon. Damn good stuff, Peach Street.

I recognized the contradiction. Here I was, still wanting to bury the truth, yet I had gone on a wild goose chase trying to hunt down that tattoo. And now here I was all excited that I remembered something about another one of those fuckers.

On the other hand, we had decided long ago to bury it.

As if reading my mind, Jonah said, "I know what we decided a long time ago. But we were kids then, Talon. Just immature kids. You were embarrassed, humiliated, and hurt, and we all understood that. Even Mom and Dad. Now we're adults, all in our thirties, and quite frankly none of us will ever be able to move on unless we all face this. Together."

I shook my head. "I don't know if I can do it."

"Do you truly love Jade?"

I wished I could lie to him. Better yet, I wished I could say "no, I don't" and not be lying. Jade would be better off for it. But I couldn't do either. I nodded. "Yes, I do."

"Do you want a life with her?"

Again I wished I could lie, for her sake. "Yes, I do."

"If you want a relationship with Jade or anyone, you have got to face this and put it behind you. And the only way to put it behind you is to confront it, accept it, and find some way to deal with it."

"Hey, guys." Ryan walked out, sporting some trunks and a towel around his neck. "Hey, Tal, I didn't know you'd be here. I just came over to take a dip."

Jonah let out a laugh. "Ryan, you have a perfectly good pool at the guest house."

"Maybe I wanted to hang out with my bros."

"You didn't even know we'd be here."

Ryan let out a loud laugh. "True enough. But you've got the good booze here."

"You, the wine man?"

"Hey, I'm allowed to have a craving for Peach Street every once in a while. Tal finished up my bottle the other night." He held out a hand. "Don't get up. I'll just help myself." He came back with a drink and the bottle. "So what's going on with you guys?"

"Well," Jonah said, "your brother here is in love."

"So I've heard."

"Yeah, but this time he told her," Jonah said.

"No shit?" Ryan said. "Good for you, Tal. Didn't think you had it in you."

It irked me when he said shit like that. Ryan was always jovial. Well, of course he was. Nothing had happened to him. I'd saved his ass that day. I pursed my lips and didn't respond.

"And I was just telling Talon," Jonah said, "that I think it's time we tell Marjorie the truth."

Ryan shook his head. "No, I disagree."

"Thanks, bro," I said. "That's exactly what I said."

"Why dredge all that shit up now?"

"Because Talon's in love, damn it, and he'll never be able to have a normal life with Jade until we all deal with this. Why do you think none of us have had serious relationships, ever?"

"I like playing around the field, basically," Ryan said. "I assumed the same for you guys."

"For God's sake, I'm thirty-eight years old," Jonah said. "It's high time I settle down. The two of you aren't getting any younger either. Don't you want kids?"

I shook my head. "Are you kidding me? I wouldn't bring an innocent child into this horrible world."

"Tal, what happened to you was awful. Heinous. Unimaginable. But it doesn't happen to most kids. Most kids have great lives, and look around you. Look at all that we have. All this is ours. We need a legacy to leave it to."

"Marj will pop out some kids," Ryan said.

"Maybe, but we need to carry on the Steel name." Jonah rubbed his temple.

"Maybe she'll have them out of wedlock." Ryan swirled the whiskey around in his glass.

"Ha-ha. I'm serious. It's time to face this, head on."

"You know, guys," I said, "this really has nothing to do with either of you. It's all on me. It's my decision."

Jonah shook his head. "I am so fucking sick of you saying that, Talon. This affects all three of us. We all died a little that day. Ryan and I not nearly as much as you. I get that. But I should've been there for you. I should've protected you. And Ryan, he's only here because of you. Because you protected him like I should've done for you. You think we don't both harbor a hell of a lot of guilt over that? You know we do. I say it's time we all move forward."

I scoffed. "It's real easy for you to say, Joe."

"You know what? No, it's not easy for me to say. Do you think I'm looking forward to sitting our baby sister down and explaining what happened twenty-five years ago? Are you kidding me? But she deserves to know how she came into this world, why she goes by her middle name, why her mother fucking committed suicide, for God's sake."

I opened my mouth to speak, but Joe kept right on yelling.

"Dad went to a lot of time and trouble and money to cover this up when it happened, but I'm wondering if he didn't do us all a disservice back then. We were never allowed to deal with it. We swept it under the rug. Then poor

Mom couldn't deal with it. So she fucking offed herself. It's time for this all to be over." He slammed his hand down on the wooden arm of the Adirondack chaise longue he was sitting in.

Ryan's lips trembled, but he did not speak. That was Ry. He accepted the fact that this was my decision. I was his big brother. I was his hero. I had saved him that day. He would never go against my wishes. I knew that as well as I knew that my name was Talon John Steel. If I fought Jonah on this, Ryan would be right behind me, having my back.

But was it worth the fight anymore? If I worked through this and came out alive on the other side, could I have a life with Jade?

Because a life with Jade was what I truly wanted. Ached for. I would never be able to live without her. She had become my obsession. As vital to me as the oxygen I breathed.

So I did the hardest thing I've ever done. I turned to Ryan, and I said, "It's time."

CHAPTER TWENTY-TWO

JADE

Colin was here? Hadn't my ex-fiancé already given me enough heartache and headache to last the rest of my life?

"Could you tell him to go away, Felicia? It's Saturday night, and I really don't want to be bothered."

"All right, Miss Jade."

A few minutes later, Colin walked out onto the deck.

"I'm so sorry, Miss Jade. He just stomped right past me. I couldn't stop him."

"Oh my God. I'm sorry, Felicia. Are you okay?"

"Of course. He didn't touch me or anything."

I eyed Colin. "Darn good thing, or I might have him arrested for assault and battery." I said the last through gritted teeth, referring to him having Talon arrested for the same. Granted, Talon had beaten the snot out of him, but I couldn't say I was too sorry. This was the guy who'd left me at the altar a few months ago.

"Why in the hell are you back here?"

"Your new boyfriend and I have a court date on Monday. Have you forgotten?"

"I struck a deal with Talon's attorney. You don't even have to be here, Colin."

"Yes, but I have a few words to say to the court. Like maybe I'm not happy with the deal that you struck."

"You're going to be getting full restitution."

"I don't give a shit about restitution, Jade. You know I don't need any Steel money. I have my own. I want to see the guy rot in prison."

"He's not going to prison for a misdemeanor assault, no matter what you do. Have you forgotten that we have an eyewitness? Namely me?"

"Yeah, also the prosecuting attorney on the case. No way should you be handling this, Jade."

I opened my mouth but shut it quickly. He was right. I had so many conflicts in this case, but my boss, the unethical Larry Wade, had insisted I take it.

"If I read the Colorado statutes correctly, he can get up to six months in prison for misdemeanor assault." Colin smirked.

"Yeah, and as the city attorney on the case, I don't think it's worth the taxpayers' time or money to pursue this any further. I'm pretty sure the court's going to agree with me."

Colin nodded. "Sure. Because Steel is a homeboy. He's probably got the judge in his pocket."

Marjorie stepped forward then. "You take that back, Colin. My family may have money, but we are decent citizens, and we don't buy people."

Colin rolled his eyes. "Do you think I was born yesterday, Marj?"

"Oh my God, Jade. How did you stay with this asshat for seven years?"

I had no clue. Seven years of my life down the toilet.

What if I had married him? He stood there, his dirty-blond hair slicked back, looking ever so sanctimonious in his pinstripe navy-blue suit and yellow tie. Who wore yellow ties anymore? *Hello, Colin? This is the eighties. We want our tie back.*

"What are you doing here now? The court date isn't until Monday, and you can easily get a hotel room until then. Why can't you leave me in peace?"

"I want to take you to dinner."

"Not that I would go to dinner with you anyway, but Marj and I are just about ready to sit down to eat. Felicia made some awesome spaghetti."

"Oh, I think you'll come to dinner with me."

"And why in hell would I do that?"

"Because if you don't, I'm going to make things really difficult for both you and Talon Steel come Monday morning."

My heart lurched a bit, but I—hopefully—concealed it, willing myself to remain calm. "Seriously? You're going to threaten me? Threatening an officer of the court? Threatening a defendant?" I looked over at Marj. "You're my witness. He just made a threat."

"That wasn't a threat, Jade," Colin said. "It was just a fact. You think this kind of thing doesn't happen in court all the time? God, you are naïve."

"If you don't leave now," Marjorie said, "I'll call the cops and have you escorted off my property."

"Simmer down, Marj," Colin said. "This is between Jade and me."

"Well, Jade is on my property and currently under my

protection."

Colin let out a snort. "Under your protection? What are you, a gangster now?"

"It's a good thing my brothers aren't here," Marj said. "They'd kick the shit out of you again, and neither one of us would stop them."

"You'd better watch what you say too," Colin said. "That sounded kind of like a threat to me."

"Just a fact." Marj curled her lips into a saccharine smile.

I shook my head. "Colin, you think you're so damned smart, but really what you are is arrogant. You don't know anything about how the law works. Now get out of here."

"Not until you agree to have dinner with me."

"She will do no such thing," Marj said.

"She has a mouth. Let her speak for herself."

"I'll tell you what. If I agree to go to dinner with you, will you be gone by Monday and just let this deal happen?"

Colin was silent a moment, his jaw clenched. Then, "All right. You've got a deal. You go to dinner with me tonight, and I won't appear in court on Monday."

"Fine."

"Jade..." Marj began.

"And Marj is coming with us."

"Oh, no. That wasn't the deal."

"The only deal was that I would have dinner with you, Colin. You didn't specify that it would be a private dinner."

"Come on, you know exactly what I meant."

I pulled my best innocent face. "I'm afraid I didn't. You know how *naïve* I am."

"Fuck this. Forget dinner. I will see you in court on Monday at nine a.m. sharp." He stomped off the deck.

Marj was gnawing on her bottom lip. "I hope he doesn't make things really bad for Talon."

I shook my head. "I don't think he can." I hoped to God I was telling the truth. "I'm the city attorney. This is my call. As long as the judge agrees to the plea..."

"What?"

This time I bit my lip. I didn't know anything about the judge in the Snow Creek Municipal Court. Could Colin buy her off? He certainly had the money, and he was mad as a rabid dog right now, thinking Talon was going to get off after beating him to a near pulp a couple weeks ago.

"Do you know the judge, Marj?"

She shook her head. "No, not well. Everybody knows who we are though."

Even if Colin couldn't pay off the judge, he could still show up in court and outline all the conflicts I had in the case and screw up the deal. I couldn't take the chance. I had to protect Talon. Without saying another word to Marj, I ran the other way through the house and caught Colin as he was getting into his car.

"I changed my mind. I'll have dinner with you tonight, if you promise to leave and not come to court on Monday."

CHAPTER TWENTY-THREE

TALON

My brothers and I drove into town to Murphy's Bar for a little celebration. It wasn't every day we decided to dig up the past so we could bury it once and for all.

I ordered Peach Street, of course. Jonah ordered a CapRock martini, and Ryan ordered a glass of his own wine.

Sean Murphy chuckled as he poured it. "You come in here and pay me for what you get for free, Ry. Now that's a damn good customer."

"We like to support the businesses of Snow Creek." Ryan lifted his glass.

Sean, being the nonintrusive bartender that he was, turned around and focused on his tasks at hand, leaving us to talk.

"I guess I'll go back to that Dr. Carmichael," I heard myself saying.

"Great, that means I don't have to get Jade to move back in to get you to go," Jonah said. "And she does come highly recommended."

Joe was the one who had given me her name a few weeks ago. "How did you come by her name, anyway?" I asked him.

My brother cast his gaze to his martini. Even in the dimness of the bar, I could see his cheeks pink up a little.

"Well?"

"I...met her at a bar in Grand Junction one night."

I cocked my head. "Are you serious? You sent me to a shrink you picked up in a bar?"

He jiggled his martini. "No, no, it wasn't anything like that. I was in the city a couple months ago, you know, at the agricultural conference. There was some kind of psychological conference at the same hotel."

"So you've met her."

"Yeah."

I took a drink. "Then how come you two acted like you didn't know each other when you saw her at the ER after I fainted?"

Joe's threaded his fingers through his black hair accented with silver. "I don't know. I didn't want to say 'good to see you again' and then not have her remember me..."

This was getting good. He *liked* her. "Okay, fine. So what happened at the bar?"

"I was down there in the evening, chatting with some of the guys, and Melanie...err, Dr. Carmichael...came in alone."

"And you picked her up."

"No, I didn't pick her up. She was alone, and she looked kind of... I don't know. You've seen her. She's a looker."

"Yep, blond and beautiful. Tall too."

That got Ryan's attention. He raised his eyebrows but said nothing.

"Anyway, there was an empty stool next to me, and she asked if it was taken. I said no. The guys I was talking to excused themselves, and then there we were. We just talked a little, and we exchanged cards. She said she was working on a book about recovering from childhood trauma."

"So you naturally thought of me."

"Well...yeah."

"And that's all? She wasn't highly recommended?"

"Actually, she *is* highly recommended. When I found out what she did for a living, I Googled her first off. She's handled lots of cases like yours. I also talked to some of the other attendees at the psychology conference. Apparently she gave a couple workshops that were very well attended and informative."

"And you had the hots for her," Ryan piped in.

Joe shook his head vehemently. "Nothing like that happened. I swear. I haven't had a woman in...well, too long to tell you the truth."

"Has her book come out yet? Maybe I'll give it a read." Not that it would matter. I had read heaps of books and research on cases like mine. It hadn't helped me recover, but it did help to know I wasn't alone in the world.

Joe shook his head. "Nope. It hasn't come out yet, as far as I know. I check every now and then."

"You check?"

"Yeah, what of it? I'm obviously interested in the subject too."

"Joe, you *do* have the hots for her," Ryan said, laughing.

"So I find her attractive. What's the matter with that?"

"Nothing from where I'm standing, bro." Ryan took a sip of wine. "So both my brothers are smitten." He laughed again.

"Yeah, she's nice to look at," I said. Of course, she was no Jade. "That really doesn't matter to me. Can she help us?"

Joe took a sip and then put down his drink. He turned and met my gaze. "Tal, you truly are ready, aren't you?"

"I said I was, didn't I?"

Joe shook his head. "I know what you said. But it's that last word you said that clinched it for me."

"Yeah? What did I say?"

"You said, 'can she help us?' Not 'can she help me?' You're finally seeing us as a team here. That's huge."

I inhaled and let the air out slowly. "I've always seen it that way, Joe. It's just..." It was just that they hadn't gone through it. Yes, they had their own demons that they were fighting because of it, but they hadn't lived the horrors. Hadn't been beaten, starved, molested. "It's just..."

Jonah placed his hand on my forearm. "I understand. I always have."

Maybe he had always understood, in his own way. Maybe I hadn't given him enough credit. I'd been so busy having my little pity party and trying to destroy myself that I hadn't been able to see it. But I no longer wanted to destroy myself. I wanted to live. I finally had something to live for— Jade. And loving Jade had opened my eyes and restored my sight. I could finally see what else had always been there to live for—Joe, Ryan, Marjorie, my ranch.

And me.

I wanted to live for *me*.

I opened my mouth to try to put this into words to my brothers, but Joe squeezed my forearm.

"It's okay, Tal. You don't have to say it."

I swallowed a lump in my throat. "Thanks," I said gruffly.

"You don't have to thank me."

"Me either," Ryan said. "I should be thanking you."

"You have, Ry, many times. You don't have to anymore."

Awkward silence reigned for a few moments, until Jonah cleared his throat. "So how do you want to handle this, Tal? You take the lead on this. Do you want to go see the doc by yourself at first? You want us to go with you? Would you rather we not go at all? We'll do this your way, won't we, Ry?"

"Absolutely," Ryan agreed.

"Thanks," I said again. "I'll go myself first. It'll be difficult, and I don't want you to see me like...that."

"Talon," Ryan began, "you don't have to—"

"No, Ryan. This is his call."

"Okay." My younger brother nodded.

"But if you guys want to go. I mean, if you feel like you have your own issues..." I let out a sigh. "I get it. I do. This has affected all of us. I haven't been able to see anyone's pain but my own, and I'm sorry for that."

"Tal," Jonah said, "I think that's the first time I've heard you say 'I'm sorry' without wincing through it." He let out a chuckle.

"I guess I'm seeing things a little differently these days."

"A good woman can do that," Ryan laughed.

"I don't know that it's Jade..." Yeah, right. They'd never buy that. "Okay, so it *is* Jade, but caring for Jade... Goddamn it... *Loving* Jade has made me see everything more clearly.

Not just what I feel for her, but you guys, Marj, myself. Everything looks different now. I know I've been selfish."

"Tal..." Ryan started.

"No, Ryan, let me say this. Just because I went through hell doesn't give me the right to be a jerk. And I've been one. Hell... I've got to tell you... God, this is embarrassing..."

Joe started to speak, but I held up my hand to stop him. I had to do this.

"When I went into Grand Junction, sometimes it was to hook up with some one-night stand, but other times..."

"What?"

"Other times...I'd walk through skid row, purposely trying to get mugged, so I could beat up the muggers." At my brothers' shocked faces, I held up my hand again. "No, don't worry. I never did any lasting damage. Heck, I didn't beat them as much as I beat that asshole ex of Jade's." I looked up to the window.

And speak of the goddamned devil. I stood, anger raging beneath my skin. "Fucking A."

Across the street, coming out of Enzio's...

Ryan and Jonah stood.

"That's Jade," Ryan said. "Is that...?"

I nodded and walked out the door, my pulse racing. My brothers were close at my heels.

I crossed the street faster than a lightning bolt and was ready to pummel the bastard, when Joe pulled my arm back.

"Easy, Tal. You have court on Monday, remember?"

Red rage flooded into me. All I could see was the malignant blur of Colin Morse with his hand on my woman's arm. This was so not happening right now. I would fucking kill him this time. Totally. Completely. Take him down like I had those enemies overseas.

I yanked my arm away from Jonah. "What the fuck are you doing with him?" I bit out at Jade.

"Talon...what are you doing here?"

"Having a drink with my brothers. What are *you* doing here?"

"We were having...dinner...because..."

I raised my fist to pummel the motherfucker, but Ryan stepped in front of me, quick as a panther.

"Don't, Tal. Don't undo everything we just talked about."

"Get out of my way," I seethed through clenched teeth.

"No, I can't let you do this."

"Oh, please, let him do it," Colin taunted. "I'm not thrilled about this deal that you guys cut, anyway. Go ahead. Hit me. Put me in a damned coma. That way maybe you'll go to prison like you deserve."

Ryan stood between Colin and me. My little brother, always levelheaded, who'd take a bullet—hell, a cannonball— for me.

"Don't let him get to you, Tal. He's not worth it. Remember what we were just talking about. You have things to live for."

"Things to live for? What the fuck?" Colin guffawed. "Come on. Do it."

"Would you shut up, Colin?" Jade said. "Look, Talon, nothing is going on. I had to have dinner with him because he..."

"Because why, Jade?" Jonah asked. "Why did you have

dinner with him? You know how Talon feels about this."

"It's *because* of Talon that I did it."

"Yeah." Colin quirked his lips. "It's because of you. She's over you. *We're* getting back together."

Jonah moved between us this time. "How old are you anyway?" he said to Colin. "Did you ever make it out of middle school? You sound like a stupid teenager."

"I ought to kick your ass, next," Jade's ex said.

"You won't get very far. I'm as strong as my brother and a hell of a lot meaner," Jonah said.

"You threatening me?" Colin advanced.

Jade grabbed his arm. "You threatened him first, Colin. Just shut up, for God's sake." She turned to me. "Could we go somewhere and talk? I swear to you there's a good explanation for this."

"Sure. We can talk after I kick his ass."

"You're not going to kick his ass, Talon," Ryan said.

Jade looked at me, her blue eyes sad and...frightened? "Talon, please. Just breathe in and out. He's not worth it. Listen to me. He's. Not. Worth. It."

At her words, her sweet hypnotic voice, my rage began to scatter. Oh, I was angry, for sure. Why was she with him, anyway? But I would ask her about it. And she would tell me. And I could be angry with her, but I didn't have to risk screwing up my future and hers by pounding the halfwit.

"Fine," I said. "Come with me across the street to the bar, and you can tell me what's going on."

"I don't think so," Colin interjected. "She's with me tonight."

Jonah stepped forward again. "Look, man, I don't know

what you think you're doing, but you're not getting what you want this way."

"Says who?"

"Says me." Jonah raised his arm.

"Not you too, Joe." Ryan caught Joe's arm in a clench. "Look, man," my younger brother said to Colin. "Do yourself a favor and get the fuck out of here. Now."

"I don't think so. You assholes don't own this town."

Ryan let out a chuckle. "As a matter fact, we do own quite a bit of stuff in this town. Now granted, you're standing on public sidewalk. So I'm not going to make you move."

"Like you could."

Ryan chuckled again, shaking his head. "I could. And the three of us together? We'd knock you into the next century. But that's not really the point, is it? I'm not going to do that. No matter how much you taunt Talon. No matter how much I would love to pummel your sorry ass."

"So now you're so civilized."

"No, dickhead. My brothers and I are *not* civilized. Far from it. We are hard-working men. We don't sit on our asses in three-piece suits all day. We work the land. Trust me, we're way tougher than you are."

"Please. You probably use slave labor to work your land."

"Oh, for God's sake." Ryan rubbed his forehead. He was finally starting to lose his cool. "You really are asking to have your ass kicked."

"Colin," Jade said. "Just leave. Please."

"Fine. I'll see you in court on Monday."

Jade turned her head. "Excuse me? We had a deal."

"I don't think so."

"You said if I went to dinner with you—"

"What?" I said, my head spinning. "You had some deal to go to dinner with him?"

"Talon, I was trying to do what was best. For you."

"Having you anywhere near him is not what's best for me, blue eyes."

"Blue eyes." Colin rolled his eyes. "God."

I turned to Colin, trying perilously to keep from shoving my fist in his face. "Look, you don't come near her again. I don't care what kind of deal you had with her. I don't care if you show up at court on Monday. What are you going to try to do? Pay off the judge?"

"I don't have to tell you what my plans are."

"Fine. Don't. Show up. I don't care. But you leave her alone," I said through clenched teeth. "Don't you come near her again."

For a split second, I saw a real fear in his eyes. Good.

"He's right, Colin," Jade said. "I don't want anything to do with you. Just leave me alone."

"You heard the lady," Ryan said. "Come on, Jade. We'll take you home."

"That's not necessary. You guys know I only live down the block."

"*I'll* take you home." I grabbed her arm.

"You don't have to. It's not even all the way dark yet."

"I'm not letting you out of my sight while this jerk is in town. I'm assuming he's staying until court on Monday, so don't expect to leave my side until then."

CHAPTER TWENTY-FOUR

JADE

Talon dragged me a couple blocks down to my apartment above the beauty shop. He took my keys from my hand, unlocked the outside door, and then lugged me up the stairs in the back.

Still holding my keys, he unlocked my door and entered. He looked around. "Pretty sparse."

"This is Sarah's furniture. I haven't had a chance to buy anything yet." I shook my head. "Why am I making excuses for you? This is it. This is what I can afford right now. You don't have to be here, you know."

"Yeah, I do. As long as that jerk is in town, I need to protect you."

"Protect me? I'm not the one who needs protection while he's in town. Apparently it's him, the way you and your brothers were all stalking him—" I stopped. I didn't need to go there. Actually, Jonah and Ryan had kept Talon from beating Colin a second time. For that I was grateful.

Talon looked around the room, his gaze settling on my unmade futon. It was still pulled out from where I had slept on it.

Would he take me there?

Of course he would. I could see the fire in his eyes. He

wanted it, and so did I.

But damn, he didn't own me. First the whole tattoo deal, and now this. He needed to understand a few things. "Talon, we need to talk."

"About what?"

"About you dragging me up here, for one, but more importantly, about you paying off Toby so that he wouldn't give me a tattoo."

"You're not getting a tattoo."

I laughed out loud. "Oh, yes, I am. I've wanted one forever, and I finally found the right image."

"Not that image."

"What's wrong with that image? A phoenix is beautiful. It has amazing symbolism."

"Not. That. Image." His eyes scorched me as he ground the words out.

And then he pulled me toward him, our chests meeting with force, and he crushed his lips to mine.

I opened for him immediately. I couldn't resist him. I was done trying. Our bodies would always respond to each other, even when I was mad as hell about other things. He was clearly angry as well, after seeing Colin. I expected an interrogation about that, and I knew it was coming. He wouldn't forget it. But for now...

Such a firm, drugging kiss—a kiss that took me away from everything that was bothering me until only Talon was left.

Talon.

My world.

For that is what he became when we were together.

Only the two of us existed on some alternate plane of the universe. Our bodies responded to each other's like no other, and we became each other. We became one.

How I loved him.

I didn't claim to know him, but still I loved him.

How was that possible?

I let my hand wander out to caress the bulge in his jeans. So fucking hard. Hard as granite. I wanted that beautiful dick in my mouth. I broke the kiss and fell to my knees, unbuckling his belt. I released his snap and unzipped his jeans. Quickly I brushed the denim and his boxers over his well-formed ass. His cock sprang from its ebony nest, hard and majestic, with a pearl of pre-cum glistening over its tip.

I licked the liquid off him, swirling my tongue around his cockhead.

He groaned. "God, Jade. God, that's good."

Would he tell me he loved me again? I wasn't expecting it. In fact, I was pretty sure he probably regretted saying it. Still, hearing those words would remain in my mind and heart as one of my most treasured moments. I considered them and thought about how much I loved him as I proceeded to give him the best damned blowjob I could.

I clamped my lips over his cock and sucked—short quick bursts of constriction. His moans forged my desire to please him. I took him back as far into my mouth as I could, until he nudged the back of my throat. I pulled back and slid forward again, sucking him, my hand on his base, pulling his skin taut.

Then I pulled back and sucked his cockhead again, short little bursts as I had before. He liked that. I could tell by his reaction.

"God, Jade, so good."

I continued my assault, nibbling on the underside down to his balls, where I trailed tiny kisses over his sac and then sucked each testicle into my mouth. I inhaled his musky odor, closing my eyes and savoring it. Savoring him. I grabbed his ass and massaged his buttocks as I continued to kiss his balls and the inside of his thighs. When I finally turned to his cock again, I sprinkled kisses over his length until I got to his head. He grabbed the back of my head and plunged my mouth downward onto him. I nearly gagged but held myself in check. I wanted so much to please him, to give him everything he wanted, everything that I could. That I *was*.

"That's it. Fuck me with your mouth, blue eyes. So good."

He moved my head back and forth over his cock, finding his own rhythm. I grasped his base with my hand again, sliding it up and back along with my mouth, helping the stimulation.

"God, baby. I want to come in your mouth so bad."

Do it, I said inside my head. I wanted him to come down my throat so badly. I kept going, sucking his cock as he moved my head back and forth, until he finally let out a big groan.

"Baby, yes, I'm coming, blue eyes."

And his hot seed spurted into my mouth. I swallowed it instantly, lapping up the rest around his head with my tongue.

His cock went limp, and it would be a while before he

could come again. That was okay, because we needed to talk.

Talon, however, had other plans. He stood, pulled up his boxers and jeans, and then turned me around and pushed me onto the futon facedown. He pulled off my shoes and pants and then dragged my lacy underwear over my hips as well.

He gave my ass a quick smack. "That's for being with Colin tonight."

I had the right to be with whomever I wanted, but damn, the sting, the intensity... I wanted him to smack my ass again. I clamped my lips shut for fear I'd cry out, begging him to spank me.

Turned out I didn't need to beg. His palm came down on my ass again. The burn turned to pleasure, bubbling through my veins and culminating in my center. My pussy was wet. The scent of my arousal was thick in the air.

Behind me, I heard Talon inhale.

"Fuck, Jade, you smell so good." He pushed my knees forward so my ass was in the air. "Such a cute little ass, and now nice and pink from my spanking. I'm going to lick you, baby."

He swept over me with his tongue. I shuddered. I was so sensitive down there. He continued licking me and inserted a finger into my pussy, finding my G spot and massaging. Damn, so good. I quivered, my blood boiling.

I was close to coming already. All he had to do was nudge my clit, and I would erupt like a hot volcano.

Bu he stayed away from my clit, teasing me, torturing me.

He continued to probe my ass with his tongue while

he fucked me with his fingers. "Blue eyes, I could eat you all night. Nothing tastes like you. Nothing so sweet, so succulent."

If words could make me come, those would've been the lines. I was on edge, so ready, so willing. He teased me to the point of almost exploding and then brought me down again.

God, touch my clit, I wanted to shout.

"You like this, baby? You like my mouth all over you?"

"You know I do," I gasped, clutching the comforter.

"I'm going to fuck you soon, baby. Fuck you hard, not gently. You need to pay for what you did tonight." He pulled back and slapped my ass once more.

And as he did so, he nudged my clit with the bottom of his hand.

I exploded, screaming, shouting. I didn't care that Sarah was next door. I didn't care if anyone was downstairs in the beauty shop. I didn't care who was on the street below. All I cared about was coming, coming, coming. As the waves of rapture surrounded me, I took flight in my mind.

Talon continued drilling his fingers into my pussy and probing my ass with his tongue as the orgasm went on and on, every cell in my body tingling, sizzling. When I finally came down, panting into the covers, I was spent.

I smiled into the comforter as I melted into the futon.

Talon's body warmed me as he slid next to me.

"You have too many clothes on," I said into the covers.

"I can take care of that, baby." The futon rose slightly when he got up. I heard the unbuckling of his belt, the soft zing of his zipper. I heard him toeing his boots off, and soon he was next to me again, his warm skin heating mine. He flopped his arm over me and pulled me to him so I was lying on my side. His cock nudged me in the back.

I smiled. "Something you wanted?"

Without answering, he slid his cock slowly into my pussy from behind.

Sweet completion. I was still spent from my orgasms, and I didn't want to move. I just wanted to lie here and feel his presence in my body.

He didn't move for what seemed like the longest time. We just lay there, joined, our skin touching, his front to my back. He placed his hand over one of my breasts, but what he did wasn't sexual. He just held me there, as he held his cock inside me.

I sighed again against the covers.

I had never felt as close to anyone in my entire life as I did to Talon in that moment.

CHAPTER TWENTY-FIVE

TALON

She gripped me so completely. The animal in me had the urge to pull out and thrust back into her heat, work myself up to another climax. Yet I held still, reveled in the snug feel of her body encasing mine. Being inside her, close to her, was so potent yet so comforting at the same time.

And something dawned on me like a light bulb illuminating over my head.

This wasn't about sex.

I was in love with her. Of that I had no doubt. But even loving her as I did, I still wanted to fuck her. I was still so sexually aroused by her.

But right now? Yes, I wanted to fuck her and fuck her good, but more than that, I just wanted to be a part of her, joined with her. I didn't want to know where she ended and I began. I wanted us to be complete in each other. One being. One body.

I kissed the top of her head and inhaled the coconut fragrance of her hair.

Maybe, just maybe, things would be all right.

"Stay?" she said into the comforter.

I chuckled against her hair. "I told you I wasn't leaving

your side until after court on Monday, remember?"

She laughed. "Yes, you did say that."

"Well, since I'm a man of my word, I'll stay." I nudged into her a little more deeply, ignoring the urge to plunge, and kissed the top of her sweet-smelling head again.

When she pushed backward, I couldn't take it any longer. I began thrusting slowly, ever so slowly, making sweet, quiet love to her. To Jade. To the woman I loved.

"Touch yourself, baby," I said against her hair.

I felt movement as she shifted her fingers between her legs. I closed my eyes and saw her, in my mind's eye, softly stroking her beautiful pussy...as I slid in and slid out, methodically, gently bringing myself to the edge.

I kept my hand on her breast but did not tease her nipple. No, this was just about the sweetness of a man loving his woman and a woman letting a man love her.

"How are you feeling, blue eyes? Ready to come?"

"Mmm," she said, her hips gently moving in circles against me. "Whenever you're ready, baby."

My skin tightened around me, and my balls inched up toward my cock. "Oh, yeah, I'm ready." I ground into her, holding my breath for a moment, squeezing my eyes shut, reveling in the tiny convulsions starting in my balls and pulsing outward.

"Now, baby," I said. "Come now."

And her pussy clamped around me, milking me, as I shot my seed into the woman I loved.

When the spasms started to slow and my cock lost a bit of its hardness, it slid out of her. She sighed against me, snuggling into me backward. In a few minutes, a soft snore escaped her throat.

I sniffed her hair once more, the coconuty goodness making me smile. Though I knew she couldn't hear me, I spoke anyway.

"Jade, I love you."

★ ★ ★

"I like it."

The boy's voice cracked as he said the hateful words. Again he said them to save his own life. To keep the cool knife that one of the masked men held on his throat from plunging through the layers of skin. As he was pounded into from behind, he said it again and then again.

"I like it."

Even as he said the words, the boy detached himself from what was happening. He had to—to survive. Why? He would die here. He knew that. He'd accepted that. Why did he say those horrid words to ensure his survival for one more second in this hellish nightmare? As if their torture and abuse wasn't enough, he had to humiliate himself by telling them that he liked it.

Because...

He wanted to survive.

So he would survive. No matter what. One day, he would find a way out of this prison.

When they were done with him, they threw him back on the blanket that had become his bed. It was tattered and gray, covered in his own filth now. How long had he been here? The boy didn't know. He had stopped counting the days long before.

Sometimes the boy dreamed while he was asleep. The dreams were always the same. He had grown big and tall, as big as his father, over six feet with broad shoulders and a muscular build. When the masked demons came for him, he overpowered them, beat each one of them. Executing martial arts moves, snap kicks, roundhouse kicks, axe kicks, knife hand punches and regular punches to their faces, their noses, their throats.

And when they were all on the ground, lying on their backs, choking on their own blood, the boy took the one with the tattoo, straddled him, and clasped his hands around the demon's throat.

"How do you like that, boy? Do you like it when I choke the air out of your lungs? Tell me that you like it. Tell me that you like it.

Tattoo gasped, struggling.

"I said tell me you like it, you fucking bastard."

"I like it," croaked Tattoo.

And the boy crushed the masked man's throat, squashing the life out of him.

He liked it.

CHAPTER TWENTY-SIX

JADE

Talon was kissing me. His lips softly grazed my cheeks, my neck, my throat.

The kiss became harder, little bites, harsh suction around my throat, around my larynx.

Still good. I sighed.

I inhaled and—

Air. I could breathe, but...restriction. Had to work a little harder.

My eyes shot open.

A jagged scream ripped from my throat.

"Stop!" I yelled, but it came out as a haggard gasp.

Talon was on top of me, straddling me, his fingers around my neck.

His eyes were glazed over. He didn't look right. He didn't look like...him.

"Talon!" I could still speak in rasps, but I feared where this might go. He wasn't responding to sound. My heart beat against my chest, my nerves racing. What was he doing? Why? Why was this happening?

I punched his arms. No response. My legs were of no use to me—from my position lying on my back, Talon straddling me around my hips, I couldn't get enough leverage to kick him with my knee or my foot.

No, I would have to depend on my arms. I hit him again and again, and still no response.

Needles danced across my skin. Panic. Sheer panic. Something was wrong. Very wrong. This wasn't Talon.

I drew short breaths as best I could, attempting to gather my will. My fingernails were short, but they were thin and sharp...and the only weapon I had. It had to work. It had to, because I didn't know what I'd do if it didn't. I reached as far as I could up his arms, sank my fingernails into his flesh, and clawed them downward, scratching him so hard I drew blood.

His eyebrows launched upward. "What? Oh my God, Jade!" He pulled his hands from my throat and stared at them, horror flowing over his features.

Quickly I inhaled, gasping. "Talon!" I shouted, my voice slightly hoarse. "What the hell were you doing?"

"Damn it!" He flew from the bed, visibly shivering. "I've got to get out of here."

I inhaled again and then again. Then I rose, scooted to the side of the bed, and sat up.

"No. You can't go. Not until you tell me what the hell that was."

He turned to me, his dark eyes sunken. "Blue eyes, I am so, so sorry."

Sorry. He'd said he was sorry, and he hadn't choked out the words. Something had changed inside him, for the better. I hoped what had just occurred wouldn't negate that.

I sat in silence as he dressed, his body moving as if

separate from his mind. Short jerky movements, his features laced with fear.

I was scared, yes, but he needed me. I went to him, not touching him. "I know you would never hurt me," I said.

"How would you know that?" His eyes smoked, turning nearly black. "I just tried to choke the life out of you."

The urge to comfort him overwhelmed me, despite what I'd just been through. "No, you didn't. Of course you didn't. I was breathing. I could speak. You just weren't hearing me. Something was going on. Tell me, Talon. Tell me what it was."

"You really want to sit here and talk to me after I just nearly killed you?"

The strained look in his eyes nearly fractured my heart. "You're not hearing me. I'm fine. You would never hurt me. I was never unable to breathe or speak. Something else was going on. I know you'd never hurt me."

"You keep saying that. But look at what I did."

"I know what you did. And you didn't hurt me."

"Are you kidding me? Of course I hurt you. Listen to your voice."

I cleared my throat. "My voice is fine. My neck doesn't hurt. I won't have any bruising. You weren't holding me that hard."

"Are you listening to yourself, Jade? I shouldn't have had my hands anywhere near your neck."

"I know that. But Talon, I'm fine. Please. We just need to figure out what was going on."

"What if you hadn't been able to stop me?" He combed his fingers through his tousled hair and then clasped his head in his hands, unable to meet my gaze.

I wrapped my arms around him, aching to console him. "You weren't hurting me, and I *did* stop you."

His eyes were rimmed with red. "What if next time you can't?"

I had been so busy trying to calm Talon down, I hadn't thought about what would've happened if he'd truly been choking me and I hadn't been able to stop him. The thought made my skin chill. Still, in the innermost chambers of my soul, I was positive he would never do me harm.

He fisted both hands in his mass of black hair. "I can't be around you anymore, Jade."

My insides bled a little. The look in his eyes was so tortured. "Has this ever happened to you before?"

He shook his head. "No, but I've never slept with anyone...before."

I jolted forward. "Really? You've never spent the night with a woman?"

He shook his head again.

"Why not?"

"I've never wanted to before."

Emotion swirled through me. This man was such a conundrum. In the span of five minutes, he could scare the hell out of me and then make me melt into a big puddle of honey.

"We can't see each other anymore," he said again.

Nope. Not an option. "Do you remember anything?" I asked. "Do you remember why you wanted to put your hands on my throat?"

He rubbed at his forehead. "I never wanted to put my hands around *your* throat, Jade. Please believe that."

"I do believe that. But do you have any idea why this happened?"

He sighed. "I dream sometimes."

"About when you were in the Marines?"

He scoffed, shaking his head. "You wouldn't understand."

"Please, I *want* to understand. I've always wanted to. Let me help you."

"I can't let you anywhere near me, blue eyes. If I ever did anything to hurt you..." Remorse and fear were etched into his features.

"But you didn't, Talon. I stopped you."

"What if you hadn't been able to stop me?"

I still didn't think he would've done me any harm, but I did have to consider that question. What if I hadn't been able to stop him? The answer came to me instantly, and in the depth of my soul, I knew it as pure truth. "Then you would've stopped yourself."

"Neither one of us can be sure of that," he said, putting on his socks and then his boots. He sat on the futon, his neck glistening with perspiration. Sweat dripped from his brow.

He was scared.

I had never seen Talon scared.

I stood, my knees trembling, and went toward him. I maneuvered myself between his legs and stroked his hair as I stood. "It's okay." I kissed his head. "It's okay to be scared sometimes. Everyone is."

"Not me." He shook his head vehemently. "I haven't been scared for twenty-five years. Until now."

CHAPTER TWENTY-SEVEN

TALON

Had to get out. Had to get away from her. *For* her. Couldn't risk hurting her.

Fear coursed through me like a bass drum beating slowly, surely...like a clock ticking deliberately...my impending doom on a timer, each sand in the hourglass one more second until I hurt Jade. How many more grains would fall until I damaged the only thing I'd ever wanted in the world?

Why would she want to be with me? I had just tried to strangle the life out of her!

"There's nothing to be scared of," she said in her calm, sweet voice.

But I knew better. I knew what I was capable of. What I dreamed about.

Of killing those three bastards.

I had thought that joining the military, commanding an EOD unit and finding and disarming bombs, possibly killing—which I had done on more than one occasion—would satisfy the need to rid the world of those three demons who took me all those years ago.

It hadn't.

I still had the dreams.

She was stroking my forearm, her touch both soothing and scathing. My hair stood on end.

I didn't deserve her loving touch.

God...if I ever hurt her...

But you didn't.

Her words echoed in my mind. I turned around and looked at her. She was still naked, her beautiful body glistening in a sheen of perspiration. Her golden-brown hair was in disarray and hung around her shoulders like tousled silk. Her blue eyes were searching, looking for something in me...something she would never find.

I had been kidding myself for too long. I could never have Jade. I could never have a life with her. I was too broken. Too fucked up. And I would never put her in danger.

I hated myself at this moment. Wanted to go find a bridge and hurl myself into the oncoming traffic below.

I'd tried taking my own life before, when I ran into that enemy fire under the guise of saving my men. Only I hadn't been killed, and I'd been touted as a hero.

Some hero. I couldn't even keep the woman I love safe—safe from that fucking ex of hers...or safe from me.

I didn't want to leave her. I had promised I would stay by her side until court on Monday morning.

"Talon"—she squeezed my forearm—"there's something good in all this, you know."

I shook my head and let out a small laugh. "What in the world could be good in all this, blue eyes?"

She smiled and trailed her fingers down my forearm, clasping my hand in hers. "You were sleeping."

I couldn't help but chuckle. I was a notoriously bad

sleeper, and when I did sleep, I was usually plagued by nightmares. Just as I had been this evening.

"Think back," she said. "Think back about how you were feeling when we had just finished making love. That slow, sweet passionate love that was different from anything else we've shared. What were you feeling right then?"

I clasped my head in my hands. I knew the answer, and I forced it from my lips. "I was feeling relaxed, blue eyes. I was feeling...*good*."

She smiled at me, that beautiful loving smile. If that smile could be turned into a sound wave and subliminally channeled across the entire planet, I had no doubt we'd see world peace.

I had been feeling good. I had been feeling so relaxed, so complete, so at peace. So...in love.

She squeezed my hand. Again. "So it's a good thing, Talon. You were relaxed, and you felt good."

I dropped my gaze to the floor. "I need to leave now."

"Please, Talon. Stay."

"How can you ask me that after what just happened?"

She cupped my cheeks and forced me to look into her eyes. The silvery-blue was misted over with tears, and my heart nearly broke.

"I trust you," she said.

My eyes filled, and one tear dripped down my cheek.

She thumbed it away. "It's okay."

But it wasn't okay. I had made the decision to get help, and I would still do that. I would not try to take my own life again. Because even after what had just happened, I still wanted to live. I didn't want to put my brothers and my sister through the agony of losing me.

I let out a huff. That last thought was true, yes, but another reason existed. Of course I didn't want my brothers and sister to suffer, but the real reason I wanted to live was standing right in front of me.

Jade. I would do this for Jade.

Even if we could never be together, just the thought of her being in this world gave me hope. Hope that I could heal. Hope that someone wonderful could feel for me. Hope that I could persevere.

I stood. "I can't stay, blue eyes. I would never forgive myself if I slipped into a dream and did something terrible to you."

She tugged on my hand. "I won't let you. *You* won't let you."

I shook my head. "I can't take that risk."

"Are you saying this is...over?" Her beautiful red lips turned down into a frown, and her eyes were laced with sadness.

I should've told her yes, it was over. God knew I had told her that many times before. But not this time.

"No. I don't think this will ever be over between us, Jade." I stroked her cheek with my thumb and threaded my fingers through her disheveled hair. "But I have to put this... on hold for now."

"Why?"

"Just some things I have to figure out." I grabbed my shirt and put it on.

"What things?"

"Things I don't have any control over right now."

"You mean what happened overseas?"

"Sort of. I'm going to get some..." God, why was the word so hard to say?

She squeezed my hand, tugging a bit.

I forced the word out of my mouth. "Help."

And just like that, a giant weight lifted itself from my shoulders. I was going to get help. I *wanted* to get help. Not just for Jade. Not just for Ryan and Jonah and Marj.

For me. I wanted to get help for me.

"What kind of help?" she asked.

I sighed. "The kind I've put off for far too long." I kissed her cheek. "I'm sorry to leave you like this. I hate it when that asshole is in town."

"Don't worry about that. He won't bother me."

"No, he won't. Because I mean to have someone watching this place and you night and day until he's gone."

"Talon..."

"No arguments, blue eyes."

"That's the most ridiculous thing I've ever heard. This has got to be the safest town on the planet."

No, it wasn't. I knew all too well.

"Besides, you can't control me, Talon."

She was right about that. As much as I wanted to control her, there was simply no controlling the little spitfire that was Jade Roberts. That was part of what I loved so much about her. But I *could* control whether Colin Morse got anywhere near her. "Don't worry," I said. "Nothing will intrude on your daily life. Besides, only one day until court."

"You'd better show up in court, Talon," she said. "This is more important than I think you realize."

Funny. She was right. I hadn't realized. Oh, I understood the law and the trouble I was in for beating the shit out of that asshole. I understood that she had gotten me a sweet deal. And I knew more than anything how it felt to be locked up. Being locked up would probably have been the end of me.

But like I had for the last two-plus decades, I hadn't let the significance sink into my brain. I had been existing for twenty-five years. Existing in a gray haze.

Now I wanted to *live*.

★ ★ ★

"Thanks for coming in on the weekend again." I sat down in the hunter-green leather chair that I remembered from a few weeks ago.

Dr. Melanie Carmichael nodded. "It's no trouble at all, Talon. I'm really glad you called."

"I'll make sure you're paid double for seeing me on a Sunday."

"Don't you worry about that. My regular fee is fine. And I will bill you."

A big lump clogged my throat. I had to finish this. I had to be honest with the therapist.

"So tell me. I'm curious," Dr. Carmichael said. "What propelled you to contact me this morning?"

"My brother has the hots for you." I had no idea why I said that. It just popped out. Joe would probably have my head, but it was way easier than telling her why I had called her.

She smiled, and her cheeks pinked just a bit. She

glowed in a lovely way. I could see why Jonah was enamored with her.

"He'd probably kick my butt if he knew I told you that, so can you keep it on the QT?"

She laughed. "Perfectly fine."

"I have to go to court tomorrow."

"Why is that?"

"Remember last time I was here, and I told you I'd beat a guy up?"

She nodded. "I remember."

"An attorney got a deal for me. I have to pay a five-hundred-dollar fine and pay the guy restitution. It avoids any prison time."

"That's great news."

I nodded.

"But I doubt that's what brought you in here."

"You are good," I said sarcastically.

"Well, it didn't take any of my education or experience to figure that out." She smiled.

Uneasiness wove a path through my brain. Jagged pieces of the previous evening mucked up my mind. Couldn't start there. Not yet. "I really don't know where to begin."

"I usually tell my patients to start at the beginning, but I'm not sure that will work for you. The last time I asked about your past, you didn't have the greatest reaction."

"Yeah, I know. Sorry about that."

"There's no reason to be sorry for fainting. But I have to warn you, you will continue to have these kind of physical responses until you work through whatever is gnawing at you inside."

"What makes you think there's anything gnawing at me?"

"Talon. I've been doing this for ten years. I can tell. In fact, I'm pretty sure a layperson on the street could tell."

"What's that supposed to mean?" My hackles rose.

"Calm down. I didn't mean anything by it. But you called me for a reason."

I clenched the arms of the chair. My fight-or-flight response was kicking in. Adrenaline coursed through me. I wanted either to run or beat something.

"That's not the answer," she said.

"I didn't say anything."

"No, but you're thinking. You're thinking you want to get the hell out of here. I can see it in your body language, in your eyes."

"So you're a body-language expert now?"

"Of course I am. I'm a psychologist."

I relaxed my hold on the chair and willed my heart to stop thundering against my chest. "All right," I said. "I'm ready."

CHAPTER TWENTY-EIGHT

JADE

"Jade"—Marj's voice was urgent—"you've got to come over here now."

The phone had rung while I was brushing my teeth, and I could barely talk through the toothpaste.

"What's wrong?"

"I found some stuff hidden in Jonah's room."

"What are you doing in Jonah's house?"

"I was curious. I'm tired of the guys not telling me anything. I knew Joe was going to be out in the pastures this morning, so I came over, let myself in, and did some digging around."

Marj... What had she gotten herself into now? "When is he going to be home?"

"Any minute. Or at the end of the day. I don't know. I don't rightly care. What's he going to do? Arrest me for breaking and entering? My brother wouldn't do that. Especially not after what I found."

"What *did* you find?"

"It's too complex. I don't want to talk about it over the phone." Her voice was agitated, disturbed.

"All right, all right." When Marj got her mind on something, there was no changing it. "I'll get there soon as I can. I just got out of the shower. I'll put on some clothes and be right there."

"You need a ride?"

"No, Talon gave me the Mustang, remember?"

"Right, good. Meet me at Joe's house."

"No way. I am *not* going to sneak through your brother's house. I sure as hell don't want to be an accessory to whatever it is you're doing. I'll meet you at the big house." Big house, meaning the main ranch house, of course. I hoped the words weren't foreshadowing...

She sighed over the phone. "Fine. Just hurry, please." She clicked the phone off.

An hour later, I arrived at the ranch house. Marj met me at the front door, Roger lapping at her heels. I knelt down and gave the dog some love.

"Since Roger's following you around, I assume Talon's not here?"

She shook her head. "He went off an hour or so ago. He texted me to let me know. Little did he know I was riffling through Joe's bedroom at the time."

"So what's the big deal? What did you find?"

"We're going to need a glass of wine for this."

"Marj, it's noon. We don't need wine. We need lunch."

"Well, it's Sunday, so Felicia's not here. And I can't wait to talk to you about this. We'll eat after. And suit yourself, but I'm having a glass of wine." She walked to the kitchen.

I followed. "Fine. Just water for me, please."

Marj poured our beverages. "We need to go to my room. I can't risk having this stuff out in case someone shows up in the house."

My heart started pounding. What was she getting at?

When we got to Marj's room, her bed was filled with scattered newspaper articles. She sat down on an empty spot and cleared another spot for me.

"Take a look at these."

I grabbed an article, and nausea overtook me as I read the words. It was about a little boy who had been abducted and never found. I put it down and picked up another one. This one had been found, strangled to death in a vacant field. Ice shrouded my skin.

"Marj, what is all this about?"

"You tell me. I found an envelope full of these articles hidden in Jonah's closet." She shook her head, her face pale, her lips trembling. "All this time I thought Talon was the one with the issues, and now I find out my oldest brother—"

"Don't finish that sentence."

"Believe me, I don't want to."

"I doubt Jonah has these for any other reason than..." I couldn't finish the sentence either. Why *would* he have them?

"I can't imagine that my brother would ever..."

"See? That's because he wouldn't." I leafed through the papers, checking the dates. "I mean, look at these articles. They're twenty-five and thirty years old. If Jonah were interested in abducting little kids, he'd be looking at present-day stuff."

Marj's features softened, and I could see the relief coursing through her. "Oh, God, Jade. Why didn't I think of that?"

"Because you were too busy freaking out. Joe is the nicest guy in the world. He would never even think of doing anything like this."

"Of course he wouldn't." Marj's cheeks flushed their usual rosy pink.

"But there has to be a reason why he has these articles."

She nodded. "Yeah, there has to be. But why?"

I smiled. "Now that you're done freaking out and thinking your brother is some kind of pedophile, why don't we go to the kitchen and you whip us up one of your gourmet lunches? I'm starving. With full bellies, we can come back in here and read through all of these and figure out what's going on."

Marj created some amazing beef stroganoff out of leftovers she found in the fridge. She finished her glass of wine and elected not to have another. A half an hour later, our bellies sated, we went back into her room.

We perused the articles and arranged them in chronological order. There were six altogether, all boys abducted between the ages of eight and eleven, except for one girl. Only one of the boys had been found. The other five children had never been found. The articles ranged from thirty years ago to twenty-five years ago. Only one of the boys was from Snow Creek. The rest were from Grand Junction or other towns in the vicinity.

I cleared my throat. "So over a span of what looks like about five years, six kids were abducted, mostly boys. Only one was found—dead, starved, and strangled, showing signs of physical and sexual abuse."

Marj nodded. "I wish I knew why Jonah was keeping these articles."

"Do you think he might have known one of the kids?

Thirty years ago he was what, about eight?"

Marj's eyebrows shot up. "I bet that's it. I bet he knew the guy from Snow Creek. But what was the boy's name?" She searched through the articles. "Luke Walker, nearly twenty-six years ago. Joe would've been twelve. But it says this kid was nine when he was taken. That would've been Talon's age."

My heart jolted. "Do you think Talon knew him?"

"Maybe. That doesn't explain why Jonah was keeping the articles, though."

"You know what we have to do, don't you?"

"What?" she asked.

"We have to ask Jonah."

"Problem with that on two counts," Marj said. "Remember how he reacted the last time we went to him demanding answers? And this time, I was snooping through his house, not just snooping through my dad's old documents in the basement."

"I know. But this is going to eat at both of us until we know what's going on."

"Let's ask Ryan," Marj said. "He's so much more easygoing than Joe, and I know he'll keep the secret that I was snooping."

I had almost suggested asking Talon, but that would have been ridiculous. Talon was less than forthcoming about most things, so even if he knew anything about these articles, he would be as tightlipped as Jonah.

"I'll text him right now," Marj said, "and see if he can come over."

I perused another one of the articles, this one about the

one girl in the bunch. Raine Stevenson, aged nine. Never found. My blood ran cold.

About fifteen minutes later, a knock sounded on Marj's door.

"I'm here," Ryan called.

"Great, come on in," Marj called back.

Ryan entered, looking like he'd just gotten out of the shower. His dark waves were plastered to his neck. "What's got you all in an uproar?"

Marj gestured to the bed where we both still sat. "This."

Ryan walked forward, and his eyes widened into dinner plates as he sat down on the bed and shuffled through the articles. "Shit. Where the hell did you find these?"

"Promise you won't get mad if I tell you?"

Ryan shook his head. "You can't ask me to make such a promise."

"He's right, Marj," I said. "If you want to get to the bottom this, you're going to have to risk angering some people."

"Fine. I found them in Joe's bedroom."

Ryan's jawline tightened. "And just what were you doing in Joe's bedroom?"

"I want answers, Ry. I found out a couple days ago that I was born premature, and my mother, whom I never knew, who died before I can remember her, changed my name. And for some reason our mother's name—her maiden name—got changed on her marriage certificate."

"What are you talking about?"

"Tell him, Jade."

I let out a heavy sigh and told him what we had

asked Jonah about weeks ago and what I had found in the Colorado records database.

Ryan stood, nodding, his signature smile absent.

"Aren't you going to say anything?" Marj asked.

"It's not my story to tell."

"Oh, for the love of God, is that all you people say?" I threw my hands in the air.

"Look, Jade, this is about...family stuff," Ryan said.

"Oh, no, you don't," Marj said. "You're not kicking Jade out of here. She *is* family as far as I'm concerned. She's my best friend in the entire universe, and she's in love with our brother."

Ryan visibly gulped, but he didn't seem surprised by Marj's revelation. Then he nodded. "Fine. These articles are simply what they are. Some psychos were taking kids twenty-some years ago."

"Why is this of such interest to Joe?" Marj asked. "Why did he save all of these? I mean God, I found these and I thought he was a pervert or something."

Ryan shook his head. "No, Joe's no pervert."

"I know," Marj said. "But why did he save all this stuff? Did he know one of the kids?"

Ryan's corded muscles tensed as he nodded. "Yeah."

"The kid from Snow Creek? Luke Walker?"

"Yeah. He was a...friend."

"Of Joe's?"

Ryan cleared his throat. "Of Talon's, actually."

"That makes sense. They would've been the same age."

Ryan nodded again. "He was never found."

"So why did Joe keep all the articles?"

"Joe was almost thirteen at the time, Talon had just turned ten. When Luke disappeared, the two of them tried to find him. I helped as much as I could, and they let me tag along most of the time. It was...kind of like a game. Junior detectives, you know?"

"What about the police?" Marj asked. "Weren't they involved?"

Ryan nodded. "Yeah. But whoever took these kids... They left *no* clues. They were smart. Genius in some ways. The kids were never found alive, if at all, so the police could never get any information about the abductors."

"You say abductors, plural," I said. "What makes you think there was more than one?"

Ryan's face reddened. "I don't know. I guess I just assumed."

Ryan was lying. His face had never turned red as long as I had known him. But I wasn't going to push it. Not just yet.

Marj apparently didn't share my reasoning. "Why would you assume that?" she asked.

"I don't know. It just seems implausible that someone could get away with so much and never get caught if there was only one brain behind it."

That seemed to satisfy Marj. But not me. He was still red. And he was still lying.

"How come you guys never mentioned Luke Walker? I mean, I'm your sister, and I've never heard of this until now."

"I was just a kid myself. He wasn't really my friend. He was Talon's. You know Joe's friend, Bryce Simpson? The mayor's son? He was Luke's cousin. Their mothers were sisters. So Joe had an interest. I just tagged along."

"Talon has never mentioned Luke Walker," Marj said.

"Talon never mentions anything."

Well, Ryan had us there.

"So what kind of things did you guys do?" I asked. "I mean, when you were playing detective."

"We talked to Luke's parents. But that didn't work out very well because they were so distraught, understandably. They didn't have much to say, and it was too painful for them to talk about. So that didn't last long. We never went back to them after the first time."

"Did your mom and dad know you were doing this detective work?" I asked.

Ryan nodded. "Yeah, I think they did. Remember, I was a kid myself. Joe would be the one to ask. He was the oldest, and he would have the best memories."

If Talon had been almost ten, his memories would be as good as Jonah's. Funny that Ryan didn't say to ask him.

"So what did you guys do after talking to the Walkers?" I asked.

"I remember going into town to the police station with Jonah and Talon. We asked to see the chief of police, because we wanted to know what was being done to help our friend. They gave us toy badges and sent us on our way." He rolled his eyes. "Jonah was so pissed. Remember, he was almost thirteen, and he considered himself a man. He demanded to see the chief, and then we were ushered out, and they threatened to call our parents." He shook his head. "Crazy stuff."

"Do the Walkers still live here?" I asked.

Ryan shook his head. "They've been gone for a while. A couple months after Luke went missing, they sold the property here and moved to Ohio, where Mrs. Walker was from. I don't know what happened to them after that."

"Do you remember their names, Ryan?" I asked.

"I was seven, Jade. To me they were Mr. and Mrs. Walker."

"It's right here in the article," Marj said. "Luke Walker, son of Chase and Victoria Walker of Snow Creek. They owned a small ranch north of town." She bit her lip. "North of town. I think that's part of the Carlton Dairy land now."

"Yeah, it is. The dairy bought it about a year later. Before the Walkers left, Talon and I used to—" Ryan stopped abruptly, his face going white.

"What?" Marj asked. "What did you and Talon do?"

"I don't want to talk any more about this." Ryan walked briskly toward the bed and gathered the articles in a sloppy pile. "This isn't any of your business. I'm taking these back to Joe's."

He walked out without another word.

"What was that about?" I asked.

Marj let out a heavy sigh. "Damned if I know. There's something that he's not telling us. And now we don't even have the articles. How are we going to figure out what they mean?"

I smiled. "We don't need the articles. Your best friend just happens to be a city attorney and has access to all archives in the state. I can pull up copies of those articles tomorrow at work."

CHAPTER TWENTY-NINE

TALON

"When I was about ten years old," I began, "a kid I knew from school disappeared."

"Was this kid a friend of yours?" Dr. Carmichael asked.

"Sort of. Not a forever friend or anything. He was a scrawny little kid whose parents ran a ranch north of Snow Creek. A real small-time operation, nothing like what we run. He was small for his age, and he had buckteeth. So of course he was ripe for the bullies at school."

"Did you bully him?"

I shook my head. "Hell, no. I hate bullies."

"Then what did you do?"

"I... I didn't really take him under my wing. He wasn't the kind of kid I wanted to hang out with. But more than once I kept the bullies from bothering him. Got my ass kicked a couple times for the trouble."

"So you bullied the bullies." Dr. Carmichael smiled.

I let out a chuckle. "I guess so. Sort of."

"So you said he disappeared. What happened?"

"Well, that's just the thing. Nobody knows. He was never found."

What a damned lie. I knew exactly what had happened

to Luke Walker. And the five other kids who went missing during that decade—that horrible decade.

"What do you think made you want to protect Luke? If he wasn't a friend, why bother?"

I cleared my throat. "It was the right thing to do."

"I know that, and you know that now. But you were a ten-year-old kid, Talon. Kids don't see things the way we adults do. So go back to your ten-year-old mind and tell me. What made you want to protect Luke from the bullies?"

I closed my eyes, trying to conjure Luke Walker in my mind. He'd been such a scrawny little thing, kind of reminded me of a scarecrow. His hair was even the color of straw. And those two front teeth stuck out. I figured he'd probably grow into them or get braces at some point.

But braces weren't in Luke Walker's future. Luke Walker was denied a future.

"I just hated the bullies. I hated seeing what their actions did to him. The kid walked around like he was scared all the time. No one should have to walk around like that."

No one indeed.

"So what did you end up doing? How were able you protect Luke?"

"Sometimes I'd wait for his bus with him. Which meant I usually missed my own bus. But Joe and Ryan would get home on the bus and tell my mom that she needed to come get me."

"And she did?"

"Yeah, she did. My mom was great."

I wished I hadn't said that. Now she was going to want to talk about my mom. Shrinks loved to talk about guys and their moms, right? But to my surprise, she continued with the line of questioning about Luke.

"So what happened to you when you protected him? Did the bullies go after you then?"

"Sometimes. But only when Jonah wasn't around. He was nearly thirteen at the time, and puberty had already started. All three of us were early bloomers. So he'd had quite a growth spurt and was heading toward six feet already, and his voice was in that middle area between high and low. He was strong from working on the ranch. We all were, for that matter. If he was around, and if his best friend was around—his best friend was Luke's cousin—no one got near Luke."

"But when Jonah wasn't around?"

"They ganged up on me a couple times. Ryan was only seven and would try to get in on it, but I'd tell him to stay the hell away and run toward home. Usually he did."

"But they obviously never did any real damage to you, right?"

"One of them broke my nose. That's where this little crook comes from." I touched my nose. "Other than that, they pretty much just knocked the wind out of me, blackened my eyes a couple times. Nothing I couldn't take."

"Was it worth it to you?"

"What do you mean?"

"Was saving Luke worth getting beat up?"

Hell, no. If I'd known what life had in store for Luke, I wouldn't have bothered. If I hadn't interfered in his life, maybe he wouldn't have been where he was that day. And maybe I would have... "Well...yeah, I guess." Was it a lie? I'd wanted to protect him at the time. Everything else was hindsight.

"You said he wasn't a great friend of yours or anything, not the kind of kid you wanted to hang out with."

I squeezed the arms of the chair. "It was just the right thing to do. That's all."

"And who taught you that standing up for the little guy was the right thing to do?"

"My dad, I guess. My grandpa. I don't know if they ever told me in so many words, but I knew right from wrong, and what those bullies were doing to Luke wasn't right."

Dr. Carmichael nodded. "So you said Luke disappeared."

"Yeah, right around the time..." My skin tightened, and blood pushed through my veins.

"Take a few brief deep breaths, Talon."

I obeyed, breathing in...out...in.

"Deep breathing has a therapeutic value," she said. "Just two or three deep breaths will calm you down."

It would take more than two or three deep breaths to calm me down, but the breathing did help take the edge off a little. I loosened my grip on the armchair.

"Joe was with his best friend, Bryce Simpson. Like I said, Bryce was Luke's cousin—their moms were sisters—and he lived in town with his parents and older sister. One time, Bryce and Joe were out at Luke's ranch. They were throwing a football around when Luke's mom came out and asked them to round up Luke for dinner. They couldn't find him."

"When was the last time they had seen him?"

Apprehension oozed through me. I hesitated for a

moment. Then, "I don't know. Joe said he had been at lunch, but then he and Bryce had run off to do their own thing. They never saw him again after that."

"So then what happened?"

"Bryce and Joe told Mr. and Mrs. Walker they couldn't find Luke. No one was worried yet. They went ahead and ate their dinner, but then when Luke still didn't show up, the Walkers called the police."

"And what happened after that?"

"The police came out and questioned the Walkers and Bryce and Joe. I remember my dad had to go over because Joe was a minor and the police couldn't talk to him without a parent present. They came home later that night, and Dad told us that Luke was missing."

"And what did you think?"

I swallowed the knot lodged at the base of my larynx. "I thought the bullies had gotten him." And indeed the bullies had. Only not the bullies I thought at the time.

"Did you tell the police that?"

I gulped again. "Yeah. I felt really terrible for not being there to protect Luke, and then I got in real trouble with the bullies for implicating them, let me tell you. As it turned out though, all the bullies had ironclad alibis, so they were exonerated right away. After that, no one really knew where to look. The police stalked around the ranch for days, looking for clues, but they didn't find anything—at least not anything that helped."

"What do you mean 'not anything that helped?' Did they find something unusual?"

Nausea rose in my throat, putrid and acidic. "Yeah." I

exhaled. "They found a black ski mask."

Dr. Carmichael cleared her throat. "That doesn't seem so unusual here in Colorado. Lots of people ski."

"The Walkers didn't, apparently."

"What about other people who hung out at the ranch? Your brother and Bryce, for example."

"The Steels have never been big skiers, believe it or not. I don't know about Bryce. But obviously the black ski mask didn't lead to anything."

I gripped the chair again in the devil's clench. Tried the deep breathing again. I had to maintain... Had to move forward...

"That's good, Talon," Dr. Carmichael said, standing. "Breathe in, breathe out. Excuse me for a moment. I want to get you some water."

"No!"

Dr. Carmichael stilled, her face unreadable.

"I... No."

"All right. A soda?"

I nodded. "That would be great. Soda. Please."

"Regular or diet?"

"Regular."

She came back with a cola. I opened it and took a deep drink, letting the cold liquid soothe my throat.

"Ready to talk again?"

I nodded.

"So what happened next?"

"A couple of days went by, and we didn't hear anything about Luke. My dad would call every day for an update, but the police didn't have any leads, and nothing had been found other than the black ski mask. Joe and I both took this kind of hard, because his best friend was Luke's cousin, and I had always kind of protected Luke, even though we weren't great friends. So one day, Joe, Ryan, and I decided to go into town and talk to the police. We rode our bikes. It's a couple hours. But we made it and walked right in there. I think it was a Saturday."

"Why didn't you ask your father to take you?"

"We did. He said no, that we had work to do around the ranch, and that he had been calling every night and there wasn't any new news."

"Did you think the police were holding something back? Is that why you went?"

I shook my head. "We were kids, Doc. Someone we knew was missing. Someone who meant something to us. We were impatient. We just wanted to know what was going on."

She nodded. "I understand. So what happened when you got to the police station?"

"Joe walked right in there and demanded to see the chief of police." I chuckled, remembering. "He thought he was such a big shot. But it was Saturday, so the police chief wasn't even in. Just a couple of uniformed officers. Of course they told us no, that we couldn't talk to anyone without our parents, and to please leave. Joe started to make a stink about it, and we were ushered out."

"And then?"

"We got an ice-cream cone and rode our bikes home. Dad was steaming mad that we had gone off and didn't know where we were. There were no cell phones in those days."

"I would guess he was quite upset," Dr. Carmichael said. "After all, a kid had just gone missing. He was probably afraid the same thing might happen to his children."

Wow. I'd never thought of that. Dad had been pretty over the top that day. Normally he didn't care if we ran off and had some fun, especially on the weekends. I didn't voice this, though.

"So you couldn't get help from the police. What next?"

"The next week we went back to school. It seemed strange without Luke there."

"But you and Luke weren't really good friends, right?"

"No."

"Then why was it strange?"

"I... I just had a weird feeling. I can't really put it into better words than that. The black ski mask..."

God, the black ski mask.

"Anyway, I wanted to go up to Luke's ranch and look around. I asked Joe and Ryan to go with me. We would get on Luke's bus instead of our own after school. Jonah said no. He had stuff to do at home, but maybe he'd go with us some other time." I drew in a deep breath. "But I was dead set on going that afternoon, and Ryan decided he would go with me."

I'll go with you, Tal. He'd put his hand in mine. I'd kept telling him he was too old for that, that boys didn't hold hands. God, the kid had followed me everywhere.

"So you and Ryan went, alone, to Luke's ranch."

I nodded, my vision blurring... If only I could go back... back...go back, not go to the Walkers' that day...

Again I clenched my fingers into the armchair... My

241

heart beating rapidly... My stomach churning... My bowels clenching...

I heaved...and blackness curtained around me.

★ ★ ★

The boy had been walking with his little brother for about an hour. Their tummies were full. Mrs. Walker had given them oatmeal cookies and watermelon when they showed up at her door. "Y'all can look around if you want to," she'd said. Her eyes were recessed and sad. "Just come back before dark. Do your mom and dad know you're here?"

The boy had nodded. It was a lie, but their older brother would tell their parents when he got home.

"This is where they found the mask," the boy said, more to himself than to his brother. The boy looked around. Nothing was visible. Even the Walkers' house had faded from view this far out. The cattle must not have grazed in this area, because the grass was tall. It brushed his knees.

In the distance stood a little shack.

"Let's go check out that building," the boy said to his brother.

His little brother nodded, and they traipsed forward.

The wood was gray and splintered, old. The boy reached out to touch the knotty surface, when—

"Talon! Auuuughh!"

He turned at his brother's blood-chilling scream, his heart drumming. Two figures had emerged from the structure, dressed all in black, their faces obscured by ski masks. Two large hands held his brother by the shoulders.

Fear and rage rose in the boy. "You leave my brother

242

alone!"

The other pair of hands lunged toward him, but before they could grab him, the boy ran into the man holding his brother, kicking at his shins. "Let go! Let go! Let go!"

The boy was no match for the grown man, and the other had grabbed the back of the boy's shirt. Still, the boy kicked, determined to free his brother. Brittle fragments of fear inched up his spine, but still he kicked, even as the other man dragged him away. He lodged one last punt with his steel-toed boot to the man's crotch. His brother fell from the man's grip onto his knees in the dirt.

"Run!" the boy yelled "Run back to the house! Get Dad! Run, run, run!"

The little boy stood, dazed, immobile.

"Damn it, I said run!"

The other man still held his crotch but got to his feet. The first one shoved the boy down onto the ground. He could no longer see his brother.

Please be running. Please get help, he pleaded silently to his brother.

The boy kicked and screamed, but two grown men were too much for him. They hauled him into the small building.

And lying on a bed by one wall, unconscious, was the boy he'd been looking for.

Luke.

CHAPTER THIRTY

JADE

I checked my watch as I stood outside the courtroom with Talon's attorney, Peter O'Keefe. Colin hadn't shown up yet, for which I was grateful, but neither had Talon.

"Have you been in touch with your client?" I asked O'Keefe.

He nodded. "Yes. We've been exchanging e-mails, and I texted him half an hour ago as a reminder."

Just then, Talon emerged at the head of the stairs and walked toward us. I breathed an audible sigh of relief.

"Cutting it a little close, aren't you?" O'Keefe said.

"I'm here, aren't I?"

He looked like hell. Though he was wearing a navy-blue suit, it was wrinkled and untidy. His blue-and-black striped tie was crooked, and his hair was a tousled mess. A tousled sexy mess, actually, but this was a courtroom. His eyelids were droopy and his eyes caved-in, like he hadn't slept in weeks. And even though I knew he didn't sleep, he didn't look normal to me.

I simply nodded. I needed to act impartial during these proceedings for Talon's sake.

I looked at my watch again. We were first on the docket.

We should get in there.

I was still on edge. Would Colin show up and wreak havoc? I wouldn't put it past him.

I sat on the prosecution side, and Talon and his attorney sat on the other side. Within a minute, the bailiff entered.

"All rise. Municipal Court of the city of Snow Creek is now in session. The Honorable Alayna Gonzales presiding."

The judge walked in, sat down at her bench, and took a seat.

"You may be seated," the bailiff said. "First case on the docket is People versus Talon Steel."

I moved to the prosecution's table while Talon and O'Keefe moved to the defense. I remained standing. "Jade Roberts for the city, your honor."

"Peter O'Keefe for the defense."

"Mr. Steel," Judge Gonzalez said, "I understand you wish to enter a plea bargain in this case."

"Yes," Talon said.

O'Keefe nudged him.

"Your honor."

I cleared my throat. "Your honor, the city is willing to accept a plea bargain for reckless endangerment along with a five-hundred-dollar fine and reasonable restitution paid to the alleged victim in this case." Who still hadn't shown up, thank God.

"And this is agreeable to you, Mr. Steel?"

"Yes, your honor."

"Since the defendant has no prior arrests on record, I see no reason not to approve this plea bargain. Counselors, I'll leave you two to work out the details. This case is dismissed." She pounded her gavel on the wooden surface.

My heart was beating a mile a minute.

Colin hadn't shown up, thank God.

I didn't have any other cases today, so I was done here. I had to go back to the office and work a full day though. And first thing on my agenda was finding copies of all the news articles that Marj and I had looked at the day before.

I moved over to the defense table and shook O'Keefe's hand. "Thank you. It was a pleasure working with you, Mr. O'Keefe."

He smiled. "Peter, please."

"Very well. Call me Jade." I turned to Talon. "I'm glad it all worked out."

He nodded quickly but didn't say anything to me. Something was off—more off than usual. And where the hell was Colin? After that scene he'd made Saturday night, I'd more than expected him to show up in court. None of this made any sense. I couldn't try to figure it out though. I had to get to work.

I headed to the building next door. I said a quick hello to Michelle and then went into my office. A few minutes later, Larry showed up in my doorway.

"How did the Steel case go today?"

"It went fine. The judge accepted the plea bargain."

"No jail time?"

I shook my head. "Nope. Given the lack of severity of the misdemeanor, I felt it was in the best interest of the people to get a chunk of the Steels' money rather than spend the taxpayers' money to keep him in jail. He's not a threat to society. This was his first offense of any kind."

"Sounds good. Though I wouldn't have minded him getting locked up. At least for a few nights."

I jerked backward. Had I heard him right? "Larry, what makes you say that? Do you have a history with the Steels?"

He shook his head quickly. Too quickly. "No. But those three boys walk around town acting like they own the place. Just because they have the most successful ranch in Colorado."

I bit my lip. Boys? All three were a head taller than my boss. "Why are you having me investigate them again?"

"I told you before. That's classified. Have you found anything yet?"

"Nothing that I haven't already advised you about. But I'll get back on it today and see what I can find."

"Great. Thanks, Jade." He left my office.

Man, something bothered me about that guy. He had a creepy vibe to him, something that went far beyond his questionable ethics as an attorney. If only I knew—

Larry *Wade*. His last name was Wade.

Wade was Daphne Steel's last name on the original marriage certificate that we had found in Marj's basement. But it wasn't her name on the one in the Colorado database.

Could there be a connection?

Probably not. Wade was a fairly common name. Maybe not as common as Smith or Jones but a heck of a lot more common than a lot of other surnames.

If I was going to investigate my boss, I'd do it at home. I wasn't sure if I could clear my cache on the city server, so I didn't want to do it here.

But my curiosity got the best of me. I had been

covering my tracks as best I knew how since I started this investigation into the Steels. I could probably begin with looking up Daphne. She had to have a birth certificate somewhere, right? If she wasn't born in Colorado, it might still be under her original name, Daphne Kay Wade.

Quickly I searched the Colorado birth records. Damn! There she was, Daphne Kay Warren, born in Colorado, and the age matched up. How in the hell did someone change a birth certificate? Whoever did this had to have left a stone unturned at some point. I hoped I could find it. I did a quick search of the national databases. A plethora of Daphne Kay Wades and Daphne Kay Warrens existed, but none of them matched the criteria I needed. She was indeed born in Colorado, and her certificate named her as Daphne Kay Warren.

As much as I wanted to start Googling Larry to find out more about him, my first priority was finding and getting copies of all the news articles that Marj had found since Ryan took her copies away.

That was simple enough. I found them easily in the local paper and in all the papers in Grand Junction. They appeared to be the same articles, so I sent them to the printer and started a file. After I put the folder of articles in my briefcase to take home, I went out to talk to Michelle.

"Did you need something, Jade?" she asked.

"Maybe. I've been doing some investigative work for Larry, and I'd like to be able to continue at home from my home computer. Is there any way to access the Colorado databases from home?"

"You can always log into our server."

Of course I could. I knew that. But I didn't want a paper

trail. "I tried that," I lied. "My computer doesn't support the logistics." I had no idea what I had just said, but I figured she'd buy it. "I was hoping maybe I could access them from my own browser."

"I'm afraid not. Not without one hell of a hacker." She smiled.

I chuckled. "That's certainly not me. Guess I'll just do my work from here. I just hate staying late."

I went back to my office. I had no idea if Larry was watching what I searched. If he was, he hadn't mentioned it.

What the hell? I got into the Colorado database and typed in Larry Wade, city attorney for Snow Creek.

Turned out Larry hadn't been elected city attorney but had been appointed two years ago when the previous city attorney resigned in the middle of his term to take early retirement. So Larry got himself appointed, and he would be up for reelection in a year.

I chuckled to myself. Maybe I'd run against him. God knew I could do a better job than he was doing. *Don't get ahead of yourself, Jade. You're still a first-year attorney.*

Real name was Lawrence Kenneth Wade. Divorced, two grown children, two grandkids. His ex-wife's name was Lena.

Nothing more about his family and certainly no mention of being related to anyone named Daphne.

I didn't know where he was born, but I searched the Colorado database anyway. There he was—Lawrence Kenneth Wade, born to Jonathan Conrad Wade and Lisa Jeanette Baines.

Jonathan Conrad Wade... Where had I seen—

I grabbed the printout of Daphne Steel's birth certificate. Daphne Kay Warren, born to Lucille Lynne Smith and...Jonathan Conrad Warren.

What were the chances that their fathers had the exact same first and second names?

My skin shrunk around me, my veins freezing. *Search Jonathan Conrad Wade.* A few hits, and I found the right one. *Search Jonathan Conrad Warren...*

Nothing. At least not in Colorado.

Jonathan Conrad Warren didn't exist.

If what I suspected was true, and Jonathan Conrad Wade and Jonathan Conrad Warren were the same person... Daphne Steel and Larry Wade were half brother and sister.

And someone had gone to a lot of trouble to cover up that fact.

CHAPTER THIRTY-ONE

TALON

"You left abruptly yesterday. Would you like to tell me why?"

I was back in the hunter-green chair at Dr. Carmichael's office. She'd made room for me on her schedule right after my court appearance.

"I hardly ever sleep, but when I do, it's plagued with nightmares."

"Interesting answer to the question I asked." Dr. Carmichael cleared her throat. "So I gather you don't want to talk about why you left yesterday. That's okay. We can talk about whatever you want to."

"I want to tell you why I came in here."

As difficult as it would be to talk about nearly choking Jade, it would be infinitely harder to talk about where we had left off the last time.

Luke's small form—I could still see it on that bed.

But I couldn't go there yet.

"All right," Dr. Carmichael said. "Begin whenever you're ready."

"I've fallen in love."

The words still seemed so foreign to me. But while

the words were foreign, the feelings they evoked were not, almost as if they had been with me since the dawn of time. I just didn't know them until now. It had taken Jade to release them.

Dr. Carmichael smiled. "That's wonderful, Talon. The first time we talked, you said you didn't have relationships."

"I didn't. At least, I never wanted to. Not until her."

"And *her* is?"

"I told you about her before. My sister's best friend. Her name is Jade."

"That's a very pretty name."

I nodded. It was a pretty name. It was perfect for Jade. It sounded like warmth and caring and giving.

"So is Jade why you came in here, then?"

I nodded again. "Yeah. I scared myself the last time we were together."

"How so?"

"We...had relations."

"You mean you made love."

I gulped. "Yes. Why is that so hard for me to say?"

"Because you've probably never made love to anyone before."

"I've had plenty of experience."

"You've had plenty of sex, you mean."

I nodded. She was right.

"So what happened? You were making love..."

"Afterward, we were lying together. And I...fell asleep."

"Okay. Nothing unusual about that."

"It was for me. I don't sleep very well. And I had never slept with another person before."

"Never?"

I shook my head. "When I was in Iraq, I shared tents with the other guys sometimes. But this was...different."

She smiled again. She had a nice, warm smile. No wonder Jonah had the hots for her.

"I would hope it was different."

I couldn't help a small chuckle at that. "I didn't mean to fall asleep. Or maybe I did. I was going to stay with her through the night and through the next night as well."

"Why?"

"It's a long story. The guy I beat up was in town, her ex. He had taken her to dinner, which really pissed me off. So I didn't want to let her out of my sight until this morning when we had court."

"But you did let her out of your sight."

"You know I did, because I was in here yesterday."

She nodded. "Why?"

"When I fell asleep, I started dreaming and..." My skin compressed around my muscles, my nerves on edge. My legs cramped up, and I clenched the chair's arm again.

"What did you dream about?"

I searched my mind to come up with something, but I couldn't remember what I had been dreaming about. I only knew that I had been dreaming.

"So what happened?"

Fear froze the back of my neck. How could I say this without sounding like a monster? "I... I'm afraid to tell you."

"Everything you say to me is in confidence. You know that."

"Yes. I know. But what I did..."

"Did you hurt her?"

I gulped, my eyes misting. "No. Or not a lot. But I could have."

"What exactly happened?"

"I woke up with my hands around her neck."

Dr. Carmichael didn't look fazed at all. Well, this was her job. Maybe she had heard worse.

"I see. And what happened?"

"Jade woke me up."

"How did she do that?"

"She scratched me. Dug her fingernails from my shoulders down to my wrists and scratched me." The scratches had started to scab up, but I felt them then, as if they were fresh. Like tiny daggers piercing my skin.

"Did she try waking you any other way?"

"I don't know. She probably couldn't scream at me because my hands were around her throat."

Dr. Carmichael nodded. "Did Jade suffer any damage from what you did?"

"Her voice was slightly hoarse. But she said she was all right." I shook my head. "And here's the damnedest thing."

"What?"

"She didn't blame me. She wanted to help me. She said she knew I would never hurt her. I mean...she woke up to find me with my fingers around her neck, and then she says she knows I would never hurt her. What kind of person would say that?"

"A person who trusts you."

I shook my head. "I don't deserve her trust."

"Well, Talon, you don't really get a say in the matter. Her trust is hers and hers alone to give. It sounds like she's chosen to give it to you."

"I'm the last person in the world who deserves anyone's trust."

"Why would you say that?"

"Because I'm..." *Broken.* I couldn't force the word from my lips. Using that word would open up a bunch of questions about things I wasn't ready to talk about yet.

But here I was, sitting in a shrink's office. I was thirty-five years old, and I was in love for the first time in my life.

Maybe it was time to talk about it.

I wasn't getting any younger, and deep within my soul, I knew I would never have a chance for a future with Jade unless I put my past to rest.

I looked up at Dr. Carmichael. "How do you get over something so horrible, so terrible, so...malicious and sick, that most people can't even comprehend it?"

Dr. Carmichael let out a sigh. "You work hard. You have to want it. And it's not enough to want it for another person. You have to want it for yourself. There's something you're hiding. I've known it since we first met. I'm willing to go the distance with you, Talon, and I'm willing to go at your pace. But know this. You do eventually have to open up about it. I will never be able to help you if you don't."

I'd heard the same words from Jonah so many times.

Dr. Carmichael continued, "You being here shows me that you do want to work through this. This is the third time we've seen each other, and you've been able to open up slightly more each time. So that's a good thing. But I know there are things you're hiding. I know that there's a reason why you fainted that first time, why you became nearly catatonic last time. I'm willing to go as slow as you need to go."

"How could that have happened?" I asked. "How could I have put my hands around her throat? I...*love* her."

"Let's change the topic for a minute. Let's talk about your love for her. How do you know you love her?"

Good question. "I...*don't* know. I've never loved anyone other than my parents and my siblings. And this is way different."

"Of course it is." She chuckled.

"It started as a craving, and then it became an obsession. I had to have her. And I thought that by having her once, I would be able to get rid of the desire. But instead, every time I had her, my desire for her multiplied."

"That sounds like lust, not love."

"That's what it was at first. But as I got to know her, I started feeling more. And then suddenly it seemed like those feelings had been with me all my life, and it took her to evoke them."

"And is the physical desire still there?"

"I want her as soon as I lay eyes on her. Every single time."

"Is she in love with you?"

"She says she is. But there's so much about me she doesn't know."

"She's put her trust in you, Talon. Do you want a future with her?"

The question of the century. And the answer was yes. "Yes. Goddamnit, yes." I wanted a future with Jade more than I wanted my next breath of air. "And I know I can't have it unless I work through my own demons."

"I think it would help to know what you were dreaming about when this event happened with Jade. Would you be willing to go through some guided hypnosis with me? We might be able figure out what caused you to put your hands around her neck."

"Hypnosis? Is that some kind of voodoo bullshit?"

Dr. Carmichael laughed. "Hypnosis is, at its center, a state of relaxation. You usually feel calm and relaxed when you're under. And quite frankly, relaxation of any kind would be really good for you."

I couldn't help a small smile. She was right about that. "I don't know, Doc. I have a hard time giving up..."

"Control?" She smiled.

"Yes, control. I guess I'm kind of a textbook control freak."

"You probably are. But just from the little bit I know about you, it makes perfect sense to me why you would want to be in control. You and I don't know each other that well yet, so you may not trust me to hypnotize you."

"I really don't trust anyone, Doc. Except my brothers."

"Do you trust Jade?"

"I've never really thought about it."

"She trusts you."

"Yeah, she thinks she does anyway. There're still a lot of things she doesn't know about me."

"You can never know everything about another person. Tell me, based on what you know right now, and based on what you feel about her, do you trust Jade?"

The answer thrust itself into my head so quickly, I knew it had been there all along. "Yes. I trust Jade."

"And are you absolutely sure that you're in love with her?"

Warmth coated me, releasing the ice from my skin. Just the thought of her... "A hundred percent positive, Doc."

"All right. Back to your control issue. When you're hypnotized, you have heightened focus and concentration, and you're more open to suggestion, but you don't lose control over your behavior. It's important that you know that. I think the hypnosis would be helpful, but it won't do any good until you're ready. So let's switch topics to something else."

"Fine with me. What do you want to know?"

"I think it's time that you tell me everything that happened when you were ten."

★ ★ ★

The boy was tied up, gagged, and thrown onto the backseat of an old brown Ford truck. He had lost track of time but thought they'd been driving for at least an hour. He wasn't sure.

He hadn't thrown up. He'd used all of his energy and will to keep the vomit from rising when one of the masked men had held a knife to his throat, telling him that if he made a noise or threw up, he would kill him.

And then the other one had...

The boy closed his eyes, wincing.

They'd forced him to watch. Forced him not to empty his stomach or his bowels.

The blood spattering, bones splintering, gelatinous goo sliming from Luke's crushed skull...

Luke. The masked men had carved Luke into pieces and stuffed him into a black trash bag.

At least Luke hadn't screamed.

He had already been dead.

The boy fought to keep from puking again. He'd already emptied his bladder. His urine-soaked jeans clung to him.

"Usually we keep them longer than this," the man holding the blade to the boy's neck had said. "We got tired of this one quickly. Those damned buckteeth of his... Didn't work so well. Besides, you're a lot prettier than he was."

The evil voice echoed in the boy's head as the truck screeched to a halt.

The boy was dragged out and his feet unbound.

"Here you are, boy," one of them said. He had a low voice. "Home sweet home."

CHAPTER THIRTY-TWO

JADE

My search for any connection between Larry Wade and Daphne Steel, other than their father's first two names, came up at a dead end.

I sighed and got ready to leave the office. Talon had looked so strange this morning, and because of what had happened last time we were together, I knew he wouldn't come to me. So I would go to him. I texted Marj quickly to let her know I was coming to the house. I grabbed the folder of the printed-out articles and also Larry's and Daphne's birth certificates and then headed to my apartment. I changed into casual clothes and drove out to the house.

Marj hadn't returned my text, so I wasn't overly surprised when she wasn't home.

I knocked, and Talon came to the door, cute little Roger panting at his heels.

"Hey," he said when he opened the door. He looked delicious in a burgundy button-down shirt and his signature jeans and cowboy boots. His hair was a mess, though a sexy mess, and the dark circles under his eyes were more pronounced than ever.

"Hey," I said back. "I wanted to come check on you."

"What for?"

"You seemed a little off in court today. Can I come in?"

"I don't think that's a good idea."

"Why not? We're in love, Talon. I want to spend some time with you. Make sure you're okay."

"I'm..."

"You're what?"

He closed his eyes for a moment. Then, "I'm...*afraid*, Jade."

"That's silly."

"I don't want to hurt you."

"You won't."

"How can you be so sure?"

"Because I *know* you."

He shook his head. "Oh, blue eyes, you don't know me."

"Then what do I need to know? Tell me, Talon. I love you. I want to know everything about you."

His facial features hardened. Up went the wall.

Damned if I was going to stand here on his front porch. I walked past him and into the foyer. I knelt down and let Roger lick my face while I scratched him behind his cute little ears.

"Have you eaten yet?" I asked.

Talon shook his head.

"What's for dinner, then? I'm sure Felicia made something wonderful."

"She left early today. She had to take her mother to a doctor's appointment."

"She never leaves you high and dry." I walked into the kitchen and opened the refrigerator door. Sure enough, a Mexican casserole sat on the top shelf, along with instructions for making it. I preheated the oven and put it in.

"Casserole will be ready in about forty-five minutes. Or"—I smiled—"if you'd rather, I can make you a grilled cheddar and tomato sandwich."

He didn't smile. Then he cast his gaze to the manila folder I had set on the kitchen table. "What's that?"

"Some stuff I brought for Marj. Where is she?"

"Not sure. Just out, I guess."

I grabbed my purse and checked my phone. Marj had responded to my text.

Sorry. Went into town to have dinner at our instructor's restaurant with some of the guys from cooking class. Sorry to miss you. Let's chat tomorrow.

"Looks like she's in the city for dinner," I told Talon.

I itched to touch him. I had been in the house for ten minutes now, and I hadn't yet caressed his skin, kissed his lips.

My body was on fire just being in his presence.

"Talon, do you still love me?"

I wanted to smack myself as soon as the words left my mouth. I was so not going to be that insecure girl who had to be told she was loved every five seconds. He opened his mouth, but I shook my head at him.

"Forget I asked that."

"I love you, Jade," he said.

Warmth gathered in my heart. As much I didn't want to be that needy girl, hearing it at that moment really helped.

I walked toward him and snuggled up to his chest. Slowly his arms came around me, enveloping me in his spicy warmth. I inhaled the crisp scent from his neck. So musky and masculine.

He stroked my back, such a tender, loving touch.

Tender and loving, yes, but still my pussy began to throb. I sighed and pressed a kiss against his bronze neck. I wanted him so much. I wanted him to grab me and pick me up and drag me to his bedroom.

But that might not happen today, and I had to be okay with that.

"Can I fix you a drink?" I asked.

He shook his head and cleared his throat. "No, I'm good for now. Do you want something?"

"No, I'm fine. Do you want to go into the family room and sit on the couch? It'll be a little while before the casserole is done."

He didn't answer, just took my hand, led me out of the kitchen, down the couple of stairs, and into the lush family room. We sat down together on a leather couch, and I cuddled against him, wrapping my arm around his chest. I closed my eyes and inhaled his essence again, savoring the heat of his body.

Maybe this was what he needed right now—to just know I was here and that I loved him. That I wasn't going anywhere, no matter what.

We sat like that for a long time...until the bell on the oven rang, signaling that the casserole was ready.

I tore myself away from him, gave him a quick kiss on the cheek, and went to the kitchen to get dinner together.

Dinner was small talk and mostly silence. When we had finished and I was cleaning up, Talon came up behind me.

"That's a nice pearl necklace," he said.

I looked down, and my cheeks warmed. I had forgotten to take off my rope pearls when I changed clothes. I let out a giggle. "I can't believe I left it on. It probably doesn't look great with the T-shirt and cutoffs."

"I think it's cute." He stood beside me and helped me get the dishes loaded into the dishwasher.

His nearness made me tingle. Did I have the same effect on him? I looked down at his crotch, and sure enough...the bulge. I couldn't help a sly smile. Yes, I had the same effect on him.

Our physical chemistry was off the charts. It always had been. But as wonderful as it was, it was nothing compared to the love I felt for him, the way I felt like half of me was missing when I wasn't with him.

I knew, as much as I knew anything to be true, that Talon would never hurt me. He would stop himself before it ever got that far. He had been asleep the other night, and once he had awakened and realized it was me, he had ceased immediately.

I wanted to prove to him that I trusted him. I looked down at the long necklace. It was a fake. A good quality fake, but a fake nonetheless. And I knew exactly what I wanted.

I set the last dish on the top shelf of the dishwasher, and Talon added some detergent and started it. When he stood, I faced him, winding my fingers around the pearls at my neck.

With my other hand, I played with my nipple through my bra.

Talon groaned. "Blue eyes, not tonight."

But I wasn't going to take no for an answer. I continued to play with my nipple until it hardened into a tight little knob poking out from my bra, and then I switched to the other one, until two ripe berries protruded against the cotton of my T-shirt. My pussy was fluttering, and I knew I was getting wet. I grabbed Talon's hand and brought it to my breast. He thumbed my nipple.

"God, blue eyes."

"Touch me, Talon. Please touch me."

He fingered my nipples through the two layers of clothing. Lust coursed through me.

"I want you," I said.

"I can't... I want... Oh, fuck..." He pulled me toward him and crushed his lips to mine.

I kissed him with all the passion I felt, letting my tongue wander into his mouth, twirling with his. We kissed hard. As sweet as it had been to sit with him on the couch before dinner, saying nothing and just snuggling, now I wanted passion, fire, unbridled lust.

I grabbed the cheeks of his ass and squeezed, pulling him into me so that his erection probed my tummy.

He groaned into my mouth, and I answered with a moan of my own. My nipples were still hard, aching for his touch, his lips. I pressed against his chest.

When he finally broke the kiss and took a gasp of air, I pulled his head toward mine, gave his earlobe a sharp bite, and whispered, "Take me to bed. Please."

He didn't answer. Just took my hand and led me to his bedroom.

I undressed slowly, provocatively, until I stood naked

before him, wearing only the long string of pearls.

Then I moved toward him, and slowly, achingly slowly, I unbuttoned each button of his shirt, even though what I longed to do was rip it off of him so the buttons went flying. When the last button was finally released, I slid the soft fabric over his shoulders until it landed in a wine-colored heap on the floor. I sat him down in a chair and removed his boots and socks. Then I pulled him up again and unbuckled his belt, still going slowly, achingly slowly.

I unbuttoned his jeans and then unzipped him. Still slowly, achingly slowly.

I slid his jeans and boxer briefs down his narrow hips and taut buttocks. Still slowly, achingly slowly. I savored each new inch of bronze skin revealed to me, skimming his strong thighs and firm calves. He stepped out of his jeans and boxers and stood before me, naked, glorious, his cock extended as far as I'd ever seen it.

I knelt before him and gave his cockhead a lick. He groaned. How I wanted to suck it to the back of my throat, to show him how much he meant to me, but that wasn't what tonight was about.

Tonight was not about showing my love.

Tonight was about showing my trust.

I took his hands and led them to the shiny pearls around my neck.

"Take these beads, Talon. Take them and tie me to the bed, facedown."

His eyes glinted with fire, smoking black in their intensity. Was he turned on by the idea? I couldn't quite tell, so I waited, biting my lower lip, bringing my fingers to my nipples and squeezing, my pussy heating.

He said nothing to me, just gazed at me, never letting the dark fire of his eyes stray from mine.

He lifted the necklace over my head. "Are you sure, blue eyes?"

I nodded.

"Verbal," he said.

"I'm sure." I walked to the bed, got on my hands and knees, and grasped two bars of the headboard. "Tie me up, Talon, and then fuck me. Fuck me like you've never fucked me before. I want you to take my ass tonight, while I'm tied up, at your mercy."

"Oh, God," he groaned. "Are you sure?"

"Positive." I turned my head and looked into his blazing eyes. "I want to be yours tonight, Talon. I want to be yours in every possible way. No one's ever taken me there before, and no one ever will again. I trust you to do it. I trust you to do it while I'm tied to a bedpost."

"No one's ever"—his voice cracked—"placed so much trust in me."

I doubted that was true. The men under his command in the military had probably placed that much trust in him. They hadn't had a choice. But I did have a choice.

"I trust you, my love," I said. "I know you would never hurt me. And I know you'll stop if I tell you to stop."

"Oh, God," he groaned again.

My nipples were so hard they poked into the mattress, and my pussy was gushing wet. I wasn't sure how I would handle not having that hard cock shoved up my cunt, but I would deal. One way or another, Talon would bring me to climax. Of that I had no doubt.

Talon came to the bed, and his fingers grazed my skin

as he tied one wrist to the bar and then stretched the string of pearls to my other wrist, binding it. It was tight, but not so tight that it hurt. I tried to get loose, and I couldn't. He had done a good job.

"Lift your ass, baby," he said. "Present yourself to me."

I complied, and he slid his warm tongue up my slit and over my asshole.

I nearly burst into hot blue flames.

"God, you're wet, baby," he said.

I sighed into the pillow. "It feels good, Talon. Eat me."

"You taste so good, baby. Always so good. Strawberries, champagne, green apples, and sex." He licked my pussy again and then shoved his tongue inside. He moved downward a bit and sucked on my clit, and then he plunged two fingers inside me, bringing me to instant orgasm.

I cried out as the waves of pleasure erupted around me.

"That's it, baby," he said, "come for me. I need you really relaxed if we're going to do this."

His words drifted around me in a sea of passion, coming to my ears in slow waves.

Funny, I hadn't been tense, or at least I didn't think I had been, but once I came down from this climax, I knew coming had been a good idea. I was definitely more relaxed now.

He got up from the bed for a minute and came back a few seconds later. "This is just some lube, baby. Makes it easier."

Something cool and wet drifted over my anus. He massaged it with his finger as another finger entered my pussy.

Lord, it felt so good. My nipples were hard, my pussy

so wet.

I gasped when his finger breached my tight rim.

"Easy, baby. Everything is good. So good. If you want me to stop, just tell me."

"I don't want you to stop."

My muscles relaxed around the invasion, and he began moving his finger in and out, in tandem with the finger in my pussy.

"How's that?"

"Good, Talon," I said. "Good." Surprisingly, I wasn't lying. The smooth intrusion into that forbidden part of me *did* feel good. Really good.

"That's it. Your ass is so tight, baby. I can't wait to put my cock in."

I was stretched wider, and I gritted my teeth, moaning.

"Just another finger," he said. "You tell me if you want me to stop."

"Don't stop," I gritted out.

"Relax. You'll get used to it."

The burn ceased a few seconds later, and the fierce sensation turned to pleasure. God, so intense. Kinky. Kinky and obscenely delicious. The intensity overshadowed his finger in my pussy. In-fucking-credible.

I had heard from others that anal sex was amazing, and though I was afraid, this was the ultimate way to show Talon that I trusted him.

"I'm going to give you my cock now, baby," he said. "The hardest part is the beginning, when I push past that ring of muscle. Breathe out when I tell you to, okay?"

"Yes. Okay." I held my breath.

He spread more lube around my anus, and then the head of his cock nudged the tight hole. He pushed against the tight muscle, but it didn't give.

"Relax, baby. Let it go."

I breathed in and let it out slowly.

And he thrust his cockhead past the tight circle of muscle.

God, the pain! I clamped my hands around the bars where they were tied and let out a loud moan.

"Breathe, baby. In. Out. The sting will stop. You tell me when you're ready."

A few more breaths, and the pain died down. I was full. So full of Talon's cock. And I wanted nothing more.

"I'm ready now."

"Okay, baby, I'm going to go in quickly. It's best that way." He pushed his cock far into my ass.

I had never felt so full. Never felt so close to anyone in my life. I had never known how intimate this act could be.

"I'm going to come out now and then go back in. Remember, if you need me to stop anytime—"

"God, no." I bit my lip. "Please don't stop." I wanted to jerk my hips backward into him, taking his cock, but because I was tied I couldn't.

He went in slowly again and then withdrew.

But what I wanted was fast. I wanted him to really fuck me. I wanted him to know how much I trusted him.

"Talon, please..."

"What?"

"More," I said. "Harder."

He jammed into me. How I longed to touch my clit. I

was on fire, but my hands were bound.

"You like it, baby?"

I nodded into the pillow. "Yes." God, yes. It hurt, yet it tantalized me, shooting prickles of pleasure outward, to every last limb. It was wrong, yet so right. How was I feeling this in my clit? But I was. I so was. I wanted to come. Wanted to touch my clit so damn bad.

"It's so good, baby. You're so tight. Feels so good around my cock."

He increased the speed a bit but still not to the point I wanted.

"Damn it, Talon," I said into the pillow. "Faster! Fuck me faster."

This time he obeyed me. He jammed his cock inside me and then out again and then in, faster, thrusting.

Thrust.

Thrust.

Thrust.

If only I could reach my clit... If only... And then it didn't matter, because I was splintering into an orgasm so intense, so rapturous, that I wasn't sure where he ended and I began.

"God, Talon, God. I'm coming! I'm coming!"

"That's it, baby. Come. Come for me."

I continued wailing into the pillow, my whole world fusing into this one intimate act with this man I loved so much.

And still he thrust.

"Tell me you like it, Jade. Tell me you like it."

CHAPTER THIRTY-THREE

TALON

I forced my withdrawal from her tight sweet body and curled into a fetal position at the foot of the bed.

Tell me you like it, boy. Tell me you like it.

How could I have said those words to her? What kind of monster was I?

"Talon?" Her sweet voice came from the head of the bed. "What happened?"

She was out of breath. I had interrupted her in the middle of an orgasm.

I couldn't answer with the truth. As much as I wanted to, I couldn't. "I'm sorry, blue eyes. Maybe I just wasn't ready for this."

"It's okay," she said. "Could you untie my wrists, please?"

I lay, still curled up, hearing her words and comprehending them but unable to move.

"Please?" she said again.

I jerked my head up. I couldn't leave her tied up when she was asking to be released. She trusted me, and no matter how misplaced that trust was, I had to honor it. Willing my muscles to move, I crawled to the head of the bed and unbound her.

She sat up, rubbing her wrists. "What happened?"

"I...told you. I wasn't ready for this." There was a grain of truth in the words. I'd had anal sex before, despite my past. But anal sex with Jade... God, the pleasure... I'd been so inside myself, inside her, feeling everything she felt, feeling the love, the trust...

She smiled. "Talon, I love you, but that's bull, and we both know it. You were enjoying yourself. Now what happened?"

Yes, I had been enjoying myself. Why had I said those terrible words to her? "I...can't..."

"You can't what?"

"Can't..."

She caressed my cheek with her soft hand. "It's okay."

I shook my head. It wasn't okay. It wasn't okay at all. I had been so close to her, one with her, and I had ruined it. My eyes filled, but I willed the tears not to fall.

"Do you believe I trust you now?"

I cleared my throat but couldn't speak for a few seconds. Then, "You're amazing," I said softly.

She smiled again.

"I..."

"What?"

"I'm not worthy of you, Jade."

She dropped her beautiful ruby-red lips into an O. "Why on earth would you say that?"

I let out a scoff. "Because it's true, that's why."

"Isn't that for me to decide? I chose to put my trust in you, and you didn't let me down. We'll try another time. It doesn't matter."

"It matters," I said. "There are things you don't know."

"I'm right here. I've got two good ears, and I'm a good listener. Tell me anything. I promise it won't affect how much I love you or trust you."

I let out a heavy sigh. "Something happened to me... Some unimaginable things."

"What kinds of things?"

My vocal cords froze. Chills dashed through my neck, and I was paralyzed, unable to speak further. After a moment or two of silence, she crawled toward me and snuggled up to my body, her skin like silk.

"I will never pressure you to say anything you're not ready to say," she said. "But I can promise you that nothing will change my feelings about you."

And in that moment—that moment where she had showed me the ultimate trust—I actually believed her.

★ ★ ★

"Last time at the end of our session, we decided we would talk about what happened to you when you were ten," Dr. Carmichael said.

I sat in the usual spot, clenching the arms of the hunter-green recliner. I nodded.

"Do you want to go there today? Are you feeling up to it?"

I couldn't help chuckling. "If I waited to until I felt up to it, I'd be dead and buried before it happened."

"I understand. We will get to it, Talon, but it's not absolutely essential that it happen today."

"So you're letting me off the hook?"

"You're not on any hook. What you say here is your choice. If you're not ready to talk about that, would you like to try the guided hypnosis today? Maybe we can find out what you were dreaming about when you ended up with your hands around Jade's neck."

I didn't like the idea of someone inside my head any more than I liked the idea of talking about certain things, but I desperately needed to figure out why I had ended up in that position with Jade. I had to, if I wanted a future with her. As it stood now, I would not spend the night with her again until I was certain I would never hurt her.

"All right," I said to Dr. Carmichael. "Let's try it today."

"Some people are more comfortable on the couch during this kind of session," she said.

The idea of being on a shrink's couch freaked me out a bit. "I think I'd rather stay in the chair."

"Why don't you pull the handle to let it recline. I need you to be relaxed, Talon, or this won't work."

I released the lever and let my feet rise. "Understood," I said.

"I'm going to dim the lights, and then we'll begin, okay?"

I nodded. *Now or never.*

Dr. Carmichael came back and took the chair opposite me. "Are you comfortable? Do you need a pillow or a blanket?"

"I'm fine."

"All right," she said. "The first thing you need to know about hypnosis is that it's more than a state of relaxation. It can be any state where you disassociate and become more focused and more suggestible. Do you ever have flashbacks, Talon?"

I fidgeted, gripping the chair as usual. I nodded slightly.

"I understand that's a difficult thing for you to admit. But I'm asking because I want you to understand that during those flashbacks, you're most likely in a state of self-induced hypnosis. I think it's necessary for you to know that before we proceed."

"I don't understand."

"There's nothing for you to be concerned about. I will guide you through your hypnosis session, and if you become uncomfortable or if for any other reason you want to stop, it's important that you understand that you can stop at any time. You will remain in control."

A shiver ran through me. I nodded.

"What sort of things trigger your flashbacks?"

"It can be anything. A glass of water on the table. Or..." My girlfriend massaging an intimate part of me. I wasn't ready to tell her that yet.

Dr. Carmichael nodded. "You're reacting to a posthypnotic suggestion when you have a flashback. Otherwise known as a trigger. In these instances, hypnosis is not relaxation at all."

"How can I be reacting to a posthypnotic suggestion? I've never been hypnotized before."

"It's a phenomenon known as environmental posthypnotic suggestion. It occurs when a person's been through a traumatic experience, and certain triggers cause them to relive the emotional and physical trauma that they experienced. For example, someone who's been shot could react to any sound that sounds like a gunshot—a firecracker for instance, or a car backfiring."

I nodded, still shaking a bit.

"I want you to understand all of this before we begin. I will do my best to keep you relaxed, but if you feel yourself tightening up, you just tell me that you want to stop. All that said, do you want to proceed?"

Was I really ready to relive all of this? Because that was no doubt what would happen. "Doc, let me ask you a hypothetical question."

"Go ahead."

"Say you have a patient who's been through a horrific experience, a childhood trauma, and it has colored his whole life. Can he recover?" I'd asked this before, but I needed to hear the answer again. Needed to know I was going in the right direction.

"Does he want to recover?"

I closed my eyes. "Very much so."

"Then he can, but he must first face what happened to him. Only then will he be able to deal with it and move forward."

Words I'd heard many times before. I cleared my throat. I needed to do this. For my brothers, for Marj, especially for Jade. And more than all of them combined, I needed to do this for myself.

"Let's do it then, Doc," I said.

"Then close your eyes, and we'll get started."

★ ★ ★

Warmth coated my face, and I shut my eyes against the sun's rays. I inhaled the scent of beach—sand, coconut sunscreen, that slightly fishy scent that was actually pleasant. The waves crashed to the shore, the sound of them soothing. I breathed in the salty air. My energy rose as the ozone swelled from the crashing waves, fueling the air with oxygen. I lay on top of a plush beach towel on a chaise longue, my knees elevated, my back relaxed.

All was right with the world. I opened my eyes. Next to me Jade sat, her lush body clothed in a silvery-blue one-piece that matched her eyes. She looked over at me and smiled, and my heart thundered. My fingers were entwined around hers.

I closed my eyes again, breathed in deeply, and let it out slowly. Tension seeped out of my muscles, and I melted further into the lush towel covering my chair. The sun's rays heated my skin, and then a cool breeze drifted over me. I moved my feet on either side of the chair and wiggled my toes in the sand.

"Are you relaxed?" came a voice from across the breeze.

I nodded my head slightly. *Yes. I am relaxed.*

Whispers met my ears, voices... Something landed on my cheek. Probably a bug. I swatted away, but still it was there, pressing on my skin.

And the whispers became louder.

"Come on, boy," a voice whispered. "You think you can take me on? Do it, boy. Show me how strong you are." And then an eerie chuckle, black and evil.

I rose from my chair to face my tormentor.

"Come on, boy. Show me what you got, boy."

I cowered, rolling into a ball to the sand.

"You think you're so tough, don't you, boy? You can't hurt me. You'll never know who I am. I'll never answer for what I did to you." And then the eerie demonic cackling again.

The cackling that brought the rage rising through me.

I stretched out on the sand. *Get up. Get up and show him. Get up and show him you're not a scared little boy anymore. Get up, Talon. Get up.*

My muscles tensed, and I grabbed hold of something... It felt like the leather arm of the chair, but when I looked down, it was just a handful of sand.

Get up, goddamnit. Get up.

I summoned my strength, called on every bit of fortitude and courage I possessed, and I stood. I stood my entire height of six feet three, and I towered over the masked maniac who taunted me.

"Decided to get tough again, boy? Show me. Show me what you've got."

I pulled my hands into fists and forced myself toward him.

For once, I noticed his eyes. They were brown, brown and evil.

With all my strength, I pushed him down and landed on top of him in the sand.

"How do you like that, boy?" I taunted. "How do you like that?"

I punched his nose, the blood spurting on my face. And

then, as he coughed and sputtered, I put my hands around his neck. His arms flopped at his sides, the tattoo of the flaming bird seeming to move as his muscles flexed.

"You like that, boy? You like how I choke you like that? Do you, boy? Tell me. Tell me you like it."

With a jolt, I was back in my lounge chair, the sun shining on my face. Jade was beside me, her hand still entwined with mine.

★ ★ ★

I opened my eyes, and I was in the hunter-green recliner in Dr. Carmichael's office.

"How do you feel?" Dr. Carmichael asked.

She was right about hypnosis not necessarily being relaxing. I had a push me-pull you sensation going on inside my muscles. They were both relaxed and tensed, if that made any sense. Of course, it made as much sense as any part of my life had in the last twenty-five years.

"I'm not sure how to answer that," I said.

"Do you remember anything about the session?"

I nodded. "I remember being on the beach."

"Yes, that's how I guided you to relaxation. Then what?"

"I felt very good. Jade was beside me. And then..."

"What?"

"A man appeared."

"Did you know this man?"

I gulped and nodded. Brown eyes. The man with the tattoo had brown eyes. Something new. "Yes. I mean, I don't

280

know his name, and I've never seen his face. He always wears a mask."

"He always wears a mask in your dreams?"

I gulped again. "In my dreams. And in reality... When I knew him."

"Was he the man you were strangling?"

I nodded. "Yes."

"I guided you back to your dream when you fell asleep with Jade. That's what you were remembering—what you were dreaming about when you ended up with your hands around her neck."

I nodded.

"So you weren't strangling her, Talon."

"I know I wasn't. I would never hurt her. But the fact is, despite that in my dreams it wasn't Jade who I was strangling, in reality, it was."

Dr. Carmichael nodded. "But at least now we know it wasn't her you wanted to hurt."

That did little to console me. "What if it happens again?"

"I don't think it will, now that we're starting to work through it. But if you're scared that it might, just don't fall asleep with her. Until you're sure."

I closed my eyes a moment. "That's pretty much what I had decided anyway."

"Now tell me about this man you were strangling. You say you knew him."

"Yes." My heart pounded.

"Is it someone from your time in the military?"

Oh, if only. People expected military personnel to

have post traumatic-stress disorder, expected them to have problems coping. If only it were that simple.

"No, it wasn't someone from the military."

"Then who was it?"

This was it, the moment of truth. The time of reckoning. Time to spill my guts.

"He was a man, one of three men, actually. He kidnapped me, beat me...molested—"

No, that wasn't a strong enough word, and I had vowed to be honest, to get through this no matter how hard it was on me.

I cleared my throat. "He... He...*raped* me." I squeezed my eyes shut. "When I was ten."

CHAPTER THIRTY-FOUR

JADE

"Hello, Wendy," I said to the receiver. "This is Jade Roberts again from Snow Creek."

A heavy sigh whooshed through the phone line and into my ears. "What can I do for you, Jade?"

"You can tell me about the relationship between Larry Wade and Daphne Steel."

Silence for a few moments. Then, "I don't know what you're talking about."

"I have reason to believe that Larry Wade and Daphne Steel were half brother and sister."

And again, silence.

"Look, Wendy, I know you don't want to get involved in this, but I care about the Steels."

"You're just doing Larry's dirty work."

"Yes and no. I'm researching them for him for classified reasons, but as you know, I have my own agenda."

More silence.

"Why did someone tamper with Daphne's birth certificate and marriage certificate? Why didn't anyone think to change her father's first and middle names while they were in there?"

"I'm not sure what tree you're barking up, Jade, but I don't know what you're talking about."

"Look, I'm not stupid. The last name on Daphne's marriage certificate is Wade. Her birth certificate notes that her father's name is Jonathan Conrad Warren. Larry Wade's father is Jonathan Conrad Wade."

Another heavy sigh. "Well, you're the attorney," she said. "Piece together the evidence."

"I already have pieced it together. What I want to know is *why*."

"I'm afraid I can't tell you that."

"Why not?"

"Because I'm not sure I know myself."

I didn't believe her, of course. In my mind's eye, I saw her stroking her cheek with her index finger. But I wasn't ready to pack up everything and fly out talk to her again if she wasn't willing to cooperate.

"All right, Wendy. I understand. If you ever feel differently about things, please call me. You have my number."

We said our good-byes and ended the call.

I shifted my focus to a couple of DUIs for the remainder of the day. I was due in court in the morning for arraignments. Besides, I had to let go of the Steels for a few hours. As much as I loved Talon and the rest of his family, I needed to escape it all, if only for a few hours. This research was taking its toll.

When I finished work on the DUIs, I got on the Internet to look at tattoo shops in Grand Junction. Maybe I'd drive into the city over the weekend and check one of them out.

Maybe find a new image. One that wouldn't upset Talon so much.

I was sipping the bottled water on my desk when Larry stuck his head inside my office.

"I'm taking off early, Jade," he said. "Did you need anything before I go?"

I pushed some documents across my desk. "Just your signature on these."

"Sure, no problem." He entered my office, clad in shorts, a Hawaiian-print shirt, flip-flops.

"Going to the beach?" I smiled.

"I wish. Nope, just taking the grandkids out for the afternoon. Do you have any plans for the weekend?"

"I might go into the city."

"Yeah, what for?"

"I'm thinking about getting a tattoo." My phone buzzed. "Excuse me for a minute." I picked up the receiver. "Yes?"

"It's a Ted Morse for you, Jade," Michelle said.

Colin's father? Why would he be calling me? "Okay, put him through." I turned to Larry. "I'll just be a minute."

He nodded, took the documents, and sat down in the chair opposite me, perusing them.

"This is Jade," I said into the phone.

"Jade, Ted Morse. I need some answers."

Would I ever be free of this family? "What do you mean?"

"Where the hell is my son, Jade? He was supposed to fly home after that court appearance. No one's seen him since he left here."

My blood froze in my veins. "He didn't show up in

court. The last time I saw him was Saturday evening."

Silence for a few seconds, and then, "I'll be in touch." The line went dead.

Where was Colin? Dread crawled up my spine and lodged in the fine hairs on the back of my neck.

Larry sat across from me, staring. "Everything okay?"

"Yes, yes. That was my ex-fiancé's father, just looking for him."

"I see." Larry scribbled his signature on the last document. "So your tattoo. May I ask where you're getting it?"

"I don't know yet. Maybe a shop in Grand Junction."

He laughed. "I mean where on your body."

"Oh. Sure. On my lower back."

"Good spot. Your first?"

I nodded.

"They hurt like hell."

"So I've heard. But I'll be fine."

He turned to leave, and my pulse raced double-time. *Don't let him go.* I needed to know things, things that only he could tell me. And now Colin had disappeared. I doubted Larry had anything to do with that, but I feared Talon might. Damn it, I wanted some answers. So I risked losing my job and my access to all the databases. I needed to start now. For my own sanity.

"Larry?"

He turned around. "Yes?"

"Before you go, I need to ask you some questions about the Steel investigation."

"Well, as I've told you, most of that's classified, but I'll help if I can."

I drew in a breath, gathering my courage. "I want to know about your sister. Daphne Steel."

His eyes grew dark, and he walked around to my side of the desk. I trembled. But what could he do? We were in a public office, and Michelle and David were right outside. I met his angry gaze and then dropped my own to the floor, berating myself for not being able to look him in the eye.

Cheap flip-flops. But something was off.

Larry was missing a toe—the little toe on his left foot.

Talon and Jade's story continues in

Possession

Coming Soon

MESSAGE FROM HELEN HARDT

Dear Reader,

Thank you for reading *Obsession*. If you want to find out about my current backlist and future releases, please like my Facebook page and join my mailing list. I often do giveaways. If you're a fan and would like to join my street team to help spread the word about my books. I regularly do awesome giveaways for my street team members.

If you enjoyed the story, please take the time to leave a review on a site like Amazon or Goodreads. I welcome all feedback.

I wish you all the best!
Helen

Facebook
Facebook.com/HelenHardt

Newsletter
HelenHardt.com/Sign-Up

Street Team
Facebook.com/Groups/HardtAndSoul/

ALSO BY HELEN HARDT

The Steel Brothers Saga:

Craving
Obsession
Possession
Melt
Burn
Surrender
Shattered
Twisted
Unraveled

Blood Bond Saga:

Unchained: Volume One

Unhinged: Volume Two

Undaunted: Volume Three
(Coming Soon)

Unmasked: Volume Four
(Coming Soon)

Undefeated: Volume Five
(Coming Soon)

Misadventures Series:

Misadventures of a Good Wife
Misadventures with a Rock Star

The Temptation Saga:

Tempting Dusty
Teasing Annie
Taking Catie
Taming Angelina
Treasuring Amber
Trusting Sydney
Tantalizing Maria

The Sex and the Season Series:

Lily and the Duke
Rose in Bloom
Lady Alexandra's Lover
Sophie's Voice

Daughters of the Prairie:

The Outlaw's Angel
Lessons of the Heart
Song of the Raven

DISCUSSION QUESTIONS

1. The theme of a story is its central idea or ideas. To put it simply, it's what the story *means*. How would you characterize the theme of *Obsession?*

2. What do you think about Talon forbidding Jade to get a tattoo? Consider this question from Talon's perspective and from Jade's.

3. Have we learned anything new about Talon's past? Discuss how this does or does not make his character more understandable and sympathetic.

4. Discuss Talon's heroism during his time in the military. Why do you think he didn't want the story to go to the national news? Was it really because he didn't want the publicity? What else might have happened during his time overseas?

5. Discuss the character of Wendy Madigan. What do you think she's hiding, and why?

6. What do you think of guided hypnosis? Do you believe it has any validity?

7. Ryan is devoted to Talon. Discuss how Ryan might be feeling, how the situation has impacted him and his

possibility of a significant relationship in the future.

8. Discuss the author's use of flashbacks in *Obsession*. How do they add to the story, and what purpose do they serve? Do they differ from those in *Craving*?

9. How do you think the Steels changed Marjorie's birth certificate and Daphne's documents? Who else might have done it?

10. Discuss Jade's role in the sexual relationship. Has it changed since *Craving*? How so?

11. Do you believe Talon truly loves Jade? Why or why not?

12. Discuss the symbolism of the phoenix and how it affects Talon in both good and bad ways. Discuss the symbolism of the single red rose. What other literary devices does the author use in *Obsession*?

13. Where might Colin be?

14. What do you think the future holds for Jade and Talon in *Possession?* What about Jonah and Ryan? Marjorie?

ACKNOWLEDGMENTS

I loved writing *Obsession*—especially because, in many ways, it poses more questions than it answers. Talon's pain is raw and deep. He's composed of many layers, and Jade has only begun to scrape through them. I hope you laughed and cried along with Talon and Jade during this phase of their journey. The ending you've been waiting for is on its way with *Possession*, but Jade and Talon will have more growing to do in the further books of the series. I won't be able to turn my back on these two amazing characters.

As always, thank you to my brilliant editor, Michele Hamner Moore, and my eagle-eyed proofreader, Jenny Rarden. Thank you to all the great people at Waterhouse Press—Meredith, David, Kurt, Shayla, Jon, and Yvonne. The cover art for this series is beyond perfect, thanks to Meredith and Yvonne.

Thank you to the members of my street team, Hardt and Soul. HS members got the first look at *Obsession*, and I appreciate all your support, reviews, and general good vibes. I have the best street team in the universe!

Thanks to my always supportive family and friends and to all of the fans who eagerly waited for *Obsession*. I hope you love it!

ABOUT THE AUTHOR

#1 *New York Times*, #1 *USA Today*, and #1 *Wall Street Journal* bestselling author Helen Hardt's passion for the written word began with the books her mother read to her at bedtime. She wrote her first story at age six and hasn't stopped since. In addition to being an award-winning author of contemporary and historical romance and erotica, she's a mother, an attorney, a black belt in Taekwondo, a grammar geek, an appreciator of fine red wine, and a lover of Ben and Jerry's ice cream. She writes from her home in Colorado, where she lives with her family. Helen loves to hear from readers.

Visit her at HelenHardt.com